1777—Danbury on Fire!

M.H.B. Hughes

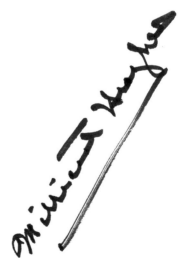

1777—Danbury on Fire!

by M.H.B. Hughes

ISBN: 978-0-578-60746-7

Map by Eugene Scheel

"Your fathers, where are they?"

Zechariah 5

**Dedicated To Those Who Went Before
and served in the Revolutionary War:**

Captain Silas Hamilton

Captain Paul Hamilton

Private John Hamilton

Private James Hamilton

Lt. Ezra Stevens

The condition of the American forces at the close of 1776 was most depressing to all save the adherents of King George. The zeal and enthusiasm which animated the colonies in the first year of the war, as they pressed on to Boston to redress their wrongs, had subsided in the breasts of many and entirely disappeared in others. The resort to arms had brought a gloomy present, with little hope and a wavering faith in a brighter future.

THE HAMILTONS
Captain Silas Hamilton, Sr. - Elizabeth Knapp
Their Children:
Silas Hamilton, Jr. md. Mindwell Benedict
(Son in story – Joe - imaginary)
Lt. Paul Hamilton – unmarried in 1777
Elizabeth Hamilton Barnum
Private John Hamilton - unmarried in 1777
Private James Hamilton – substitute engaged 1/1778 James died 1778

The Lockwoods
Peter Lockwood md. Abigail Hawley (d. 1749)
Peter Lockwood md. Elizabeth Lambert of Wilton (d. 1762)
Their Children:
Lambert Lockwood (b. 1757)
Gould Lockwood (b. 1762 d. unknown)

Peter Lockwood (d. 1775) md. Hannah Shove Starr of Danbury
Note: Hannah Shove Starr's previous husband left money to set up the Danbury school system. Colonel Cooke, Captain Silas Hamilton and another citizen had charge of the project.

The Stevens
Lt. Ezra Stevens - Ann Barnum
Their Children:
Anna Stevens and Anner Stevens married the Hamilton sons, John and Paul

The Benedicts

Judge Thomas Benedict	Mathew Benedict	Daniel Benedict
His Children:	His Children:	His Children:
Judge Thomas Benedict, Jr.	Mathew Benedict, Jr.	Lt. Lemuel Benedict
Joshua Benedict	Capt. Noble Benedict	Amos Benedict
Thaddeus Benedict, Esq.	Jonah Benedict	Sarah Benedict Cooke
Mindwell Benedict Hamilton	Zadock Benedict	

*Amos Benedict b. 1757 graduated from Yale in 1774. Aide to G. Washington d. 2/1777 in Danbury, after smallpox inoculation.
**Sarah Benedict Cooke was married to Colonel Joseph Platt Cooke.

The Knapps
Mr. and Mrs. Benjamin Knapp
Their Children:
Sarah 13
Mercy 10
Noah 6
Urana 1

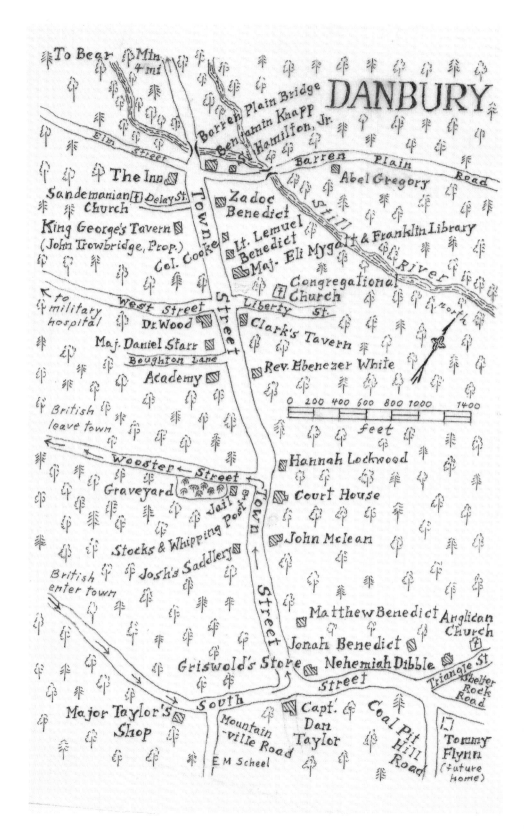

DANBURY

To Bear Mtn. 4 mi

Elm Street

Barren Plain Bridge

Benjamin Knapp

Sq. Hamilton, Jr.

Barren Plain Road

Abel Gregory

The Inn

Sandemanian Church

Delay St.

Town Street

Zadoc Benedict

Still & Franklin Library

King George's Tavern (John Trowbridge, Prop.)

Col. Cooke

Lt. Lemuel Benedict

Maj. Eli Mygatt

River

north

to military hospital

West Street

Dr. Wood

Liberty St.

Congregational Church

Clark's Tavern

Maj. Daniel Starr

Boughton Lane

Academy

Rev. Ebenezer White

British leave town

0 200 400 600 800 1000 1400
feet

Wooster Street

Hannah Lockwood

Graveyard

Jail

Court House

Stocks & Whipping Post

John McLean

Josh's Saddlery

British enter town

Matthew Benedict

Anglican Church

Jonah Benedict

Griswold's Store

Nehemiah Dibble

Triangle St.

Kheller Rock Road

South Street

Major Taylor's Shop

Mountainville Road

Capt. Dan Taylor

Coal Pit Hill Road

Tommy Flynn (future home)

E.M Scheel

Author's Disclaimer of Full Responsibility

First of all, this book is a novel. Many things contained in it are true, but many are invented. Snips from old letters and descriptions reinforce the true feelings and deeds. I did not compose those words.

All of the adults existed, lived in Danbury (or didn't), and retained the professions the books claim. The three young folk – Joe, David and Isaiah — are fictional.

That the Hamiltons left the farm is fiction. The pacifist beliefs portrayed in Silas Hamilton, Jr. and Mindwell Benedict Hamilton may be pure invention, but a large portion of the population believed as they did. Danbury in those times is represented by historian James Bailey as being half Tory and half Patriot, but common sense says that the middle ground existed. Church wars involving Reverend Baldwin, the Sandemanians and Reverend White formed a powerful local dynamic in a world with no social services and steep financial decline.

I used supposition to explain actions, even down to the clothing they wore and what was in their pockets. This is true of the horse rental business to explain Captain Hamilton's many land purchases.

Family relationships as depicted in the family tree pages are factual, although brothers and sisters not mentioned in the book are left out.

Lambert Lockwood's job and past present accurately, but all histories of the Lockwood family declare the disappearance of Gould Lockwood to be unexplained. This mystery found a possible answer in the death described in the book.

That these people made our country is undeniable.

M.H.B. Hughes

Chapter One

Thursday, April 24th, 1777
at Four o'Clock of the Afternoon

I jumped to be the first boy to escape class, and barreled out through the Academy's heavy oak door. Then I wondered what my hurry had been. Job-hunting had occupied me every day after school for the last two weeks. Yesterday, the bartender had laughed me out of the Inn, the rebel tavern near my house. The Inn had been my last choice, due to the rebel clientele. I had assumed that I rated as kitchen-boy material, worthy of actual money. Wrong.

Stopped dead on the stone step, I remained stuck in the mud of my own mind, too downhearted to move.

David Weed yelled, "What's slowing you down, Joe Hamilton? Out of the way!" He grabbed my shoulder and pushed, but I didn't mind. David always found me after school, ready for our short daily walk — him to work in the Clark's Tavern kitchen and me to haul the tavern's kitchen garbage home to our two sows.

I didn't answer, just started up Town Street, fuming. Tomorrow school would be out and I had no job. Would I still wear the same too-small clothes and shoes when school began again in fall? In Danbury, Patriot boys work for Patriots, and Loyalist Tory boys work for Tory bosses. My parents and I are "pacifist," the basic meaning of which is "not getting along with anybody in town." We want America to be its own country, but not a country cannon-balled into the ground.

The war. The revolution. So what? My real problem was the war in my family. The war that made my father leave the family farm. The war that made us poor. The war that made everyone poor, or made them look like it, anyway. With the new "dollar" losing value every day, any Patriot adult who got hold of a dollar bought land or animals as fast as he could. Even just a chicken. And those animals were sacred, bought only to breed or produce wool or eggs. My father called that "investment."

I kept on walking as David moved up beside me. We listened as schoolmates behind us planned a ride to the town cow pasture. I would not be included. Tories decorated Tory ponies, and Patriot ponies bore a row of smaller Patriots, often four or five, all holding on for dear life. That I did not have access to a pony counted, too. My grandfather owned thirty horses. Surely, one of them must be too old or too lame or … oh, well, nothing I could do.

Then misfortune approached, as it did 'most every school day. Isaiah-last-name-unknown didn't attend The Academy, but he hung around us the way a fly hangs around meat. Probably expelled from an outlying school like Wolfpits. The nearby settlement looked about the way it sounded.

Isaiah thought I was a Tory and I couldn't prove I wasn't. I never answered him back the way I wanted to, 'cause I'm fair-sized for thirteen, but two extra years of eating made Isaiah out of my weight class for fighting. My relief when Isaiah sighted in on two genuine Tory boys didn't last long. Those educated tongues spit out a furious hail of curses, causing Isaiah to ricochet back toward me.

"Well, if it ain't Little Tory Boy Hamilton! You got pigs at home, I hear tell, Little Tory Boy."

This direct focus on what my family owned did not sound good. The crowd suddenly stopped talking as Isaiah took the stage, and our audience gathered.

"I jus' love pig fat drippin' into the fire. My mouth be waterin' already." Hands over green-mottled teeth indicated laughter. That or drool.

Shaking with amusement, Isaiah leaned closer to me and snorted like a pig. "If the Big Raid happens, I'll end up rich and you'll end up robbed!"

Isaiah made a showy pause, finger in the air while he pretended to think. "On second thought, just keep them smelly pigs. Your peace-lovin' Daddy won't be needing his fancy horse no more. At midnight, I bet I could grab that nasty nag right out'n your broken-down shed."

Stung by the threats, I took dead aim and let fly, "Your weight would break any horse's back. What day are you going to join up, fat rebel boy? Got a gun already?"

The two Tories applauded my new bravery, clapping hands over their heads. I loved it when older boys liked my act, so I readied more ammunition.

"Just throwing your weight around?" I challenged.

Isaiah walked closer to me, puffed up a little bigger than usual. I didn't flinch, since David had my back.

"I can claw up a gun and a horse any time," Isaiah sneered, "'cause I takes what I wants. I don't care where I gets it from, neither." Rebel confiscation activities gave criminals free rein to snatch anything and blame "Patriotism."

"Do you ever do anything, or just boast and steal?" I shot back.

A shiver surged around the group, such as occurs before a fight. Isaiah preened for the two girls, who made faces of disgust before they edged away.

An odd thing happened then. The bullying look drained from Isaiah's face as he motioned us closer. His voice turned low and confiding. "I turn sixteen on Sunday. I gots to enlist, and I wants to fight, but I ain't doin' it for free. The Continentals offer twenty pounds bounty money now."

To the Hon. John Hancock, Esq., President of Congress. State of Massachusetts-Bay, Boston,

December 30, 1776.

It was found necessary to make an addition of twenty pounds to the Continental bounty, in lieu of the additional wages that were intended, said bounty to be given to each effective man enlisting to serve three years, or during the war, and payable in two equal notes, issued by our Treasurer, on interest, at six per cent., payable in four years from their dates.

"Why do the rebels offer pounds instead of rebel dollars?" asked a Tory boy. "No takers on their own worthless paper? Plus, they likely won't pay 'til the year 1800!" He and his friend slapped each other's well-dressed backs.

Isaiah issued a dirty look. "The Patriots will give land away after the war, too!" Isaiah stuck up his nose, as proud as if he already owned a whole farm.

"Not worried about starving while you wait? After the last war, the king promised my grandfather Hamilton three thousand acres. He got nothing!"

Given at our Court at St. James's the 7th Day of October 1763. in the Third Year of our Reign.

GOD SAVE THE KING

And Whereas, We are desirous, upon all occasions, to testify our Royal Sense and Approbation of the Conduct and bravery of the Officers and Soldiers of our Armies, and to reward the same, We do hereby command and impower our Governors of our said Three new Colonies, and all other our Governors of our several Provinces on the Continent of North America, to grant without Fee or Reward, to such reduced Officers as have served in North America during the late War, and to such Private Soldiers as have been or shall be disbanded in America, and are actually residing there, and shall personally apply for the same, the following Quantities of Lands, subject, at the Expiration of Ten Years, to the same Quit-Rents as other Lands are subject to in the Province within which they are granted, as also subject to the same Conditions of Cultivation and Improvement; viz.

To every Person having the Rank of a Field Officer—5,000 Acres.

To every Captain—3,000 Acres.

"I ain't worried," Isaiah stated, hands on hips. "Folks hire substitutes and pay up front. That's twenty pounds hard money while I wait for the government lot."

Trying to rile him up, I chanted, "Plus, you get to be first in line for smallpox!" These words had originated with my mother, but they worked as intended.

Isaiah tossed a rude gesture in my direction and stalked off toward downtown.

Judging by the faces of my schoolmates, we all felt like ignorant children for lacking financial plans. The three oldest Patriot boys turned away from the group, frowning faces whisper-close, while they evaluated Isaiah's plan. One had been headed to Yale College, but his course might change in a hurry.

The girls seemed mystified, "Joining the Continentals pays money? They say the British hire German troops, but why is this any different?"

David inched closer to me and murmured, "God almighty, Joe Hamilton, could Isaiah get twenty pounds two different times?" Twenty pounds counted as a family's rent money for years to come. Or a down payment on land.

I shrugged. "Better for the Patriots to invest in gunpowder than Isaiah."

"What if the slug does steal your dad's pigs? Everyone knows Isaiah's dad robs barns and sheds all the way from here to Wilton." Thieves were as common as acorns since the money system had become so confused that Spanish coin was accepted in every shop.

"If Isaiah leaves for the army right away, we're safe," I answered.

"What if he leaves with your father's fancy stallion? He could be over the state line into New York in an hour."

"If he steals the stallion, he'll be cantering his own coffin," I said.

The beast's lack of interest in human life had become the town joke. As the stallion reared sky-high, pawing the air, the comment always came, "Si Hamilton's the best rider living in Danbury. He'll be the best dead one, too!"

As soon as we got well away from the group, David Weed grabbed my arm, revealing a face of unhidden joy.

"Joe, guess what happened!" He almost whispered, choked by some deep excitement.

"I can't guess," I replied, feeling as dull as my job prospects.

"What Isaiah said is true. I'm going to be sixteen in August, and they'd make me enlist. The Committee would get tough with my father if I didn't."

"You want to sell your life for twenty pounds?" I asked.

"Me? Ha!" David answered. "If I work for a doctor, I enlist, but they won't call me unless they have to. Young Dr. Starr is starting practice now. I'll heft his bag and drive his black pacing pony on calls. Plus, he'll let me hold down patients when bones are set."

Driving the doctor's sharp-looking pony might be fine, but broken bones did not appeal to me. Nor did the idea of disease passing from person to person to doctor.

"Say, Joe, how old are you again?" David had a purposeful gleam in his eye.

"Thirteen," I said. "Too young to go to war as your substitute."

"Maybe you'd want to be my substitute in the kitchen at Clark's? I was thirteen when I started there. I didn't tell Mrs. Clark yet that I'm leaving right away. She might not be angry if I have a replacement. Not that every boy in town wouldn't want to work there!"

True enough. Clark's tavern turned out the best food in Danbury. Their tavern counted as Patriot, but everybody went there for a midday ale while looking at the free newspapers, even my father, although he never stayed long in that Patriot climate.

"Do I want your job?" I yelled. "Yes!" My whole life lit up as bright as the April afternoon. Three crows in a nearby tree cawed approval. I stepped out faster, but David's hand pulled me back.

"Joe, wait! Let me tell Mrs. Clark first. I can explain where you fit in. Don't worry. It's logical — you'll get the job. Just slow down." He galloped down Town Street, leaping in the air with exhilaration.

The thought of working all summer in the cheery tavern kitchen sent warmth all through me. My first job! I'd garner only a few pennies, but it would add up. I peered at the holes I had cut in the shoes I wore. My toes might curl like a pig's tail if I kept wearing them. But when school started in the fall, I might have new ones, paid for with my own money. I had been saving already, but only had three pence so far.

I took a 'specially free breath in belief that life would improve when I worked where a chunk of toasted brown pork fat might not be missed. Maybe I could eat the leftovers at closing time.

Tight shoes or not, I skipped twice around a pile of horse manure in the middle of Town Street. My main problem in life now solved, I took off at a slow jog toward my new job.

Chapter Two

Thursday, April 24th, 1777
at Half Five o'Clock of the Afternoon

Approaching Clark's tavern, I tucked in my shirt and pulled my jacket sleeves down. During the last year, my life had unraveled in a real way. My pants now functioned as knee breeches, while my shredded sleeves ended half a foot before my hands showed up. Not that I was much different from other boys. The war had made us all poor. The rebels had strict rules on who could sell what and where they could sell it.

I walked into the tavern kitchen, just like every other day, but my heart pounded. I would still have to ask for the job, no matter what David had arranged.

Pots of stews and beans blasted luscious warm vapors throughout the superheated kitchen. At four o'clock, Farmers wanted their hot meal and hot gossip before heading home to evening chores. Clatter joined chatter in the nearby eating room. Anner Stevens rushed in, ladled a plate of beans and ham, grabbed a spoon and hurried into the bar. David stacked an armload of wood next to the fireplace. He grinned and headed back outside.

Old Mrs. Clark rolled out piecrust with a rolling pin, finally uttering an icy, "Good day, Joe." She didn't look up at me and smile the way she usually did. The way I had expected.

"G'day, Mrs. Clark. David's starting work with Dr. Starr now. He says his job here is open." A long speech for me, but she never looked up while I was saying it.

"David's of an age to choose his life's work, but it causes a bit of a problem for us, I will say." No smile lifted her mouth. She looked weary and irritated, eyes red and wrinkles creeping around them.

"Could I have his job? Please? I need it!" I held my breath.

Before old Mrs. Clark could answer, Lt. Clark's wife swept into the kitchen. Sharp and pretty, she ran the bar with an iron hand, being the wife of the owner. No penny got away from her, as she freely and frequently announced.

Mrs. Clark's usually pleasant countenance flashed me a withering look. "Sorry, but working in my tavern will not happen, thank you!"

"I'm old enough for kitchen work," I protested. "I was thirteen last fall." My voice rose to a squeak I didn't like.

Young Mrs. Clark favored me with her full attention, a powerful stare more becoming in a witch. "It's a matter of principals, Joe. My principals. It's not you; it's your parents. They left the church without joining another one. Refusing to support a church is against the law."

At that day no class of citizens was more conspicuous for patriotism than the Congregational clergy of New England, and among them Mr. Baldwin was noted for his zeal and signal ability. Almost all writing for the public prints at that time was done by the clergy.

"I don't understand," I croaked out of a dry throat. "What does church have to do with a kitchen job?"

Old Mrs. Clark had kept quiet, but now she slapped her pie-crust into its dish and stood upright. She wiped her hands on her formerly-white apron, and swiped her curly gray hair back under her still-white cap. "Joe, the churches support the poor of the town. Congregational, Anglican, even the Sandemanians contribute their share. Your parents don't share the burden with the rest of us. Because of the war, the burden grows every month. That's why your father pays those hefty fines."

My skin had turned cold and clammy, as vague fears washed over me.

"Thank you, Mother Clark, for explaining the facts of life to this young man, apparently a little late," commented her daughter-in-law in an acid voice. "Lt. Clark and I feel no obligation regarding the upkeep of the renegade Hamilton couple's family!"

The tavern owner gathered her apron and skirts, sweeping her tall and pretty self out of the kitchen's heat and back to the bar. I heard her trill, "A good day to you, sir! What would you like? A shrub? A cider, perhaps? Just got in fresh ale from the country!"

"Fines?" I repeated, moving closer to the old lady, to make sure she heard me. "What fines?"

"Yes, fines. Didn't you know?" She frowned at me with obvious concern at my ignorance of a town basic.

Still, how was it possible that wanting peace cost money? Father had led us out of the Congregational Church during one of Reverend Baldwin's anti-British sermons. When the Reverend enlisted in the Continental army after the fourth of July last year, then sickened of putrid fever within a week, Father declared that preaching war went against God's will.

Old Mrs. Clark sighed. "You know, Joseph, you'd better think for yourself about what's going on in this world and in your family."

Desperate, I tried to think my way out of this situation. I soon landed on a way to make the Clarks change their minds. Become a customer, as I often was in the past

"Mother said I should buy a pail of ale," I said and headed into the bar.

As I waited my turn, I picked out the voice of the town clerk, Major Taylor, as he mentioned my grandfather. "Saw Captain Hamilton an hour ago, spending plenty of dollars at the blacksmith's. Usually those boys just trim hooves themselves and don't bother to shoe. Must mean action. Maybe troop movement."

An answering croak came from my mother's older brother, Judge Tom Benedict. "Premature, sir, premature. We have no genuine reason to believe the British plan any actions."

I walked up to the bar, avoiding young Mrs. Clark, and addressed Anner Stevens. I knew my Uncle John was sweet on her. Miss Anner made special point to smile at me any time we met.

"My mother wants a pail of ale, please. I'll bring the pail back tomorrow."

But Mrs. Clark intervened. "I'll take care of this." Mrs. Clark's arms crossed in front of her and her foot tapped the floor.

My face went hot. I knew what would happen next. It had happened on Monday at the baker's.

"Joe, your uncle, Lawyer Benedict, paid your family's account on Christmas. I have not seen a penny since. Four whole months. It's time to shut off your family's account. Your father angers the Loyalists by opposing the king and he angers the Patriots by opposing the war. This might not be an issue if the question of payment did not arise. Payment each month!"

The snap of the flames in the fireplace became the only sound in the room. Everyone else had stopped talking and started looking. At me. Slowly, I understood that our conversation had ended. Shying away, I dodged back through the kitchen door.

I avoided old Mrs. Clark's direct glance, but I thought she looked sad, as if she felt forced to go along with family policy.

"Sorry, Joe," she muttered as I fled.

I grabbed the slop pail and backed out the door, grateful for the cool breeze hitting my boiling hot face. I seethed with embarrassment. Now I would have to return here, tomorrow and every day, because we needed the tavern's garbage to feed our pigs. My parents had turned me into the boy that nobody wanted around.

My mother had set me up for this. Why didn't Father buy ale himself? Then I understood. What had happened to me had happened to him.

Account not paid.

Ale or cider wouldn't be a problem if we still lived at the farm, where my uncles ground cider aplenty with fruit from our own apple trees.

No account needed.

Well, maybe an old bottle of cider still hid somewhere in our house. Or something.

Chapter Three

Thursday, April 24th, 1777
at Five o'Clock of the Afternoon

My teeth clenched 'til my jaw ached as I started the short walk home. "Just bite the bullet," Mother used to say when I had a scrape or hurt. I bit it now. I kicked hard at the same pile of manure where I had skipped before. It scattered into dust and flew across the street. The same crows cawed, and I yelled bad words I'd heard while watching the blacksmith shoe my father's horse.

A year ago, I had still admired Father for refusing to turn traitor, but the results totaled up to be bad. People in Boston lost homes due to battles. Now, with no battles at all in Connecticut, my parents and I had lost *our* home, the big farm at Bear Mountain where my Hamilton grandparents and my uncles lived. If I still lived there now, I could pick a mess of greens for supper, to be loaded with butter and larded with pork chunks. Then I could fish in our own pond.

Both my parents' families couldn't imagine anything but a war for America to gain freedom from English control. My father said intelligent people should find peaceful solutions rather than destroying our country. Schoolmaster said that, too, although the boys living in the house where he boarded told us that he was a rabid Patriot at heart.

Hoof beats approached behind me. The riders hollered at each other across the extra horses they led. I leaned into the street, happy to eavesdrop on my own family.

"Paul, I still think the fellow's a fraud," Grandfather chuffed. "Just a blow-hard."

"Who could think up things like that?" protested Uncle Paul. "*Part* of it has to be true."

"Oh, it don't make no difference where boats start from. It's where they land. If the wind's bad, they tack ever' which way. Anyways, this blacksmith trip may pay off sooner than we thought, if those fellers are right."

I jumped into the middle of Town Street, deciding to stop them, even though there was always a risk of Father catching me. When Grandfather began renting out militia horses, we still lived at the farm. Father called Grandfather a traitor for fostering war. Uncle Paul shoved Father into a wall. When Grandfather declared that he and my uncles were Patriots and *Father* was the traitor, we moved into town. I wasn't supposed to talk to the traitors.

"Don't jump out like a haunt! Lord a'mighty mercy, Joseph!" my grandfather shouted. "Whoa, whoa down, now." Grandfather pacified his nervous equine flock and gave a thoughtful look at me. "Heard you was lookin' for a job at The Inn yestereve."

My heart sank – the Danbury gossips had blabbed about my expulsion from the Inn, laughed out for being "a pacifist spy."

Grandfather's half-frown merged into a seductive smile. "Lots of work for you out on the farm. How about that, hey?" The ice-blue eyes crinkled at the corners. Grandfather must figure me for desperate. Every time we met on the street, he always tried to lure me back to the farm. I turned to my favorite way to distract any Hamilton.

"Grandfather, what's that new horse? I never saw it before." Grandfather's favorite horse had been a rangy gray, but now he sat aboard a stout and ugly mud-colored nag.

"Got my new rentals all fresh-shod today. Come on back to Bear Mountain and we'll fit you up with an old beast. Know you want one, Joe." An enticing smile followed the sales pitch.

He hit at my weakest spot. I had always wanted a horse, for sure. Now I was big enough, but I lived in town and didn't *need* a horse. Or so my mother said.

"Yes, sir," added Uncle Paul, assuming the same expectant expression. "I might let you shoot my new long gun. Got these new-fangled 'rifling' grooves inside the musket barrel. Makes the lead fly straighter than ever before."

This kind invitation did not sit well with me.

"You know my father doesn't want me to go out there with you." I was conscious of their real motive — to lure me into disobeying my parents and maybe running away.

Grandfather cleared his throat and said, "Uh, Joe, about your father … uh, he'll be taking a little trip real soon." He stared at the mud-colored horse's ears.

"Oh, where?" I asked, mystified.

The old man's ice-blue eyes snapped to my face and his voice took on the sound of command. "Lookahere, Joe, you got to put the facts together. Times have changed. Ever' man has to do his part for the common good or else — Whoa! Whoa down, you devil!"

The horse on Grandfather's right side had bitten the mud-colored horse, and an equine rebellion featured eight hundred pounds of horse jerking on each of the frayed ropes clutched in his leather gauntlets. Uncle Paul hollered to Grandfather to get a move on. With yells of "Quit it, you hellion!" and "Dang you!" the herd moved off in the direction of Bear Mountain with never a backward glance.

I walked on and chewed over why Father would take a trip. All Hamiltons were present and accounted for. So were Mother's relatives, except … yes, *Jonah Benedict*, that had to be the answer.

Last fall, the British had captured Mother's favorite cousin and imprisoned him in New York City. Father must have won the dangerous and difficult assignment of springing Cousin Jonah from the Sugar House prison. Father might have a good chance at success. The British couldn't arrest Father for rebel activity, which could not be said for anyone else in my mother's family.

After hearing at Christmas that Jonah was starving on a prison ship in New York harbor, I never saw my mother look happy again. Father might become a town hero if he could rescue Jonah. I wanted to hear the plan as soon as I reached home. This exciting news cut down my disappointment about the job.

Next subject — Grandfather telling me to face facts. I didn't *know* any facts. Up until now, I had been happy to know nothing but school learning or who won at marbles. Other boys talked about war all the time. Their fathers and brothers were involved in it, often with bad results. Every time my uncles went away to war, they soon came home again.

I considered war to be an adult business, since people made money from it. George Washington favored soldiers riding to battle and then sending the horses home with their owners. The result: no dead horses, which were in short supply. This was how my grandfather and uncles began their rental business. My great-grandfather had been in good health when they began. Now the Hamilton farming and rental operation was two men short.

Footsteps startled me from these deep thoughts. I whirled around, delighted to see Lambert Lockwood approach. Meeting him on the street 'most every day formed the brightest spot in my life. Lambert fired off a brilliant smile full of the whitest teeth in town.

"Why do you shamble along, Joe? Move out like a soldier! How do you fare on this fine evening?" He looked older than twenty tonight, courtesy of a black tricorn hat, fit for church.

"Mrs. Clark just kicked me out of their tavern for trying to get a job," I said. "I don't want to talk about it."

"I'm off to The Inn," he said, followed by a sigh. "I don't want to talk about that, either. A couple of strangers just came to town, telling an interesting story. We can't figure out what's true and what isn't. People spread war rumors based on nothing, like the Salem witch trials. Speaking of trials, I heard about your father, Joe. I'm here if you need anything."

Word about Father's mission must travel fast. It would be a trial by fire, to get a prisoner away from the British.

"I'll be busy while Father's gone," I said. "I get to be man of the house and do the trading at Griswold's store. Father trades eggs there."

"Won't your mother do that? Aren't the hens usually the mother's?" Lambert's expression said trading eggs wasn't manly.

Now I would have to admit a thing I never admitted to myself.

"My mother doesn't leave home. Women she meets say mean things. Anyway, I like going to Griswold's. I don't know how long Father will be gone, but thanks for offering your help."

With a wave, Lambert turned left into the tavern yard of The Inn.

Luscious smoke from the tavern's kitchen chimney followed me half way home. How I longed for a good feed! The vision of old Mrs. Clark's hot ham and egg pies lived on in my mind. I didn't want to be anywhere except in a kitchen full of food. Home wasn't like that at all. A one-pot dinner was about where our eating stopped.

By the time I reached our cottage, on the corner of Barren Plain, I had tired of banging the pail against my shins and stopped to look at the house. The lime-washed white cottage still didn't seem like home to me, even after nine months. And the cottage wasn't ours. We lived there, but I had stopped believing that rent money changed from Father's hands into Mr. Benjamin Knapp's.

Soon the church might soon be supporting *us*.

Chapter Four

Thursday, April 24th, 1777
at Half Six o'Clock of the Afternoon

I dropped the garbage pail by the shed door and went to the backhouse to pee. Instead of feeding the sows, I ran to the cottage, anxious to hear about Father's trip. Imagine going to New York City, where the biggest battles happened last year!

The ones the Patriots lost.

I entered the back door, hoping to overhear the adult version of the adventure. A glimpse of the front room caused me total alarm. Father sat at the table, both hands covering his face. As he caught sight of me, he wiped his face as if it had been wet, maybe with sweat, but I feared worse.

Mother rested her forehead against the glass of the only window. She looked stunned, as if she had hit the ground hard. She had been in a strange state for several weeks. I had asked Father if she was sickening. Seemed to me, folks who dropped down on the bed with fever got better. People who sickened slow died.

Father had told me not to ask questions.

Now he studied me in a new and intent way. I sorted through my recent activities, wondering what I had done wrong.

Of course.

"Um, no, I couldn't get it," I said, shrugging and looking at the plank floor. I couldn't help feeling guilty for the lack of ale. Without it, there wasn't anything to drink. The rain barrel had moss in it.

"Didn't get what, Joe?" His look was blank.

I feared that opening my mouth might bring out the full story. Finally, he muttered, "Oh, ale. Right."

Father rose from the table, but looked pained. He ended by levering himself up with his hands. He seemed about to speak, but showed no hurry to get on with it. I pretended I didn't see any of this.

Father put one hand on my shoulder and turned my chin up with the other. I had a feeling that life had slid further downhill since this morning. What had I done?

Mother walked over to us and said, "Your father wishes to speak to you, Joe." I looked at her, trying to figure out what was going on.

Why hadn't she said, "Your father and I…?" The hand on my chin forced me back to looking at Father.

"Joe, today your grandfather threatened to have Major Taylor read me The Articles of War."

"I don't understand," I said. "What would Major Taylor read? And why would anyone read papers to you?" My father could read and write just fine. Mother could read, too. Her Bible, anyway.

"The rebels can't attract enough men for their fake army, so they wrote a law paper called 'The Articles of War.' If an officer or a town clerk like Major Taylor reads it out loud, a man can go to jail for refusal to enlist. The Committee of Inspection enforces it."

A Proclamation by the Governor and Council:

April 12, 1777

The quota or proportion of the army is not yet completed in Connecticut, and the time swiftly approaches and is almost arrived, when, without more vigorous and successful efforts, all is lost.

The Committee of Inspection controlled Danbury like an iron net. Grandfather Hamilton and my Uncle Tad Benedict were members. The rebels had stolen all the public offices — mayor, militia leader, town lawyer, both judges. All of whom were my mother's brothers or cousins. Every single relative had gone rebel right down to the bone.

Father let go of me and I whipped around to catch Mother's expression. If my grandfather had threatened my father with jail, one of them had to be crazy, and I needed her to tell me which one.

Then lightning struck. Was this the little trip Grandfather had mentioned? The jail subject, mentioned first by Isaiah, fired through my brain like Dr. Franklin's electricity.

I had only dreamed up the imaginary rescue trip an hour ago, but it seemed so logical that it had to be true. A rich and powerful family like Mother's would never let a family member die in enemy hands. Maybe this was an "either-or" from my grandfather.

"Aren't you going to fetch Jonah?" came right out of my mouth before I could stop it, producing a violent reaction from both parents.

My mother let out a sound, right through the hands over her mouth.

My father yelled, "Who told you such a thing?" Both of my parents looked appalled. How had rescuing Jonah Benedict from the British become a bad thing?

> Corporal Jonah Benedict was a thorough patriot and took an active part in the war. He was before Ticonderoga in August, 1775, and was commissioned sergeant by Captain Noble Benedict, November 10th, 1775, at Fort Johns.

"I, uh — I … I just couldn't imagine why you would go on a trip." I needed to sit down after all this. In fact, I wanted to throw myself on the floor from frustration.

"Who told you I was going anywhere?" Father demanded, just as intense as before.

Now I would catch it, for sure!

"I met Grandfather on the street and he said you were taking a trip." I wanted to yell and smash things, all at the same time. I felt furious with my grandfather for telling me such a half-truth that it became a total lie.

Catching my breath, I recalled Lambert's quick remark as he connected a trial to my father. He had known the truth, too. How had I ignored Isaiah's taunt about Father's not needing his horse anymore? Everyone in town must know, except Little Boy Joe! Curse the rebels and their awful Committee! I grabbed a chair back so I could clench my fists without anyone noticing.

"I swore I wouldn't enlist and I won't!" Father declared, still looking me in the eye.

Jail or enlist would be a toss-up. Either way, Father would lose his mind within a week. I might lose my mind, too, since I could see the jail and the graveyard behind it every time I looked out of the tiny schoolhouse window.

I wanted to try reason, the way my mother did. Not that reason ever worked.

"Why would the rebels want you, if you don't want to fight?" I asked.

"The Patriots force recruits to fight. An officer would shoot anyone who wouldn't face the enemy." Father inspected his hands as if he had never seen them before.

"Father, Uncle Paul is an officer." His younger brother wore a Continental Army uniform, although all he had was the coat.

"Son, I refuse to take part in this ill-considered, so-called war. Those with different ideas will bring disaster down on our heads, as I found out this afternoon. You need to be away from this invitation to incineration. Somewhere far from here."

I again checked my mother's face. She looked sympathetic as she touched my shoulder with hands so icy that I felt them through my shirt.

"Maybe it would be for the best, Joe. We don't know what's going to happen," she said quietly. "You wanted a tavern job, to be paid in pennies and burnt chicken wings. Maybe a genuine job, an apprenticeship, would be the thing to do now."

"Now? Why now?" I begged. "I'm only thirteen."

Father's ash-gray face turned red as he shouted, "Because the British are going to invade Connecticut!"

I closed my eyes and almost sank to the floor. My father must have slipped right over the edge. Mother bowed her head, arms pressed to her body as if she felt pain.

Father stuck his face down in front of mine. "Two riders galloped into Danbury two hours ago, saying forty boats sail toward Connecticut shores, in a direct line for us. They're tacking against the wind, but closer every minute. Forty boats! That's armed forces, not merchants!"

From what Judge Tom had said at the tavern, and what Grandfather had told Uncle Paul, I didn't think anyone believed the story of an invasion. Lambert had sounded more impatient than worried. This tale about boats could never be true.

"How can you fear boats? We're twenty miles from the water!" I shot back.

"Grow up!" Father shouted, a shower of spit following his words. "Those rebel fools stockpile guns downtown in their alleged commissary. If the British find them, they'll snap the neck of this town. Everything we've built here will turn into ashes and be gone forever. Moving you into a safe place is the answer … in Vermont, maybe." Father paused to consider his splendid scenario.

"What is this?" I muttered. "Last month Mother spoke of Yale

College!"

Father grabbed my shirtfront, and his voice turned to ice. "In the War against the French, I was a boy of fifteen, taking care of my father's horse. I saw Indians scalped by white men for money. Indian babies jerked from their mothers' arms and thrown away, because baby scalps weren't worth anything!" I have never stopped dreaming of it. War and atrocity were my college. That's where I learned to stay away from this criminal war!"

> The English, however, passed acts through their colonial assemblies. Even before war was declared, on June 12, 1755, Massachusetts Governor William Shirley offered £40 for Indian male scalps and £20 for female scalps. The following year, on April 14, Pennsylvania Governor Robert Hunter Morris "declared war and proclaimed a general bounty for Indian enemy prisoners and for scalps." The bounties to be paid were £130 for a male scalp and £50 for a female scalp.

This was getting to be too much for my mother. "Husband, you and Joe should feed the animals. You can speak of your plans there." With a vague moan as he pulled on his hat, Father complied, giving a corresponding groan as he stepped down onto the stone step.

Exhausted, I followed.

Chapter Five

Thursday, April 24th, 1777
at Six o'Clock of the Evening

As I exited the back door, I reconsidered my position. Apprenticeship could lead me out of this madness. Masters bought the apprentice's clothes. Their family became your family. Other apprentices became your friends. You might live by a lake or the sea — increasingly important as summer approached. Maybe apprenticeship wouldn't be so bad.

In our school, boys stayed until they graduated at fifteen or sixteen. Direct to college was the usual Academy student's future, well equipped with Latin and Greek. Or they apprenticed with doctors or lawyers where those languages came in handy on Day One.

I give and bequeath the sum of Eight Hundred Pounds money out of my estate to and for the use of a Publick Scool to be kept in the first or old Society in Danbury to be Paid to a Committee within two years next after my Decease to be appointed by the sd Town of Danbury for that purpose and to be by the sd Committee for the Time being and their successors in said office under the Direction and Inspection of the Civil authority and Select men of sd Town of Danbury for the Time being Improved for the only use and benefitt of one Certain Scool in Such Part of the sd Society as they shall think Proper to Effix the sd Seal to be Constantly kept by a Learned and Skil full Scoolmaster well able to instruct children and youth in the various branches of Good Literature and in the English Greek and Lattain Languages and in vulgar arithmetick

Comfort Starr, who departed this life May 11 1763

Witnesses: Deacon Joseph Peck   Thaddeus Benedict   Eli Mygatt

Still, I didn't want to leave Danbury for a reason I wasn't planning to mention — certainly not to my parents. A girl.

"Mr. Knapp would let me apprentice for him," I offered, pointing down the river toward our neighbor's leather tannery. "His apprentices run off faster than deer. Plus, he's not a rebel." Mr. Knapp, small and cheerful, would be a joy to work for, even if the job was … well, revolting.

Father shook his head. "Joe, those apprentices run off because Patriots pick fights with boys who work for Tories. Fingers break. Teeth get knocked out."

The reward posters downtown no longer seemed funny. No way to fix teeth. Ever. Boys said George Washington had wooden teeth. Ugh.

"But I want to stay here," I said. On a good day, whining brought actual reasons instead of "Because I said so."

Father pounced on the same old answer. "The rebel commissary warehouses guns. Guns attract attention. Attention attracts destruction."

Father had insisted that the rebellion would fizzle out, adding that the "Declaration of Independence" had become the "Admission of Starvation."

I wanted to let Father hear his own words. "You said the war might be over soon. You said not enough Patriots remained to put on a decent skirmish."

Before he could answer, I noticed Father's saddle, thrown down in the doorway to the shed. As I picked it up, the wooden frame shifted inside the leather. Shifted in multiple pieces. Wooden saddle frames shattered when a horse reared and fell over backwards. New scuffmarks covered the top of the leather seat. Another man in Danbury never walked again after such an accident. I imagined the horse's massive weight, churning its steel-shod hooves around my father's body as the dreadful beast fought to rise. I examined my father, as I had the saddle. This powerful and athletic man moved slower than Old Lady Clark.

A year ago, Father had spotted a lame and starved colt, ridden by a traveler. Despite the man's warnings, Father traded an old rental horse for the sad case of creature abuse. The gelding he traded did not belong to him, but to Grandfather. The Hamiltons were accustomed to training and reselling horses as safe mounts for anyone; their usual source of money in peacetime.

Father had healed and fed this new beast, which ate better than we did. And received new shoes every six weeks. Now, the eye-rolling stallion appeared to be as fine a horse as ever existed — but it didn't sell. Its mind had turned killer — ready to buck, bite or rear at any opportunity.

I held out the saddle. "Did this just happen?"

"At noontime, when I mounted after a stop to relieve nature."

"Can it be fixed?" I asked, still examining him head to toe.

Father shook his head. "Huh! Needs a new frame. Only good ones come from England, so you know what that means."

It had seemed stupid for the rebels to cut off the main source of fine furniture, clocks, everything of real craft or value. Our family didn't buy special things, but why couldn't we, if we needed them? The Patriots didn't see it that way. Americans could no longer trade with England.

"So nothing can be done to fix it?" Riding with a broken saddle fork could dig raw holes in an animal's back, making a vicious horse worse with every step.

Father snorted again. "Danbury's supposed saddler ran off to join George Washington's gang of thieves."

He was talking about Josh Benedict, another of Mother's cousins. Josh had been the only relative that I could visit undetected because his shop was right near school. Now his saddle shop sat empty, with a sign in the window. Josh had enlisted.

Father flexed the saddle and listened to the crunching sound it made. He mentioned God in a negative way. "A sheepskin under the saddle might help. Another expense, but the accursed nag will kill me if I don't exercise it every day."

"Grandfather might have a sheepskin." Free was free, the way I saw it.

Words shot out of Father's mouth like pellets from a fowling gun. "Get this straight: we do not ask Captain Hamilton for anything. I will not be any more beholden to him than I am now."

In much the same good will, the stallion kicked the wall. Father matched the beast's mood, hurling the saddle onto its rack, making the extra noise that angry people make. After few glances at both horse and saddle, reason brought Father to a truce with the Patriot side.

"Listen, Joe. This Lockwood person owns every horse appurtenance in existence. The wastrel is probably over at The Inn right now, swilling ale. Run down there and snag a sheepskin, however you can get it."

I understood that "no money involved" was the best and only

way. Grateful to leave, I started for the street, but a low growl sounded behind me.

"Joe! Beware of your grandfather: the old trickster will offer you a horse, a saddle, anything he can think of. Next, you'll be invited to be orderly for your Uncle Paul. Then welcome, son, to hell on earth!"

I wished I could look him in the eye and not feel guilty, because this had already happened. But I had no plans to attend a war.

"No answer? Is that because your Uncle Paul has some new-fangled gun? Like to know how digging grooves in a rifle barrel makes the lead fly straighter — another Patriot myth, I'd wager. Go on, admit you admire your Uncle Paul."

"I, uh …." I pictured my uncle's sharp, intelligent-looking face and his sharp, intelligent-looking horse. Yes, I did admire Uncle Paul, but I wasn't going to admit it.

"If you take anything from them, anything at all, your grandfather will have you by the throat. Then forever after, your mouth will speak no words but the words he puts into it. Understand?"

"Yes, sir," I whispered, the only possible answer.

Father drew himself up straight, eyebrows raised. "And tell me, Joe, why would your Patriot friend Lockwood, a grown man, take a sudden liking to a young lad like you?"

I just looked at him, trying to figure out where he was going. I didn't like this strange questioning.

"Well, I'll tell you why, son." He produced a grudging, scornful smile. "You're the replacement for the brother he got killed."

A lurch of hurt hit me. My new friendship had not been strong enough to bring out that Lambert had a brother.

Father directed his thumb toward the dust at our feet. "Just don't get mixed up in rebel business or you'll end up the same way."

I shifted from foot to foot, longing for those feet to get away fast.

A snort and a whinny reminded Father of his beast and he waved me off on my errand.

I started running, but I had to stop and consider what had happened in real life. A few boats sailed somewhere. If Father's panicked rantings constituted fact, people would be running down the streets yelling. All looked quiet enough to me.

Why did Father hate Lambert? Did he just repeat evil gossip?

Deep relief washed away my confusion as I took off to find Lambert Lockwood.

And the truth about a lot of things.

Chapter Six

Thursday, April 24th, 1777
at Six o'Clock of the Afternoon

My recent job-hunting encounter at The Inn had been unpleasant, but I loved passing by this cheerful place. Not seeing much cheer at home, taverns always attracted me. Mostly younger men hung out at The Inn, where conversation and laughter flowed outside on warm nights. I loved hearing men laugh in a way my father never did.

Tonight I could walk right in, head up, and act just like a grown man. If the bartender said anything, I had *business*. Such as it was — borrowing a sheepskin.

I had first met Lambert Lockwood outside the Inn on a frosty February day, after I connected with a certain red chestnut mare tied at the hitching rail. Steam from the horse's breath warmed my numb fingers as I stroked the white stripe down her muzzle. When Lambert appeared, we started to talk as naturally as if we knew each other. I had never seen him in town before, but now I often met him, proceeding to or from his house on Town Street, near the Academy. His cheerful laugh even improved school days. He knew all my uncles on both sides of the family, but as a rebel, he ignored my father, which didn't bother me.

Since Josh had gone, Lambert counted as my own and only adult friend.

Lambert conveyed the military bearing of an officer, even in civilian clothes. He had lost his own clothing in the war. The fine outfits he wore now had belonged to his dead father. His fresh white shirt looked sharp under a canary-yellow vest and dark blue wool coat. His white teeth and dark hair always appeared fresh-washed, rather unusual in a grown-up.

Closer to the tavern, my nose sucked in the mouth-watering air, suffused with applewood smoke accented by pork. Smelling pork or chicken were about the only choices. The rebels had confiscated all the extra cattle a while ago, leaving only milk cows and baby calves. Rebel cattle herds grazed near town, guarded at all hours by dour men with sets of long-barreled horse pistols ranged across their saddle pommels.

At first, I thought that the usual tavern dinner crowd had not assembled yet. Then I noticed at least twenty men huddled as close as frightened sheep. They resembled a church before a funeral — bleak faces, with whispers circulating like the breeze. Tobacco fumes mingled with chimney smoke, adding a mystic air of witchery to the April sunset.

Lambert leaned against the weathered wood siding near the open door, chatting with Dr. Wood. When he caught sight of me, he hurried forward, but not looking pleased, the way he had an hour ago.

"What brought you here, Joe? I am busy this evening." His silken voice now sounded harsh and disturbed. His face, usually a flickering stage of animation and amusement, had condensed into business-like stone.

"My father needs your help — and I do, too, sir." I had never called him sir before, but this seemed like the time to start.

Pushing me back to the street by my elbow, Lambert halted at a stone mounting block, now looking more hurried than angry. He gestured for us both to sink onto the mossy old stones, still warm from the late afternoon spring sun.

"Your conversation was important?" I began, feeling small. Not that I am small, but I saw all too plain that Lambert did not want to be seen talking to me.

"We grow more concerned about the informants who dine here tonight," Lambert said. "At our expense, may I add."

"Are they the men who told about the boats?" This should provide me with a yes-or-no answer on that subject.

The object of the expedition was kept secret by those in command. The next morning, from a point of observation in Norwalk, the fleet was first discovered by our people. Its destination was, of course, a mystery. The fleet passed Norwalk and stood in for the mouth of the Saugatuck River. In that harbor, it dropped anchor. It was now four o'clock in the afternoon of April 25th.

"They *say* they're Patriots, but it's hard to tell what they want — to tell the truth or a free meal." He soon relaxed into being my friend again. The startling sapphire eyes resumed their usual glitter.

"What happened? I only saw you an hour ago." He pulled his legs up, arms around his knees.

"My father needs a sheepskin to go under his saddle. His horse fell and shattered the frame."

"Joe, your father must get rid of that awful beast before it kills him. God's truth."

"I just want a sheepskin for under the saddle. Do you have one or not?" I didn't mean to talk back, but hadn't my father been trying to get rid of the awful beast for months? Everyone in town knew that — and knew why he couldn't.

"If I have a sheepskin, do you have the price?" Lambert questioned with a smirk.

"No!" I snapped back, even more irritated that I had landed in the same unpleasant position of inability to pay.

"I didn't think so." Lambert radiated smug superiority as he rose to his feet. "I shall donate a sheepskin to the accident victim, payment reserved for an unknown time. We must fetch it. Come on."

I had never been invited to Lambert's home before, so I trotted along, just as if nothing unpleasant had been mentioned.

As we went down Town Street, Lambert startled me with, "Is your father going to sign for the local militia or the state crowd, where nobody would know him?"

I bit my lip. "How would I know?" I answered, angry at the repeated teasing.

I cautioned myself to restrain further backtalk. I had no one else to turn to.

"Father wants me to choose a trade, but I've never thought about it before. Now I have to choose by tomorrow!"

Most boys in Danbury did the trade their fathers did, but I didn't know what other choices existed. We didn't have all trades in Danbury. No newspaper, no bank, no gunsmith, no carriage-maker. Kind of sad, really. Those things came from England or New York. Or they didn't come. Last year, two boys left to learn banking in Philadelphia. Father had to explain to me what a bank was.

I had never considered what trade I would do. All Hamiltons farmed and raised stock. Anything else they learned was a winter-time activity only. Father knew how to weave, but hated it. The cloth he and Mother made last winter sat unsold in Major Taylor's shop downtown. Since he had no farm anymore, Father was up against a wall as far as earning a living.

That could happen to me.

"I don't know what to say," I answered. "I like horses, but black-smiths get kicked by colts all the time. Are you still in the army or militia?"

"I work for the Patriot commissary, a hardware store for the army. Tomorrow I visit the new artificer regiment to check our order for the military hospital. Want to come with me and see ten trades, all in one place?"

Had this been a real question, a genuine invitation? I began to glow inside.

"A what kind of regiment?" I had heard this word, but still couldn't say it.

"Ar-ti-fi-cers. Tradesmen enlist in the army, but they make things – harness, ox-yokes, boots. The camp formed last month. It's sort of secret. It's only about five miles away."

I could feel my father's disapproval of any visit to a Patriot army site. How far would he go? Father hadn't hit me since I was five and got spanked for re-baking bread in the fire. Still, to go with Lambert seemed worth any risk.

"Of course I want to go!" I said. I skipped a few steps out of excitement, making Lambert grin. I resolved not to skip any more. Not if anyone could see me.

We walked behind Mrs. Lockwood's imposing gray house, finding an equally imposing barn. Lambert pulled open the barn door and ushered me inside. "Meet Pomp, the Lockwood general manager!" Lambert called, as a smiling curly head popped around a wooden stall post.

A laughing black man said "Lambert, who you friend?" Pomp's smile radiated good will and his voice contained both joy and a heavy African accent. His short, curly hair emphasized the light shone from his eyes at the sight of Lambert. I had seen him before, talking to Mrs. Lockwood's slave Jeda and raking gravel.

"Now here's a first class animal!" Lambert stroked the alert and lively muzzle sticking out over the stall door. As well dressed as her owner, the mare's legs showed four white stockings. She must run as easily as an arrow flies through the air.

"How did you find Desire? She cost a lot, my father says."

"A Tory in Norwalk sold her to avoid confiscation. He didn't want her to go to the army. Their Committee of Safety takes everything, just the same as the Committee of Inspection does here."

Patriots call confiscation supporting the cause of freedom. Other people call it stealing. The Patriots took all the lead doorknockers in town and melted them into bullets. Just one example.

Lambert raised her muzzle to touch his face in a kiss. "Desire is my little girl. Only six years of age and such a badly behaved child!" Lambert said, caressing the "little girl's" soft ears.

It Lambert had fallen off, my father would have told me, probably every day. Which made me wonder just what kind of bad behavior Desire did. Each time I saw her ridden, her reins hung loose as she paced the street in a most dignified manner.

Lambert found his sheepskin among the rolled bundles hanging from the ceiling beams. He bowed when he gave it to me, turning the deed into a ceremony. He should have been a knight in a Shakespeare play.

When he opened the barn door, ready to leave, I recalled Father's accusations about rebel gun stockpiles. I wanted to conduct an investigation, though my main investigation concerned Father's sanity more than the rebels' equipment.

"Lambert, do the Patriots stockpile guns here? How many do they have?"

"Joe! Don't speak of such things!" Lambert said. A warning finger flew to his lips. Pomp's eyes popped open to reveal an excess amount of white. Even the mare turned her startled eyes to me, the cause of the excitement.

He looked around before whispering, "None. Mr. McLean sent them all to West Point for safety. Today."

The Patriots wanted war against the British, so they sent the guns away. I almost laughed.

"Are the militia guns stored in the Commissary?" I couldn't leave it alone.

"The men keep them at home or hide them," Lambert said, speaking fast. He took hold of my sleeve and gave me a sharp push, but I had to know if my father's wild ideas told true. I clamped my fingers onto both sides of the narrow doorframe.

"What about the powder and ball? Is it dangerous to store gunpowder? Or does it need the spark from the flint to explode?"

Lambert's patience snapped in spectacular fashion. "Powder can't explode if it doesn't exist, can it? Are you satisfied now? *No* guns, *no* powder, and *no* flints, neither!"

"The militia has no gunpowder?" I couldn't resist verifying

these admissions. "Or flints?"

"We used all our powder last training day." Lambert mumbled. "As to the flints, who knows why we don't have flints? We just don't."

I plunged on into deepening waters.

"Colonel Huntington's troops that came for smallpox inoculation – do they have flints and powder?"

Patriot army troops had deserted last year when tales of smallpox circulated in Boston. Dr. Franklin opposed the procedure, so my parents did, too. My cousin Amos Benedict died of inoculation. The military hospital however, had a new regiment coming for it every month.

In Session, CT. General Assembly February 21, 1777.
A letter received from Gen. Washington of the 10th of February, Stated… that he had determined to inoculate all the new troops… that he had given directions to Gen. Parsons to superintend the inoculation of the continental troops in Connecticut.

"Colonel Huntington is ordered to leave Danbury on Monday," Lambert said. "It's hard telling, General Washington says one thing and General Parsons says something else. Well, he left here on Tuesday, so we are 'general-less,' so to speak."

From Gen. Sam'l Parsons to Gen. Geo. Washington April 22, 1777
In the course of this Inquiry it appears to be the General Expectation of the Tories that the Enemy will soon land on the Coast about 20 Miles from this place and attempt to secure or destroy the Magazine of Provisions &c. here—…. As the stores here are of great Importance I think it is highly necessary a strong Guard should be kept here—however the Necessity for Men is so great at Camp I shall forward them On to Peekkill….

I accidentally eased my hold on the doorframe and another shove propelled me into the street, faster than I wanted to go.

Lambert almost disjointed my arm as he pushed me down the street. "Don't you go repeating any of this, you hear? Especially not around any Tories – or your father. We don't know about *him*, do we?"

"We?" I choked out, indignant at being included in the Patriot whirlpool that sucked men and boys into in an army with no gunpowder. And no guns, unless you brought your own. As well as your own flints.

Bullets? I didn't dare ask. Doorknockers were in short supply.

Now here I was, mixed up in rebel business — just what my father warned me about. Knowing real secrets is dangerous. You might tell without knowing what you'd done.

The way Lambert had just told me.

How could the Patriots believe in an unarmed army? Were the boat stories just more lies and tricks, meant to lure the reluctant rebel troops to fight? Did the Patriots only guess at things, the same as I did?

When we reached the tavern, I forced out words I had prepared. "Lambert, my father said you lost your brother. Could you and I be brothers? And could you tell me the truth about the war and everything else?"

He halted, his body still leaning in the direction of the tavern. Then he turned and stepped toward me. The lanterns of the building lit the evening fog, and chimney smoke swirled behind him like the molten brimstone flames of a hellish underworld.

"The truth, hey? I already told you more of the truth than I should have told anyone." A pause followed, during which I held my breath. "Agreed, Joe, we'll be brothers. Come here tomorrow after school. We'll ride out to camp together and talk as brothers do." Then Lambert's friends signaled and they all disappeared into the tavern for their dinner of roast pork and spies.

I clutched the rolled sheepskin to my chest and started walking. Time to think about tomorrow made an arrow of fear shoot through me. A new and embarrassing problem lay in my future.

I had accepted an invitation to ride without having a horse.

My walk home slowed to a crawl while I counted over such ponies as I might borrow. The end-of-school ride was tomorrow, meaning nothing doing. I ignored the Number One Answer, the pony mare belonging to Sarah Knapp, next door. I had a good reason. Sarah and I weren't on speaking terms.

Chapter Seven

Thursday, April 24th, 1777
at Half Seven o'Clock of the Evening

The rank odor of two overfed sows welcomed me back to our shed. Although the horse lived there, one stall did not elevate it into being a stable. The smell labeled the building as a pigsty, even though the sows lived outside under a lean-to roof.

Father stood against the fence, gazing at the two porkers. When they farrowed a fleet of piglets next month, our immediate money problems would cease. We would be in possession of money on the cloven hoof. Of my parents' three "investments" — cloth, horse and sows — the future piglets seemed the only one likely to pay off. Maybe I'd get a piglet to play with — not as a pet, as a future ham.

Father stroked the sheepskin just as gently as if the sheep still resided there. He nodded full approval and laid it across his crushed old saddle. His selection of a handful of corncobs indicated afternoon chore time. I knitted bunches of hay onto the three-tined hayfork while I collected the courage to submit a few questions.

From what I heard at school, formal Patriot operations had ended with last fall's loss of Fort Washington in New York. Minor Patriot wins could never make up for that one huge loss, which had allowed British warships up the Hudson River

"If nobody wants to fight any more, how can the Patriots continue the war?" I asked.

Corncobs thumped into an old wooden bucket and Father leaned against the stall planks, watching the horse eat. "Every town has a Committee of Safety or Inspection to drive the war forward. The old Indian-fighter captains like my father front for them, and the militia leaders go along to justify having a militia. The church pounds the war drum, too. The brains behind it are lawyers like your mother's brother Tad. Her other brother, that snake-in-the-grass Judge Tom, pushes from behind, keeping himself 'impartial.' War profiteers, that's what they all are — because otherwise, this supposed revolution would be a lot more successful than it is."

"What about Town meetings? Don't the Loyalists speak up for the law?" I asked. I dumped moldy old hay into the pigsty to give the sows a dry corner. Father followed me to their pen, which surprised me. He usually preferred watching the horse to talking to me.

"Tories vote, but the results of those votes never reach the General Assembly. Afterwards the Loyalist businesses suffer, as the rebel pawns shun law-abiding folks and perform their evil contracts."

Father perked up. "Speaking of contracts — this apprenticeship is not punishment, but a tool for success in life, should anything happen to me. Take your uncle John: in bad weather, he's learning to build furniture. What interests you?"

"I just don't know," I said, maybe sounding more forceful than necessary. After swallowing a few times, I said, "Lambert Lockwood rides to the artificer camp tomorrow. I could see many trades at once. Of course, it is but 'rebel pawns performing their evil contracts.'"

I had resumed a normal voice, pleased once again at parroting Father's own words. I received the frown I had expected, but I walked closer, to make sure he produced a yes or no answer instead of stamping away.

He uttered a resigned sigh. "If it's necessary to reach a quick decision. Who knows where those boats are now?"

Boats again. Once Father got an idea wedged into his brain, he never gave it up.

"There's just one thing," I began. Maybe Father knew of an old pony to borrow. Most likely, his answer would be, "Don't go."

But Father was off and running with his usual disapproval of Patriots.

"Their revolution is so wonderful that these rebels back out as quick as they can. Twenty years old and your friend Lockwood *retired* from the Patriot army? A handsome fool who acts the hero, but his real act is stacking crates in their alleged commissary. It's what reward he got after he crawled home from New York in disgrace."

"Lambert fought with the Danbury militia," I declared. "He's a lieutenant, too." I realized while saying this that I had no idea what had happened in New York. The Patriots lost, but Lambert couldn't be held responsible.

Father's teeth reminded me of a snarling watchdog. "Calls himself 'lieutenant' now, does he?" The raised eyebrows and slow, measured speech formed a clear accusation of lying.

"He never told me that," I said in my own defense, "but I heard two men call him lieutenant."

"Whose body did he crawl over?"

Trying to distract him, I said, "Father, is Lambert's mare faster than your stallion?"

The idea worked, but Father's anger melted into a sly and shimmering satisfaction so fast that I sniffed more bad news on the way. "What does it matter how fast it runs, if the beast is out of control? Last militia training day, Lockwood's mare shot past the captain and kept on running out Elm Street. The creature would have carried your grand hero over a cliff. And for such a runaway, he spent his whole inheritance, I hear."

The rant stopped when he caught movement at our landlord's house next door. Sarah Knapp had opened the door of the big house. The sound of a baby wailing drifted across the yard. She looked right at us and then looked away. My usual luck.

Last fall, Sarah's mother became too weak to care for her little brother and sisters, causing Sarah to drop out of school. For a while, she waved and called greetings, but friendship slipped away with the leaves of autumn. Now, after staring right at me for an entire minute, she shut the door. Girls.

Her father was Benjamin Knapp, a Loyalist Tory and the only person willing to take us in when we left the farm. The rebels had made very exact laws about who could move into towns. I think Father had thought it would be easy to rent from men he knew. It wasn't, so we remained in the tiny cottage, originally meant for servants. Now the Knapps needed a servant, but we still lived there. And Sarah Knapp, at thirteen, had become the household servant.

Father frowned at the sight of Sarah. "You two used to ride together every day, but I never see you speak now. Did you offend that girl?"

He shot an accusing look that gave me the slow burn. "Did you say something that she might not have told her parents?"

"I didn't do anything," I said, my face now roasting hot. "It isn't *my* fault. It's *her* fault." Maybe I only imagined that Sarah Knapp and I used to be best friends. Last summer, we would lead her pony around town with her little brother and sister aboard. Our mothers made us do it, but we loved it anyway. We'd look for thieves or counterfeiters busy receiving lashes at the town whipping post. Later, Sarah and I rode double through the lanes. We galloped close to old ladies and heard them predict our future in hell.

I wanted to forget Sarah Knapp and her pony, but the nagging transportation problem needed a solution. Father had started for the house. I rushed in front and turned to face him. "Lambert Lockwood plans to *ride* to the artificers. On his *horse*," I said, with heavy emphasis on the four-legged word.

Father remained silent as he walked around me – a game he could play, but I could not.

"What could I borrow to ride?" I begged, now forced to hurry as his back moved away from me.

"Two problems solved. Borrow the Knapp girl's pony. You've ridden it before," and he gestured over his shoulder with his thumb.

"She most likely wouldn't let me take Pony," I said as I skittered to catch up again. "Why would she do a favor when she has ignored me for months, not to mention two minutes ago?"

"It's Mr. Knapp's decision, not hers," Father said, his voice growing harder. "Learn to do what is necessary to achieve your goals. Don't let a childish dispute disturb you."

A childish dispute indeed. Lot he knew about it. Although, come to think of it, I didn't know anything about it either.

I had little choice but to follow him through the old kitchen, where his loom and Mother's spinning wheel sat unused. Fighting with Grandfather Hamilton meant no more wool came from the farm. It didn't matter, since no one bought the flannel cloth he had made last winter. The war scared everyone. Continental dollars carried so little value that they bought nothing. Even the Patriots demand that taxes be paid in British money.

Mother felt about the same as usual. I could tell by the lack of dinner plans. No pot heated in the glowing coals, no fresh bread smells lingered in the air. She wandered from window to door to table, touching things, but not *doing* anything. Being a Pacifist ate away at her, not to mention whatever sickness might be eating her alive. She used to spin, used to cook. For the last two weeks, she had stared at her Bible, but the pages didn't turn.

Two weeks. What had happened two weeks ago? How could she

catch disease when she never left home?

"Wife, Joe understands that apprenticeship would be a life choice — not just to keep him safe, but to have a fitting trade. He also understands that Danbury is in danger."

Although I did not understand that at all.

Fear consumed my father the way a fire consumes dry wood. Mother had blamed his experiences as a boy in the War against the French. That war had ended before I was born.

"Just let it be, husband," Mother said in a dead kind of voice. "Constant talk about war only stokes the fire."

"That's what I've been saying all along," Father said, nodding approval at the mention of fire, one of his favorite fears. Then he explained the artificer camp visit, ending with, "Your son is now grown too proud to borrow a pony from the neighbor child, so he may not be going anywhere."

"Go and ask at the Knapps, Joe," Mother said. "Since you and I have been placed in this unfortunate position, we must take responsibility for ourselves." Mother looked, not at me, but at Father. The air around her commenced to crackle with suppressed opinions and strangled anger, different from her usual weak agreement with anything he said. I looked at her, hard. Her pale face contained a new expression — silent and smoldering determination.

The cottage grew dark as dusk approached. Father pointed at me and to the fire. Taking the hint, I fed in a few sticks and muddled around with the iron poker before going to the woodpile outside. When I returned, the flames blazed, lighting my parents' haggard faces. Mother came to life a bit, stood and looked around, as I dumped a heavier log atop the kindling.

Father fetched the jug of ale from two days ago, sticking out his tongue in disgust after he smelled it. A dusty, but half-full jug of cider promised better. Mother slapped pewter plates down on the table and dumped last week's rye bread ends onto a piece of wood. My heart sank when she produced the box of dried herring. Father loved them. Bloaters, he called them. Mother served them right out of the box. Cold and dry, no cooking needed. I wished they had removed the insides. The heads, too.

Father plunged a fish into his mouth before jamming the heel of a bread loaf in after it. He followed with a slug of cider. Mother made no more progress at eating than I did. Five minutes passed without a word, during which Mother picked at her bread, turning it into crumbs.

I stared at the blind fish eyes before me. I could not eat one. Father ate three, head first down his throat, fins and all.

Mother looked up. "If you are not going to the Knapps, Joe, eat the meal God gave you." That determined look settled on her face again.

Sarah Knapp or sardines. What a choice.

Chapter Eight

Thursday, April 24th, 1777
at Seven o'Clock of the Evening

"You will conquer your childish pride, young master!" Father's chair skidded away from the table as he snatched at my shirt collar and ushered me out the door. This felt not all bad from my point of view. If Father borrowed the pony *for* me, I wouldn't have to ask Sarah for anything.

"You say you want to go to that rebel place, and go you will. Your trade must be decided by tomorrow." Like driving a sheep in front of him, Father herded me over the stile steps separating our yard from the Knapps.

Mr. Ben Knapp rested on a bench outside his roomy horse barn. After dinner, he and Father would sit there, discussing the problems of Danbury. Mr. Knapp looked ready for church or court. He always changed clothes after work to rid himself of the disgusting corpse smell from the cowhides in his leather tannery. Then he went to one of the nearby taverns, purchased dinner for his family, and carried it home in a tin pail, his ale pail in the other hand.

"Ah, Master Joseph! To what do we owe this rare honor?" Mr. Knapp beamed at me.

Sarah slipped out of the house and ran to her father, giving me opportunity to examine her. Close up, she looked a lot older than thirteen. Not exactly older. More like a miserable thirteen.

Her new face, all its former cheer faded, made me wonder where the girl I remembered had gone. In truth, she looked about to cry. The crying baby in the house gave both reason and example.

"Sarah, look who's here," said Mr. Knapp, pointing at me as if

I were indeed a prize sheep.

"Oh," she said. Her head turned, but only as if she heard a noise in the street. She wrapped an arm around her father's waist and rested her face against his tan vest. His arm slid around her. She looked ragged — not her apron or skirt, but *her*. A face that hadn't seen the sun yet this spring. A face that might not smile when it did see the sun.

Father pulled me close, too, but he held me by my left ear. "Joe must ride with a grown person tomorrow, but he has no mount. Might he borrow your pony?"

"What's your answer to Mr. Hamilton, young miss?" asked her father, holding Sarah away from him.

Her face lifted with a thought. "Could Joe watch Noah ride the pony right now? Noah and Mercy pinch each other and fight. Then the baby cries. I can't stand it," she said.

When I nodded, Sarah made for her house without waiting for any other answer. I had served her purpose. And she hadn't said one word to me.

I wouldn't mind riding double with little Noah. A comfortable seat on an energetic beast is not easy without recent practice. Falling off the pony on Main Street would be a disaster.

Noah dashed outside, jumping with joy. "Joe! Joe!" His little arms went around my knees, as I struggled through the barn door. Mr. Knapp untied the pony and reached for the little bridle, hanging on a wooden peg.

"Going visiting, are you, Joe?" Mr. Knapp slipped the bit into Pony's mouth and adjusted the bridle. I had always liked this sprightly man, as nice to young folk as he was to adults.

"Yes, sir." I stopped there, not wanting Mr. Knapp's Tory ears to learn about the artificer camp.

"No animal of your own in sight, lad? Your grandfather owns such a wide *range* of beasts." Mr. Knapp did not sound approving. How did he know what horses Grandfather owned?

"No point in asking for a pony in our family," I said, which was the truth, for sure.

"No, I suppose not," Mr. Knapp muttered.

He dropped the reins over Pony's head and held out his cupped hands. "Here, Noah! Up you go." Noah's foot bounced from the hand and he sat safely aboard. Unconcerned, he trotted away, reins flopping.

Mr. Knapp looked proud, saying, "Now that he's six, he rides by himself just fine. Keep an eye on him, Joe, or he'll fetch up a mile away from here."

Angry at still being on foot, I watched the pony's tail bounce up the quiet lane toward the tannery. My too-tight shoes pinched in new and amazing places as I began a slow run. I felt every stone as I wondered how long those shoes would hold together.

The sun had slipped toward the horizon before we returned. An ecstatic Noah jumped from his steed and raced to the back-house. I led the little mare into the barn through gathering shadows and turned her out.

When I returned, I stopped moving as I reached the door-way and poked my head out, just to look around. If Father and Ben Knapp were still there, I wanted to overhear their talk. What adults said to each other might be far different from what they said to me. Would my father be talking about the boats to Mr. Knapp? Or was that a ploy to get me onto the apprenticeship road?

The two men stood by their bench in the half-dark, clutch-ing each other's arms the way ladies do. Every word resounded in the still evening air.

"Why this needless fear and worry?" Mr. Knapp sounded as if he were soothing a crying child. "If British troops do come here, England plans no injury to her loyal citizens. Of course, those trai-tors-in-chief, the Committee of Inspection, had better hit the road, your Captain Hamilton included. A noose hangs ready for those petty tyrants."

"Do you truly believe we're safe from attack, Ben?"

"British leaders are gentlemen, decent men, but stockpiling of guns in our town must stop. We have to suffocate this revolt be-fore an explosion occurs. Glad you never joined that lot." Mr. Knapp laid his hand on Father's shoulder.

Father's voice softened as he declared, "Separation from England must not come by killing the British soldiers who saved us from the French. When American leaders didn't know how to lead, the British Army came to our side, taught us, and paid us to save ourselves. Your children and my children will thank us for opposing another devastating war. No destruction in Connecticut: not on our watch, anyhow."

"Whatever happens," came Mr. Knapp's calm and reassuring voice, "We'll watch out for each other's families like brothers, will we not? Give me your hand on it."

They clasped hands and remained so, looking into each other's eyes with perfect trust.

My father had a new brother, too. This one was Tory.

Chapter Nine

Friday, April 25th, 1777
at Nine o'Clock of the Morning

The morning sun radiated its dreamy warmth right through my jacket and shirt as I slipped out the door, ready for the last day of school. Violets flooded the grass, and clumps of bluebells surrounded the bridge and the stone wall that ran the length of Town Street. Even the ground smelled fresh for my walk to the Academy.

Today would close with the usual end-of-term gingerbread and lemonade feast, but what did I care? Nothing could be better than seeing a real army camp and riding there with Lambert Lockwood.

Friday morning passed in a haze of expectation. My only worry revolved around Lambert riding a saddle awhile I perched atop slick and shiny fox-colored fur. Pony was a carthorse for the tannery, plus a children's plaything, never meant for long distance transportation. Still, why didn't they have a saddle?

The schoolroom morning droned on, mostly with summing up and giving a few small awards. Schoolmaster was unfair, since each of the two girls won an award, and I did not.

I decided during the morning to choose my trade by how happy the men in that trade appeared to be. The actual work of apprenticeship would drag on all day, every day. Like school.

At noon pause, David Weed wanted to commiserate about my lost tavern job. I passed him a dried apple, hoping he would chew it and keep quiet. Today I was the one bursting with news.

"Hear this," I said. "My father says I should apprentice, too!"

"What trade will you learn, Joe?" David turned bright-eyed with interest.

"I don't know, but I might find out soon. Today, maybe." I turned my face to the sun. I no longer cared whether the apprenticeship worked out well or not. I just felt through with my parents' dismal outlook on life. Maybe my mother's snappish attitude indicated that she felt about through with it, too.

David's interested smile disappeared. "Say, Joe?" His question sounded anxious. "Is your family going away?"

"No, *I'll* be the one going away." Silly boy.

"I mean, if the British army comes here. You know, the boats…."

The boats. Lambert had no fears about them, and he knew all about spies. Mr. Knapp wasn't worried. This boy's mother and my father must carry the same madness in their heads.

"Wouldn't seeing an army on the march be a sight to remember for the rest of your life?" I asked David. "Even if the tax money paid to England goes for horses and uniforms, it would still be beautiful. What if we get into a war with the French again? They'd help us, the way they did before."

"Where does the money for Patriot soldiers come from, Joe?"

"It looks to me like the Patriots don't *have* any money. Or they print it. Dr. Ben Franklin was a printer. Maybe I should learn printing," I speculated, just to make him laugh

We passed our last school afternoon by reading a play from our one Shakespeare book. The best part was where King Richard yelled, "A horse! A horse! My kingdom for a horse!" I liked the horse idea, but not King Richard, who seemed to have it in for folks my age.

My after-school adventure began when I arrived at the Knapp's barn. Going to the artificers excited me more than anything I could remember. I retrieved the pony bridle from its peg and walked out to bring Pony in from her paddock. I put the reins around her neck, already worried about bridling her. I had only done it once or twice last year. Sure enough, the afternoon soured as I attempted to place the bit in her mouth. Whenever I pressed the metal bit against her teeth, she threw her head in all directions. Her final opinion included slashing at my leg with her front foot. The bone hurt like fire. This equine had changed from furry to fury.

The battle ended when the little beast smacked me with her head, almost breaking my nose. Holding my hand to my stinging face, I checked for a nosebleed. Then I hit the jagged edge of tears.

I closed my eyes from embarrassment as I tapped on the Knapp's front door, maybe harder than I should have. I shifted from foot to foot while I waited. I hated asking for Sarah's help.

Mercy, Sarah's ten-year-old firebrand sister, reached the door first. "What do *you* want?" she demanded, as rude as ever. Her cap and apron sat askew. A dark smear lay across her face, perhaps apples cooked with spices. Robins could have nested in Mercy's snarled hair.

"Could Sarah show me how to bridle the pony?" I asked, my voice cracking.

My appearance kindled a firestorm in the form of Noah, who skidded around the corner of the kitchen door. Careening through the door, he raced outside, barefoot. "Joe! Joe, can we ride again? Please! Let's go!"

"Who is there, Mercy? Child? Who knocked?" called Mrs. Knapp from her room.

Oh, good, now I had bothered a sick woman. I might hear about that.

"It's only Joe Hamilton! He wants to ride the pony!" bawled Mercy at the top of her lungs.

"Joe?" Sarah came flying down the stairs, slamming into me as she reached the doorway, plummeting both of us back outside. We grabbed onto each other to keep from falling.

Mercy danced to the door, pointing and laughing with evil glee. "Here's your gentleman friend to visit! Just like you wanted!"

Sarah jerked the door shut in her face as I stood there, dumbfounded by Mercy's teasing remark.

"What do you want now?" Sarah demanded, breathless with irritation. Her white apron and hands exhibited the same smears as Mercy's face. "Just take the pony and go where you're going." Her finger pointed towards Town Street, and her expression suggested I use all possible speed.

"I couldn't get the bridle on, no matter what I did." I hoped that being humble would produce the best result.

"Noah!" shouted Sarah, as she bounded off the stone doorstep in search of the escapee.

I followed her angry progress toward the barn, but when we arrived, a happy Noah emerged, leading the bridled pony. Sarah grabbed the rein, pointed at the bit in the pony's mouth, and shot me a glare that could have melted horseshoes.

Noah stood by the pony's side, his raised hands imploring me to lift him.

If Sarah wanted me to feel embarrassed, I could turn it back on her. "Sarah, why do we never ride together now? We could ride after your father comes home at night."

"Ride together?" she shrieked. "On what? We grew. Both of us together would be the same as a grown-up man. You just tell me: where is Arthur?" She faced me, coming closer than I liked. Who knew what angry girls might do?

"Where is what?" I wasn't sure what she had said.

"My horse! My new riding horse that my father bought me to make up for leaving school."

"*What* horse?" I had never once seen Sarah on a real horse.

"Why don't you ask Captain Hamilton, *what horse*? Your grandfather. He's the one that did it." Sarah looked to be in a rage. She whipped off her cap and hurled it to the ground, letting down a mass of uncombed auburn hair.

"*What* did my grandfather do?" I asked.

"I hope those Committeemen rot in hellfire, and your grandfather is most welcome to go with them!" Having had the last word, Sarah swept her cap off the ground, then yanked Noah's arm hard enough to disjoint it. The little boy turned a sad and accusing face when he saw me prepare to mount Pony.

Once safely aboard, I turned toward the road, passing the Knapp's house. Sarah still stood in the doorway, her face without expression. Then the green paneled door swung shut, the polished brass lock giving a dignified click. I just shook my head. Why had Sarah Knapp formed such hatred of my grandfather?

And what horse was she talking about? Had it ever existed?

Chapter Ten

Friday, April 25th, 1777
at Four o'Clock of the Afternoon

I reached Lambert's house with my fingers twisted in Pony's mane, gasping for breath, but at more or less the correct time.

"Good afternoon, sir," Lambert called, as he led Desire out of the barn. Pomp held the saddle in place while Lambert swung aboard and took up his reins. Then Pomp swished the dust from Lambert's knee-high black boots and watched us leave, smiling like a proud father.

Lambert turned to admire me on Pony. "Did you just get this creature? You're making progress in life!"

"She belongs to Mr. Benjamin Knapp's daughter." I wondered if mentioning a Tory might be offensive. In Danbury, it was hard not to say the wrong thing.

"You should have an animal of your own. Your grandfather must have fifty horses."

"*Fifty*?" I repeated. "He only had thirty horses last year, when we left the farm."

"When Captain Hamilton pays sympathy calls, whoever he visits pays more."

"What do you mean?" Grandfather had told me to wake up to facts. I intended to find out every fact I could, from now on. Every fact about everyone in town.

"Last Christmas, your grandfather visited the families whose soldiers sat in prison in New York. His holiday greeting would be an offer to buy their beasts. Neighbors waited a decent amount of time, not wanting to appear convinced that the soldiers would never return. They would offer three times the price the widow had received. But the horses were already sold."

I remembered only a smiling Grandfather, wearing a shapeless farmer hat, while he introduced baby lambs and calves. He would plop me onto the backs of broodmares with foals trailing behind and then lead us around the pasture. His eyes gleamed the palest blue, bleached almost white by age and sun. And perhaps by the things he had seen.

I had loved him once. When I was little.

"Lambert, my grandfather's only an old farmer who rents horses, right? How could he have any power to make people do things?"

"After the war against the French, your grandfather proved to the bigwigs that he could deliver the goods. *Any* goods. He set up the whole school system for Danbury, eleven schools, built the buildings, hired the teachers. On the Committee of Inspection, some men think, and some men do the deeds. Your grandfather does the deeds." Lambert smiled with the over-kindly smile of patient people who answer stupid questions.

"*What* deeds?" A suspicion arose in me that those deeds possessed a life of their own.

"He goes from farm to farm, inspecting. If he finds boys, he recruits them. If they won't enlist, he inspects their homes for extra blankets or shoes. When Captain Hamilton collects, he often has, uh, *friends* with him." I suddenly imagined the arrival of Grandfather and my three uncles. Pleasant, reasonable — carrying the force of Patriot law. Resisting would be impossible.

I compared Grandfather's "deeds" with Isaiah's preparations for enlistment.

"What if those men or boys *do* enlist?" I asked, as we turned left onto South Street, and right again, out Shelter Rock Road.

"About the same thing. But, Joe, he *has* to do it. Our troops leave bloody footprints in the snow and eat dogs, when they can find any. There's not enough weaving or shoe-making in all the colonies to keep our men warm and dry. There's not enough guns. There's not enough of anything. That's why I left off fighting and why Captain Stone started the artificer corp.

Ct. General Assembly
In session March 20, 1777
...was directed to purchase 20,000 weight of cheese ... provided he should be unable to purchase the same, and (supply was) found in the hands of any person, more than was sufficient for their family's use, he was authorized to seize and take the same for the purpose aforesaid, and pay them the price fixed by law,

After this speech, I wondered about the Knapps. Had an inspection occurred? But I had never seen any horse there except Pony and the ancient gelding Mr. Knapp rode.

The empty, pale green hills of Shelter Rock Road spread out before us like food on a plate. Two oxen dragged a plow far in the distance, but the rocky ground retained no furrow. So far, war had torn no furrows in Connecticut, either.

Sweat beaded on my face. I had occasionally trotted an old rental horse around the pasture at the farm. I had ridden behind my father and grandfather, but I had never ridden *with* a grown person. Trotting or cantering might be my downfall, in every sense of the word.

I decided to slow my companion down by asking questions. "Lambert, do you fear the British coming here?"

Lambert glanced sideways at me. "Tomorrow is payday. That's all I worry about." I sniffed real concern.

"You fear you won't get paid?"

"Sometime government money doesn't come, so Dr. Wood pays me with his own money. Dr. Foster spends *his* own money on hospital equipment. He says Congress owes him $20,000."

"So the Patriots have no guns and no money," I declared, saying it like a final decision.

Lambert remained silent.

"Do Patriot soldiers ever receive the money they're promised?"

"Soldiers join on promise of future payment only."

Lambert's words seemed to make him angry, and he started his mare into a brisk trot. From then on, all I saw was his methodical rising in his stirrups to avoid the painful bouncing. I grit my teeth in silence as I bounced along.

I longed for a saddle — or I thought I did, since I had never ridden one.

Chapter Eleven

Friday, April 25th, 1777
at Five o'Clock of the Afternoon

I let out a sigh of relief as Lambert slowed to a walk. With no warning, he dodged around an angled turn and behind a giant rock. If you didn't know the way, the rock concealed the tracks of anyone who had turned off the road there. Our mounts picked along a rock-strewn trail that twined between the gray granite ledges of a ridge. An army camp in the middle of nowhere had to make noise, but I heard only the tweeting of the robins and the calls of the jays.

Startled hawks flew overhead as we crested the hill. Then the path dropped into a shadowy valley. Another world revealed itself when we reemerged into the sun. Here smoke rose, mingling with the smell of new-sawn wood. Combined with the aroma of the pine trees overhead, the perfumed air filled me with a desire to race into the artificers' camp as fast as Pony could canter.

Tents appeared, a collection painted in golden yellows, dirt-color tans, or the scarlet red of fall leaves. Hammers and adzes attacked iron and wood with happy violence. Men shouted orders, threats and greetings, while bits of song drifted like the smoke. Picket lines of horses and oxen waited in a ring around the camp, many asleep standing up.

Our horses' ears pricked forward with the same keenness I felt. My nose extracted one more enticing smell. "Is that bread baking?" I asked. The scent floated on the air, so layered and powerful that it must fuel all the energy in camp.

"A squad of bakers arrived this week," Lambert replied. "Their ovens must be well tuned by now. Captain Stone can ship bread to soldiers in other states. Hard bread is still bread. You just soak it in water."

"Sounds like prison fare," I muttered. One more mark against enlistment.

"Captain Stone, sir!" Lambert gave a sharp salute as a workman in tattered clothes flashed a delighted smile.

"And a good day to you, Lieutenant!" Captain Stone returned the salute. Sure enough, a captain had acknowledged Lambert to be a lieutenant.

Taking any excuse to stop work, several men yelled, "Hey, Sergeant!"

"I thought you were a lieutenant." My father's absolute fury at hearing me use that title still made me wonder.

"I'll explain later," he answered. Although he could have explained right then.

Stacks of rough chestnut and ash lumber surrounded a dozen wagons in various stages of construction. Pegs in holes fitted the boards together and iron braces attached the sides to the bottoms of the wagons.

"The wagons will carry the bread?" I asked.

"Plenty of food sat available for Valley Forge last winter, but no wagon transport system existed."

While we let our horses stroll around the camp, a bass voice started a chant.

"Like church singing class, only better!" I said. "The foolery we used to do in the church every Sunday night was the best thing! Now I'm not allowed to go. There isn't even a minister there anymore, but the singing class goes right on. I wish I could go."

"Just tell your parents. Stand up for yourself!" Lambert said. "Young folk do have rights. '...life, liberty and pursuit of happiness,' you know. Just what the Declaration of Independence said."

I didn't answer. That I had rights was news to me. I couldn't tell if stating what I wanted meant disobeying. But I was beginning to wonder.

"See the ox-yokes over there?" Lambert pointed to crude posts, hung with wooden yokes ready to fit to ox teams. "You could saw and whittle and carve."

"Forget oxen," I said. "They walk slower than stock-still. Once I saw a man driving one horse and two oxen. How the horse could stand it, I don't know. I only like two things, horses and food." Lambert laughed, which was what I had wanted.

It was the truth, too.

Picket lines surrounded us. Assorted carthorses stood tied to linked ropes that led from tree to tree.

"I could be a teamster. And there's packhorses, too." Packhorse parades, the horses sporting ribbons of their company's color, walked regular routes, delivering goods. Most roads weren't wide enough for a team. A downed tree would stop a freight wagon cold.

"Do you know how to drive horses, Joe?"

"No, but I could learn. Then I would eat in all the different taverns along my route."

"You'd be sucking bread crusts out of your pocket! Then one day, in New York or Pennsylvania, an officer would threaten to horsewhip you unless you hitched your team to his cannon. Usually, his previous team is dead. You'd never see your animals again."

The idea of seeing dead horses horrified me. It seemed a good way to lose your job.

Lambert dropped the conversation to wave at a soldier and point to a pile of goods awaiting shipment.

"What did you buy?" It looked like boards wrapped in rope.

"Forty cradles."

"Cradles? In a military hospital? Cradles are for babies." He must be teasing me.

"Cradles are hammocks with wood frames. They hang from the hospital's ceiling beams, leaving the floors clear to see rats or bugs. Or blood, in case something's dripping. We have to be ready for wounded, you know," Lambert explained.

"What wounded? No battles ever happened in Connecticut," I answered.

"Men and boys talk of 'going to war.' They can't imagine that war is coming to them. Joe, the Patriots are not going to give up. Ever. It's only a matter of time until —" Lambert stopped as the artificer approached to discuss delivery and payment.

Left to myself, curiosity drew me closer to the horse picket line. Two men joked as they brushed down a team of stout dark bay horses, both sporting long black manes and tails. I walked Pony closer to the team, whose soft warm eyes promised undying effort. Until they were killed in action, if Lambert's predictions came true.

Sharp little ears snapped to attention, and one beast snuffled a half-whinny. Next, my own two legs flew over my head as they followed my body through the air. The rotation completed when I smacked into the muddy ground. Sharp surprise. Sudden impact.

Sprawled in dust well churned with natural products, I tried to breathe. I became frantic, making horrible gagging noises until one bit of air was followed by more. A raft of sniggers accompanied the grinning attention of a dozen soldiers, including one who clapped.

After a long minute, I dragged myself to my knees, checking bone-by-bone for anything cracked. A man jumped forward and lifted me by my armpits. I prayed that when he dropped his hands, I could keep my feet. My mind and body felt too shocked to do anything, except try to put one foot in front of the other. My fall had jarred a shoe loose. I hopped like a frog while I put it on again. More clapping.

Pony had rushed to the team. When the three touched noses, great snorting and squealing broke out. A teamster retrieved her and was decent enough to snuff out his laugh before handing over the reins.

I wiped the dirt from my hands onto Pony's fur – her punishment. I had been rattled so hard that I couldn't dream of mounting again. I walked back to Desire, still with no idea why the safe old pony mare had dumped me.

To my irritation, Lambert burst out laughing. "Joe, isn't this animal part of the team Mr. Knapp bought in Cornwall last fall?"

"I never saw them before," I said.

"Well, *I* saw Ben Knapp drive them through town the day after he bought them," Lambert stated. "They would have made friends with your pony that first night. As fine as those hay-burners look, your grandfather must have been on their trail within five minutes. Bought them same as the others I told you about — for any price he chose." Lambert looked satisfied at unraveling the puzzle, but it all carried special meaning to me.

"If Mr. Knapp didn't want to sell, he should have said so," was my curt reply. I hadn't recovered enough to be polite.

"He *had* to sell them whether he wanted to or not. The Committee could jail a man for refusing to relinquish horses during wartime."

"Could Sarah lose Pony if a Patriot wanted her?" I looked around, just to see what eyes were looking back.

"I don't think she has a good reputation as a mount right now," Lambert answered.

"If I have rights, don't Tories have rights? Can't Mr. Knapp go to court?"

"The court is solid Patriot, through and through. He can go to court. Judge Benedict and Lawyer Benedict will be as polite as can be.

Then the case is continued for six months. Then it will be continued again." Soul-deep satisfaction beamed from his smiling face. He turned away, walking Desire along the line of tents. I followed, rather more dispirited than before. Until I saw the saddle racks.

Lambert indicated a dark red tent and its occupant. "Here's a man you should meet, Joe. Maybe the saddler's knife and awl are your future."

A man with curly brown hair to his shoulders looked up from his leatherwork. "Good morning, Lieutenant." I liked his smile. I liked the man's whole face. I liked that he called Lambert "Lieutenant."

"This young gentleman is in need of a trade, Private Gorton. His family provides militia horses." Lambert smiled as brilliantly as a tin salesman.

"Must be the Captain's grandson, eh? Interested in the art and science of saddle-fitting, are you?" He gestured at the three new saddles sitting atop a sawhorse. "Want to produce a few like this for your country?"

"Yes, sir." My own swift words surprised me. Maybe it came from envying the saddle shop Cousin Josh had given up so easily. If I had owned that saddle shop, the Patriots would have had to blast me out of it with cannon. On cold Connecticut winter days, I had felt so happy to stop on my way home and suck in the leather smell of new reins, breastplates and saddlebags.

A survey of future customers produced higher mathematics. If Captain Silas Hamilton rented out fifty horses, fifty saddles and bridles formed part of the deal. My parents might not be popular with the Patriots, but *I* would be, for sure. Saddlery would solve all of my problems. Learning my trade here would be the best place imaginable, less than half an hour from Danbury.

The imagined clientele gave me a big grin. "Could I apprentice here, with you?"

I had conveniently forgotten that Private Gorton was a rebel. No matter what the answer was, my parents would have none of it.

Daniel Gorton .... In 1777 joined Major Paintor's regiment of artificers for three years, at fourteen dollars per month. Remained through the winter at Bethel, a little east of Danbury, Conn., which has just been burned...

"Ah, that's another matter, young gent," the saddler said. "This is an army camp, not a tradesman's shop. Only take those as finished the full seven years of apprenticeship."

I gave him a fishy look, since Private Gorton didn't look old enough to have done seven years himself.

"I can see what you're thinking, but yes, I apprenticed when I was fourteen, about your age, I guess."

The saddler put an arm around my shoulders and pointed out a soldier working in the next area. "We had another feller who *claimed* to be a saddler, but we converted him to the harness making trade. No skill needed." The man heard the jab and cast a joker's glance our way. I was thrilled to see a well-known face.

"Josh!" I yelled out. Half-hidden under his floppy hat was my cousin Josh Benedict, the disappeared saddler of Danbury. He darted over and swung me right off the ground. I did not find it manly to be dangling in the air, but a good kick in Josh's shinbone dropped me back to solid ground. I then received a clap on the back that almost drove me into the dirt. When I looked up, we just grinned at each other and kept on grinning.

"Hey, Joseph! How did you get here? And with the elegant Mr. Lockwood! Turning Patriot are we, Joe?" I didn't care what teasing I got, I was so thrilled to see him. He was twenty-three and married, but he still acted young, like me.

"Your sign said you enlisted, but you're still here!" I shouted. Josh was real family, the family I had missed. Overjoyed was only a small part of it.

Josh pulled me in tight, a thing my father never did anymore. "Artificers belong to the army, so that part's true. I can help the Patriot cause right here, without fear of smallpox or cannonballs."

"You don't make saddles anymore?" I asked.

"Wagon harness was in short supply. I do what will make the biggest difference to our troops. One wagon will bring food for a hundred men. Watch this!" He sharpened his knife before shaving the edge off a rein over twenty feet long. The rein led from the bit in the horse's mouth back to the driver's hand. A thin place could bring disaster.

"I came here to choose my trade, Josh. I wish I could apprentice with you," I said, longing to stay in camp with him.

Josh stopped his work and searched my face. "Joe, don't run away to war. It's a dreadful business. I'll teach you saddlery when the war is over," he said.

"You would be my master for my whole apprenticeship?"

"Of course I would. We need to pull our family together again. My father and your mother, brother and sister, shouldn't be on opposite sides." Josh's father was my uncle, Judge Tom Benedict.

The sun had drifted over the mountain, leaving Josh's worksite overtaken by shadows. He took the planks of his cutting table apart and put his wares away. We rejoined Lambert and the saddler.

"How does leatherwork sound to you, Master Joe?" asked Lambert, while giving me a boost onto my mount.

"I don't know ... fitting horse trappings would satisfy me just fine, but ...."

"But what?" demanded Lambert, looking anxious to head home.

"Father wants me to learn a trade *now*. Josh would teach me after the war's over, but I have to apprentice right away. And Father wants me to leave Danbury."

"Then let your father search out a master saddler," Private Gorton said. "Plenty of fine men out there. Learned in Norwich myself."

"Where's that town?" I asked. Maybe I could find my own master saddler.

"By New London, on Long Island Sound's waters. Beautiful to see the ships flying all sail."

If it was by the sea, it had my vote, for sure.

Lambert remounted and I turned to say good-bye to Josh.

"Joe, wait." Josh leaned in close to me and murmured, "If trouble comes to Danbury, tell your mother not to worry. I'll be safe at Stony Hill."

I tried to understand what trouble he meant and what the tiny settlement of Stony Hill had to do with it. The connections soon floated to the top.

Boats. And Josh's wife came from Stony Hill.

This answer arrived with a shock. "You mean, if the British come, you're going to *hide*?" Patriot soldiers hiding with their in-laws only confirmed the bad things my father said.

"The artificers form the backbone of the army," Josh explained. "Tools and tents may be destroyed, but *we* have to survive or the whole army will sink." The saddler nodded agreement. All three men looked serious as death.

"The militia could never defend Danbury," explained the saddler. "Any child knows that."

No words came to me, just a sinking feeling. This particular child had already figured it out.

Joel W. Church, a pensioner … swears that he knew Captain Levi Stone during the war of the revolution …he knows that said Stone was captain of the artificer corps from March, 1777, to August, 1779. That he had thirty or forty artificers under his command; that said company was raised under the quartermaster's department; that said company was raised by said Captain Stone, under the direction of Major Wood, a quartermaster general.

Chapter Twelve

Friday, April 25, 1777
at Six o'Clock of the Evening

Lambert and I turned our horses' heads back toward Danbury, passing the camp's open-air kitchen, which featured a steaming iron cauldron the size of a washtub. Men formed a line, and the warm evening breeze carried the powerful scent of beef stew as it sloshed into each passing tin plate. Army life appeared like a cheerful fellowship, complete with meat.

The saddler arrived and perched on a stump in the center of the company. Bringing out a fife, he commenced a concert such as I never imagined. The men clapped and called encouragement. Having lived without music for many months, I hated to leave.

Lambert waved as we passed by. The wave reflected back to us in smiles and a few salutes. I hoped none of those smiles resulted from my muddy fall.

An early owl hooted from a nearby tree and a wolf howled in the distance. Answers came from wolves on other hills. I had never seen a wolf, but I wanted to, for sure.

"A fine end to our day. You found your trade and your cousin, too." Lambert looked pleased with himself, as he 'most always did.

I decided to cut to the heart of my problem, even if it was embarrassing. "Father may wind up in jail due to the law about enlistment. I have to find an apprenticeship right now."

"You could learn about leather in a cobbler's shop. Mr. Knapp's brother is a cobbler."

"Father says Patriot boys might knock out my teeth if I work for a Tory. Is there a Patriot cobbler?"

"Hardly. Our last Patriot cobbler should hang by the neck until — well, you know...." Lambert assumed a sour expression.

"What did he do? Was he a criminal?"

"I met that scum of a cobbler, Enoch Crosby, in the Danbury militia. He seemed wonderful to me when I was but seventeen years old. So open, so full of common sense. I was too young to see the truth. Crosby ran off last year, to spy for the British. A shoot-on-sight, if there ever was one." Lambert blew out a breath between his teeth.

"I hate to admit it, Joe, but when Enoch Crosby turned traitor, it hurt me worse than my own father's death. I couldn't believe it." He sighed, as if the subject hurt him still.

"He had no family here?".

"No, he came from New York. Typical spy behavior — fool people into trusting them and have no strings to trace. Funny thing was, Captain Hamilton was fooled as much as anyone. He thought Enoch Crosby was his best friend in life. Can you beat that? A British spy."

"Wait a minute! Nobody could fool my grandfather."

"Joe, part of growing up is discovering that criminals can be nice and smart, too. The Patriots caught him twice, but the scoundrel escaped. He moves as free as the air that blows over your face. Why? Because whoever meets him trusts him immediately. If Crosby ever comes back here, your grandfather had better watch out for the hangman's noose. The old man would forget to be afraid. He loved Crosby; always rode with him, if he could. I'll put a bullet through that lying spy, if I ever spot him again. No questions asked"

What a strange story. If I ever saw Grandfather again, I'd check this story out, for sure.

Cream and copper clouds, lit by the sinking sun, made a glorious pre-sunset. A barred owl of massive wingspan flapped down from a towering sycamore, flying low and slow, sailing the grassland, in search of an evening victim. The owl sank toward the ground, then powered aloft, wings flapping in victory, a baby rabbit drooping from its claws. The speed and accuracy of the attack impressed me. The slow search for opportunity, ending with the instant decision to kill. Maybe spies make those same decisions.

Lambert pointed up the road. "Looks like a late delivery for the camp."

An ox cart approached on the narrow country road. Riders could move along the road's edges, but a heavy freight cart had to stay in the hard center tracks to keep moving. We pulled over while the overloaded vehicle drew closer.

The swaying bulk of the wagon emitted clanks and screeches, causing our mounts to shiver with suppressed fear. Two oxen crawled along, while bedsteads and cherry chests rocked against a polished walnut desk. Poking out around carpets and feather bedding, a tall-case clock looked lost without the dignity of its former home. Three children topped the load, jabbing each other and giggling.

"It can't be her, it can't be," Lambert whispered, as he reined Desire to face the newcomers and eased closer to the track, an activity not favored by his fiery mare.

The driver and a lady occupied the wagon seat, the lady's identity half-hidden by an elegant hat with a plume. Her arms lay crossed atop a leather hat case. The stark white face kept an expression of wooden politeness, but her lips did not open until she drew even with us.

"Good afternoon, Lieutenant Lockwood." The woman displayed a familiar frozen attitude. Her face resembled my mother's appearance during the last several weeks. Mother had seemed quite like this lady, her face gone as rigid as a painting.

"Missus McLean, ma'am, where are you – ah…*going*, thus arrayed?" Lambert sounded like a part in a Shakespeare play, but his face had mildewed to a greenish color.

"This invasion talk compels action before it's too late. With a house full of fine items imported from London, I —" she began.

"From the *Oppressor*, ma'am, items imported from the *Oppressor*," corrected Lambert.

"Yes…, the Oppressor," the lady mumbled, repeating his words as if too weak to resist.

"When may we anticipate your return home?" Lambert used warm and elegant speech, as if he conversed with a queen.

The lady's frigid eyes cut back to us. "I shall *not* return to Danbury." The mouth shut. The chin lifted. Her attention shifted back to the road ahead. She gestured to the driver to keep moving.

The oxen ground onward at their worm-like speed. The children waved. And so the wife of John McLean, head of the Continental Army Commissary, fled her distinguished home. Lambert looked devastated, mouth open and eyes staring like a dead rabbit's.

"Lambert, are the British coming to Danbury or not?"

Why was I always asking this question? The answer was always the same, whether from Patriot or Tory.

"No."

But all evidence seemed to point in another direction.

"No guns remain, and the Continental troops leave town on Monday. As for the rest of the Commissary, how could a few Brits remove two thousand tents, boxes of boots, barrels of hams?"

"Ham is the kind of crime I'd support," I said. "In truth, there's nothing to fear?" This had to be settled in my mind.

"If the British just ride through the countryside, it only means more business for taverns. British officers don't permit their troops to run wild. The generals in command are often noblemen. Men like that don't destroy little villages like Danbury."

"I suppose not," I mumbled, while thinking that destroying villages might be *exactly* what generals did. Or how they got promotions. Still, Lambert agreed with the opinions of Mr. Knapp and my father, which took away what little worry I had.

Lambert's horse picked up a slow jog, but trotting didn't bother me so much now. Maybe it's true that nervousness makes people bounce when riding. I relaxed into a deep happiness about my life and the promise Josh had made. And here I was, riding along next to Lambert. This day had turned out better then I'd ever hoped.

I liked how Josh wanted to bring our family back together, the way we used to be. My parents seemed like splinters knocked from a larger piece of wood. Splinters so fragmented that they might not fit back into place.

We reached Lambert's house and said our good-byes. I rode on alone, smacking and scratching the dust off my breeches. I rode past Lt. Clark's tavern, noting Colonel Huntington's horse, Captain Noble Benedict's horse, and Judge Tom Benedict's servant watching them. I speculated on their conversation and decided they were all asking each other about — boats! A boy had to laugh.

When I saw a man approaching the tavern on a lathered horse, I thought only of how people are so thoughtless about their beasts.

Chapter Thirteen

Friday, April 25th, 1777
at Seven o'Clock of the Evening

Great consideration went into my report at home. I could not mention Josh. Or my fall. Or seeing Mrs. McLean. Which left only my apprenticeship.

Father and Mr. Knapp once again sat on their bench, holding their end-of-day meeting. "Learn anything in that infernal camp?" asked my father.

"Let the lad talk, Si." Mr. Knapp put out a hand to shush him.

"I decided to take up saddle-making. Would that suit you, sir?"

Father's face flashed relief. "A classical trade, financially appealing in peace or war. A fine decision, Joseph, I'm sure." A peaceful smile of closure settled atop his perpetually worried face.

Mr. Knapp patted his arm to indicate Tory approval.

"A grand idea, Joseph, and I'll be the first to commission a saddle from you," he said, as I turned into the barn, I felt myself rise in value in Father's eyes and in my own opinion. I now had a future in an important trade.

When I returned from tying Pony in her stall, Father cleared his throat five or six times. Most likely, this indicated a chore I wouldn't want to do.

"Joe, Mr. Knapp's sheep will remain in his barn tonight. We can help him shear their wool in the morning. The girls are coming out to herd the sheep into the barn for the night."

My heart jumped as I saw a chance to tell Sarah about the team I had seen. I still needed to verify just what had happened.

"So, Joe, you can help us now, and in the morning you can hold the sheep for the shears."

I lit up at the thought of sheep-shearing. Grown folk perceived it as nasty, smelly work. I counted wrestling sheep as the best fun in the world. I had learned at the old Bear Mountain farm, when the sheep were bigger than I was.

Following my usual plan for extortion, I heaved a deep sigh and nodded, "I guess...."

"Good lad, Joe. A bit of the real coin might transfer from Mr. Knapp's pocket to yours. Shall we say a quarter-penny?"

I smiled.

Sarah and Mercy darted out of the house into the almost-dark. We moved the herd inside after much running and screaming on Mercy's part. I felt beat out, but new energy poured into me at the thought of revealing my secret to Sarah. I had no chance to talk to her until we finished. She drifted through the warm dusk, following her sister home.

I eased up next to her and whispered, "I saw your team of horses today."

Sarah jerked to a stop, sucking in her breath, which all came out again at once. "You found them? Where? Are they all right?" Her clenched fists pumped in excitement.

Just the thrilled reaction I wanted.

"They're at a Patriot camp, both of them. I saw them today." She bounced in place, stuffing her fists into her mouth. We walked on, coming closer together. She moved toward the stile and I could see that she wanted to hide this conversation from her father, though I wasn't sure why.

"Their names are Arthur and Merlin. Dad meant Arthur to be my riding horse, to make up for my leaving school and having the baby to deal with. I never rode Arthur once before – well, before he was *taken*. And just guess who *took* them both?" Her voice swung between spite and pleasure at my discovery.

"Someone stole them?" I decided to play dumb.

"Father rented them out to plow a field the day after he got them. That night, he *said* he sold the horses, but he sounded like they had died. I thought he concealed a deadly accident. Then I overheard him talking to Mother. Your grandfather confiscated them. Old Captain Dan read him a law about it, and paid him four pounds for the pair and their fitted harness. Robbery, my father called it."

"They're all fat and shiny," I said to distract her. "They both recognized your pony right away. Then Pony threw me in the dirt and my shoe came off."

"No!" Sarah covered her mouth, but burst out laughing anyway. After a minute, she said, "Joe, tomorrow I have to do laundry in the big laundry kettle in the yard. If you start the fire, we could talk about the horses and you could ride Pony again, if you want to."

"If you show me the secret to bridling her," I said. Sarah had suggested tomorrow's plan all on her own. Maybe this war was over!

Sarah giggled and scurried into the house, exchanging pretend slaps with Mercy on the way. Maybe she looked back at me when she got to her door. I think she did.

Back at home, Mother stirred a pot, while Father put out wooden trenchers for dinner. Not real trenchers, just slabs of wood we could burn in a few days, when they got too greasy.

"What about all the boats?" I asked, anxious to cross them off my list forever.

"Gracious heaven!" Mother snapped. "The British may come here, but it's not an Indian raid. It's a government mission. Control yourself, Joseph." She poured fresh ale into our pewter cups in such a hurry that she slopped it on the table.

I wondered if she believed one word she said. I also wondered where that fresh ale came from.

To silence further talk, she plumped down into her seat and shoved a mountain of fresh rye bread chunks toward me. A brown glazed stoneware bowl held hot beans to dump on the bread. The biggest plus turned out to be a fair-sized chunk of fried cod. The salty and buttery crust on that fish tasted marvelous. After a second helping of bread and beans, I declared it the best dinner we had eaten in a long while. A steely look entered Mother's eyes.

"It's the least I could do for you, since your father will be leaving us when he goes on his 'trip,' as you quite accurately termed it, Joseph."

Father snorted and moved to the fireplace. He set to sharpening his hand shears for the next morning's work. I gathered the courage to ask, "If there aren't any boats, do I still have to go away?"

Mother shot Father a dark look, which he didn't see.

I decided that this was time to ask a question that had lurked in my mind. "Did you know Enoch Crosby, the spy?" I asked. Mother raised her eyes to the ceiling.

"Being against war is one thing, betraying your friends is another," she said. The nastiness of her tone was something I had rarely heard.

"And he was Grandfather Hamilton's best friend?" I asked, wondering if Lambert had imagined that.

"Lockwood's right about that," Father said, not looking up from his work. "Only time I saw my old man fail in judging a person," The regular slush-slush of the whetstone filled the silence.

"Couldn't he come back to Danbury and turn his former friends in for treason?"

"No, son, actually, he couldn't. Enoch Crosby would be shot dead the minute he entered town. I'm no rebel, but I don't approve of him hoodwinking people."

"Did you know Enoch Crosby, too?"

"Glad he saw the error of his ways politically, but he was a liar. That's all I can say." Father stared into the fire, then sighed before he gestured at the logs on the hearth. I put on a new backlog and raked around with the tongs.

"'Course, the truth is, I miss him still," Father muttered.

"Joe, listen to me. Nothing may happen this time, but war can rekindle next month or next year. Truly, apprenticeship is the way to go. When the threat is over, back home you come. I'll check who might know a master saddler, maybe in Pennsylvania. Quakers are pacifist and also do quality leatherwork."

"New Haven must have fine saddlers," I suggested. I still wanted to visit the ocean.

"Not New Haven, of all places! That overbearing hothead Benedict Arnold runs that snake pit of traitorous fools."

I had my fingers crossed, but wished I had the two rabbit's feet I kept in the loft. If only I had found a paying job, Father might not have started this campaign. Yes, I wanted to apprentice, but I wanted to do it *in* Danbury and *with* Josh Benedict.

Rather than start him off again, I left well enough alone, content to daydream about earning money, wrestling sheep, and talking to Sarah. I climbed the ladder to my loft feeling better about life than my recent knowledge of grown-up facts might indicate.

I shucked off my outer clothes and rolled myself up in the coverlet Grandmother had made. Maybe I'd see her before I left town. Not maybe. I would visit the farm again, even if I had to walk.

For once, I had real plans of my own, long term and short term.

Our schoolmaster told this riddle:
    Question: "How do you make God laugh?"
    Answer: "Make plans."

Chapter Fourteen

Saturday, April 26th, 1777
at Four o'Clock of the Morning

I emerged from a deep sleep like rising from a pond's dark waters. The night chill gave me the shivers after yesterday's summery warmth. No dim glow of dawn lit the space where the ladder came through the floor. The steady pounding on our front door demanded action, though not from me.

I couldn't tell who kept yelling at my father to open the door. Cowering under my bedquilt, I listened. Could it be the summons for Father to go to jail? Was it "just" my grandfather or was other evil afoot? Could a nearby house be on fire? I sat up to listen.

Identifying the coarse voice of my father's cousin, the militia drummer, came as a relief. "It's an alarm! Open up!" His drummer's fist continued pounding until Father negotiated the fifteen feet to the front door. I ran to the ladder, where I could see and hear better. Sitting on the floor, I rewrapped the quilt and settled down to listen.

"Si! It's a total invasion! Man from Compo just came through. The thing is… the thing is …." His voice weakened from the effort.

"Is *what*?" Father demanded as he yanked the door open. When I looked down the ladder, Mother had walked up behind him, her hair hanging down her back. I couldn't believe she would let Father's cousin see her in nightclothes.

"It's not the twenty-five or fifty men we thought," the drummer choked out. "It's six cannon and over two *thousand* men. The British commandeered horses and wagons. They'll tear the town apart!" He paused to catch his breath.

"Your alleged commissary collected guns and made no secret of it. What result did you expect?" Father snarled.

"That would be *your* attitude, wouldn't it? Today you'll find out which side of this war God is on!"

"God? That preachy Reverend Baldwin mixed up rebel business with God's business. Got his just reward for it, didn't he?" The Patriot minister's ghost still preached war in the First Congregational Church. They never found a new minister who preached enough war to satisfy Danbury Patriots. That left only Reverend White, who had suffered ejection for preaching peace. He had started a new church of his own.

"Be reasonable," Father's cousin pleaded. "Send your wife and the boy to safety."

"I am informed that the British will not hurt peaceful citizens," Father insisted, "which is *not* you and your ilk!"

"My 'ilk?'" screeched the drummer. "My 'ilk' is *you*, you fool! We're both Hamiltons and citizens of this town!" His face had turned red and he could barely sputter. The door slammed shut in his face, as hard as my father could slam it.

The drummer had to pass our house to reach Danbury, but I had never seen this fervent Patriot at our door on any other occasion. His brown militia coat, powder horn, and short dagger-type sword indicated full preparation for a military event. His long gun rested diagonally across his back, but carrying it while beating a drum had to be painful. He never carried his gun and sword on training days.

I crawled back to my hay mattress, where I curled up in my quilt again. The quilt and my family had lasted through the war against the French. We'd all last through this, too. After a while, my heart stopped pounding from being waked up that fast. All of this invasion worry sounded foolish to me. England had owned America for over a hundred years. Why would they destroy what they own?

Just to make sure, I repeated, "Nothing will happen to peaceful citizens." several times. The drummer might be frightened and angry, but what he said went against the opinions of everyone else. If my father had stopped worrying, that was good enough for me.

All the same, it gave me a funny feeling to recall the panic in Mrs. McLean's cloud-white face as she mentioned leaving town before it was too late.

Too late for what?

When a pot banged downstairs and I heard a slow grinding noise, I jerked awake again, surprised that it was well on into morning. I heard Mother announce that this was the last of the coffee beans she had hoarded. I thought about getting up and peeing in the chamber mug, but it felt too warm under the quilt, so I didn't move. Besides, I could eavesdrop on their usual conversation over coffee. What would they say about our midnight visitor?

A poker stirred the fire and wood thumped on top. Eventually, Mother began to talk. "Husband, I heard horses galloping on the road this morning. Were people fleeing Danbury?"

"Neighbor Knapp stated last night that this is a peaceful mission. People should mind their own business and not cause trouble by running around with swords. Coffee boiled yet?" His tone shifted for the better after the smell of coffee wafted up into my loft and cups clinked. While never too sure about the taste of coffee, I loved the smell.

"The way I see things, Wife, the British approach offers real possibilities." Father sounded thoughtful and positive. "That accursed stallion might sell to a British officer if I ride out where they observe his gaits. Perhaps I would show some jumps over the stone walls. Few living in *this* town could ride that horse – none, if their wives know they plan to try." Slurping followed.

Selling the stallion to an unsuspecting victim sounded like the best idea Father had invented lately.

I heard Father stand up, ready for barn chores, but more was to come. "I have a charitable mission for you today, Wife. Neighbor Knapp at last admits that the girl Sarah needs adult help. All of Mrs. Knapp's Tory friends have decamped to Canada because of the economy. The children's clothes are in a sorry state and their every meal comes from a tavern. Joe and I will help shear their sheep this morning — a fine time for you to visit Mrs. Knapp and assess what's needed. What say you?"

"I am relieved to hear this. Neighbor Knapp kept denying that help was needed. That poor girl. I can roast the two fowl that don't lay eggs, plus make a cornmeal pudding." She paused. "I hope we won't have to flee."

Father stamped his foot in a way that was truly comical. I bet he shook his fist, too.

"No 'fleeing' will occur in this house. Anyone 'fleeing' will be those who subscribe to the rebel drivel, such as your sainted brothers, the infamous Judge Thomas Benedict and Tame Town Lawyer Tad." He stamped outside and slammed the door for the second time this morning.

Good. Safe for me to ask Mother what she thought had happened last night. I climbed down the loft ladder, dropped from five feet up, and landed on my feet with a resounding thunk.

Mother jumped and spun around, looking terrified. She forced out an artificial smile, which twisted her face in a way no one could want.

"Joe, did you hear last night? About the British coming here?" I could see her hands shake.

"Yes, ma'am. When might they arrive? Can we watch? And is there anything to eat?" I could feel her disapproval of my happy attitude.

"Take a dried apple for now, but johnnycake will appear later." She didn't answer my question about our invasion visitors, which was good.

"Joe, will you feed the hens for me and gather the eggs? By the way, all the baby chicks went to your Aunt Elizabeth yesterday while you were at school."

"She bought them? With money?" Father's sister must have felt sorry for us. Then I wondered why that was my first reaction to a simple sale of chick babies.

"I hated to do it," Mother added, "but we'll be good for a little while. Starting with paying the baker yesterday, your father also paid the bill at Clark's. Your Aunt Elizabeth is a good soul. She knows what I go through."

I wasn't sure just what Mother meant. Was she not in total agreement with Father?

"I'll make skillet cakes for your breakfast and to take next door. Perhaps I should do an extra batch in case of invasion…."

Her "invasion menu" made me choke back a laugh as I headed outside to the backhouse. I loved spring. Nobody used the close stool in the house in warm weather and I rarely had to empty it. Dropping it was my absolute nightmare, a nightmare most familiar to those with only one set of school clothes. I hoped the soft gray-green leaves of the plant we used after our backhouse business would grow fast and lush. Corncobs were just too rough.

My plan for the morning consisted of finishing my own chores and completing the sheep shearing as fast as possible. If my plan worked, I could help Sarah finish her laundry chores with the same speed. If the British *did* come, we could watch the parade together. "Together" meaning without Noah or Mercy.

Hammer blows broke the morning silence while an early mist lightened into a sun-filled spring morning. Father affixed fir saplings above the fencing on the horse pen. On Wednesday, his beast had leaped the five-foot high fence and run out North Street. For allowing his horse to be a public danger, Father had to pay a fine. Another fine.

My morning chores included Mother's hens. Six corncobs ran through the sheller, the results dropped into the hand grinder, producing chicken feed for both victims and survivors of the coming chicken roast. Then on to general barn work. Five cobs dropped into the trough for the horse, and I forked in hay. The two sows got the second half of the tavern's kitchen leavings. Three wooden buckets of water from the rain barrel finished off my tasks in record time. I was afraid to clean the stallion's stall with him in it and left that to Father. I brushed stray hay and other products from my canvas trousers, glad to begin the fun part of the day.

I hopped over the four-step stile into the Knapps' yard, anxious to challenge the sheep and to hear the latest British parade information.

Sarah and Mercy wore outgrown clothes due to dirt forecasts. Both girls' knees almost showed. Sarah and Mercy played with the lambs instead of grooming them, but I plied the currycombs as fast as I could. Mud would dull the shears and slow the shearing. Not sure if the ewes liked my speed, since the combs were only blocks of wood with nails sticking out.

Our fathers came in, both wearing leather aprons to repel misaimed shears and sharp cloven feet. Father always seemed glad to help Mr. Knapp, since it disguised our lack of rent money. Both men had their own shears and sharpening stones. They would take turns shearing and sharpening. I twisted the sheep around to the correct angle for shears to work, moving as the work progressed. As the sheared ewes dashed around the barn, Mercy rolled up the fleece and stuffed it into a cloth bag. Being out of practice, nothing went quite right at first, but after a lot of noise from lonely lambs and angry ewes, speed improved.

"Ben?" Between sheep four and sheep five, Father appeared to ponder a brand new idea.

"Yes, Si? What is it?" Mr. Knapp pointed to the ewe he wanted next.

Father sounded trusting, but tentative. "Ben, if this all goes *wrong* — I mean, if one of those filthy rebels starts shooting, what would happen?" His calm had not evaporated. He just looked cautious.

"The rebels couldn't be that stupid." Mr. Knapp sounded decisive, as befit a successful merchant. "I already sent word to the Loyalist leaders that we need to add a parade aspect to this event, just to ensure that the scared rabbits remain peaceable. It's in everyone's best interests. Lord Howe's policy is not to make the rebellion worse. Violence must be stifled, however. The British might search for Committee members. The *Hartford Courant* published all the names, you know. Including your father's."

All the names on the Committee of Inspection included Grandfather and Uncle Tad Benedict, plus a couple of older Benedict cousins. I suddenly saw the Hartford newspaper as equaling the wanted posters posted downtown.

Five, six, seven … We had almost finished. Sara and I kept looking at each other.

Dew was still on the grass, so it wasn't late, maybe only a little over half-way through the morning. I wondered how long doing laundry would take.

"Si Hamilton!" Harsh words drilled through the morning air.

Mr. Knapp peered around the edge of the door. All he said was, "Speak of the Devil!"

Chapter Fifteen

Saturday, April 26th, 1777
at Eleven o'Clock of the Morning

A rumpled, shapeless figure sat lodged in the saddle of a grimy and burr-covered pale gray horse. Clumps of hair hung in the old horse's mane and tail. The skirts of the rider's long coat formed a tent over the saddle. Five more saddled horses trailed behind on ropes, like privates following their sergeant. Captain Silas Hamilton, my grandfather, had come to call.

Grandfather didn't resemble the smiling man I had known when I was little. Nor even the man I had spoken to on Thursday. This old man looked bloated and rumpled, his face clouded by beard, his eyes lurking under his hat brim. The pale blue eyes now had red rims.

"Those tea-taxing red-coated English devils are on the way here right now," Grandfather announced, his eyes and yellowed teeth gleaming.

"What do you want from me?" Father asked in an iron voice. Silhouetted against the barn door, his slouched attitude showed zero respect.

I just stood there, hands at my sides, looking at this almost unknown person. Only the well-known horse face of Tom looked back. Mostly, I tried to look away.

My mother appeared and made her way to the top of the stile, where she remained transfixed, as if an Indian arrow had lodged in her back, forward motion ended by agony.

"You're coming with me today, son," the Captain announced. His fiery gaze intensified into the evil eye alert as the eye of a general.

"I am going *nowhere.*" Father's toneless voice could have cut the letters on a tombstone.

"Major General Wooster comes from New Haven with General Arnold. General Silliman left Norwalk with his militia. War is here. You will ride with me, just as you did as a lad. You don't have to fight, just work behind the front lines, run messages and help with the wounded." The voice sounded businesslike, the voice of a captain laying out the plan for experienced troops.

Telling you what you would do. Or else.

"You old fool; you're not *in* the army anymore," Father dared. "You're a war profiteer and that's *all* you are. I'm not fifteen anymore, to be ordered about like a dog." My eyes bugged out to hear this. I wondered what would happen to him for acting so disrespectful. Then I remembered that jail was about to happen to him.

War had seemed like an adult game played in costumes, like theater. We didn't have theater in Danbury and we didn't have war, either. Now, here came my grandfather, talking about wounded and prepared for a battle right here in town. War must be blowing across the heavens like snow or rain. And landing on everyone.

The sudden clatter of steel-shod hooves sounded like a regiment as three riders hit the Barren Plain bridge at a fast trot. My uncles, John and James, both privates in the militia, rode with Uncle Paul, who was in the Continental Army. Each led four saddled horses and headed toward town. All carried long guns. Uncle Paul wore his new rifle slung across the back of a brown uniform coat. None of them wore boots, just shoes with cloth leggings wrapped from ankles to knees. All eyes remained focused down the road.

Grandfather had demanded that my father help with wounded, but what wounded did he mean — my uncles? I always thought of dying as just people disappearing — you didn't see them again. Now I pictured my uncles lying unconscious in a field where everyone else had galloped away.

Grandfather gathered his reins. "The militia forms downtown and will ride this direction to meet the generals in Redding. You will join us as we pass or you'll be in jail and I will see to it that you are." The reins shortened. A half step backward prepared all of the animals for a turn.

My mother's hands covered her own mouth in a useless effort to stifle Father's lightning-fast retort.

"The militia will be coming *out* of town? Your militia is running away?" Father's voice could have struck sparks from one of the flints the Patriots didn't have.

The voice that answered was like a Mohawk arrow: primitive, hardened, brutal.

"Your brothers should risk their lives while *you* go scot free? Sedition is a crime — resistance to lawful authority. You just committed it. The Danbury Committee of Inspection will attach this property and everything else you think you own. You have one hour."

The six horses turned as one, headed past the ford and turned onto Town Street. None of them looked back.

More adult nonsense, because it had nothing to do with Father. The house and shed belonged to Mr. Knapp, not to my parents.

Not wanting to hear Father rage and Mother cry, I intended to delay going indoors as long as possible. I started for the bridge, where traffic had become heavy, moving in only one direction – north, the opposite direction from the waters of Long Island Sound.

David Weed and his little sister trotted by on a pony, cloth bags of possessions tied in front of them and a rolled blanket across the girl's lap. Mrs. Weed and David's grandparents followed in a wagon. I searched faces in the other wagons that clattered by, piled with wooden trunks and bedding.

Sarah slid up next to me. "Don't the rebels look scared? Look! There's that little Taylor girl, covered in mud." Sure enough, Major Taylor's little girl sat on the tailgate of a wagon, hands and skirt a muddy mess. A woman so ancient she appeared already dead lay on a featherbed, holding Mrs. Taylor's hand. Major Taylor, as town clerk, had signed every one of the Patriot proclamations posted downtown. No wonder he was leaving.

Mr. Knapp approached Sarah and gripped her shoulders. "You're wanted in the house!" She looked at me and shrugged as her father led her away.

I, too, might be in trouble if I didn't follow my parents inside, so I abandoned my post with heavy footsteps. I had walked a few steps when a cart came up the street, going like the wind. Holding the reins was young Mrs. Clark, long whip at the ready, and gloved hands showing off her tight grip on the leather. The dappled pony was a classy gray, as handsome as the owner. The two Clark children sat deep in the cart box, looking frightened for their lives.

> Amidst this scene of fear and sympathy, of hurry and flight, a Mrs. Clark, wife of Capt. James Clark, a woman of singular fortitude, remained after the inhabitants had retired, to dispose of her family and secure her goods, and was, in fact, the last whig female that left town upon the entrance of the enemy.

When I opened the cottage door, I thought to find a snake pit of misery, but all appeared strangely calm. Father sprawled in a chair at the table. Mother wandered around the room. No sobs, no curses.

"I wondered how long it would take for this to happen." Father sounded too beaten to be angry. "I'm called to heel like a dog, whether for jail or battle or whatever he invents. Just like my brothers. The old Indian-fighter will kill us all before he's done." He looked at his own down-at-heel shoes, as if wondering how far they'd make it. He took the long strips of cloth that he wore instead of boots, and wound them around each leg. They prevented the stirrup straps from blistering his legs.

Mother strode from here to there, more active than usual, maybe trying to diffuse the tension of the one-hour deadline. "The British tax now and the Continentals tax later," she said. "Everything will end just like the English civil war a hundred years ago. Thirty years of war to rid themselves of the king. Then the chaos and violence forced them to choose another king."

"Thirty years of war? How long is this revolution going to last?" I asked, almost in shock.

"The war may have gone to sleep, but it might awaken with a vengeance," Mother said. "If these visitors start a genuine confrontation, we'll all be in deep trouble. I hope they just take the guns and leave. Oh, why can't all of this be over?" She shook her whole body. Like a horse shaking off the rain.

"Good riddance to the power-mad," Father scoffed. "When their weapons are confiscated, Connecticut may be cured of the disease of revolt. Our families may lose everything as a result of their decisions, idiotic instead of patriotic. Peaceful change is the right way."

Father tilted his chair back and turned his face toward the cobwebbed ceiling. Mother looked less satisfied with the situation. A lot less. Her lips had sucked almost all the way into her mouth.

Anxious to help, I reached over the chimney shelf for his musket. I noticed the wooden stock that rested against his shoulder had split. It counted as more of a blunderbuss than a musket, anyway. My eager hand returned to my side when I noticed Father watching me.

"Are you going to get ready?" I asked, becoming a little nervous about the time limit. Time was close to running out.

"I'm not going anywhere." Father's simple statement gave me a vision of the trumpet sounding the Last Judgement and Father refusing that invitation, too.

"But Grandfather will —" I had forgotten exactly what had been said, so I retired to a corner, where I sat down on the floor and recounted word by word, what Grandfather had threatened.

Father forced a half-real laugh. "What an actor my old man is, Wife! That bit about confiscating everything we own. When the cloth and the stallion sell, he'll be paid in full. I don't know why he doubts my honesty. I know better than anybody what I owe, I just can't pay."

"What exactly do we own, free and clear?" Mother's voice was tarnished by misery.

"What do we own? *Half* of a horse worth fifteen pounds, *half* of the wool flannel Major Taylor's store," Father listed. "The sows will farrow soon. Maybe get a dozen piglets, all of them owned by *us*."

In other words, two sows made up the sum total in the "free and clear" department.

"I hoped that cloth would sell by now. Nothing had better happen to it," Mother threatened.

"Who could be more trustworthy than Major Taylor?" Father reassured her.

Accurate, as far as it went. Which wasn't far.

"Um…I saw Major Taylor." Neither of my parents paid any attention. "Just now, I *saw* Major Taylor," I repeated, louder than before.

"You didn't go anywhere today," my mother contradicted, without bothering to look at me.

"Major Taylor just drove by here in a wagon, headed out of town. He was following Doctor Foster. I saw them."

Three quick steps brought Father toe-to-toe with me. He looked far more alarmed than before. "You tell me exactly what you saw. *Tell me!*" Father demanded in a low, strangled voice.

Both hands on my shoulder produced only a slight shake. Before it got serious, I spilled the story.

"An old lady lay in the wagon bed. Honest, he drove the wagon.

Mrs. Taylor was in there, too, and their little girl."

Father backed off and turned to Mother to vent his fury. "All these Patriots *do* is run. My flannel cloth is probably still in his abandoned store, just begging to be stolen. I'll fetch that cloth right now, before months of spinning and weaving go wasted!"

Father jerked a set of rusty spurs from the wall and mashed them onto his boot heels. I wanted to tell him not to wear the star-like metal rowels. An accidental kick could make the rowel drill right through the horse's hide and draw blood. Then the beast could rebel and rear over backward. Again.

"But what will Captain Hamilton do?" asked Mother.

"I was going to jail anyway, wasn't I? My old man is going stupid from old age, you know that, Wife? That nonsense about confiscating this house! Looks like he forgot that Ben Knapp owns the place."

"Captain Hamilton never forgot anything in his life." Mother sounded sharper than the spurs.

I had reached a more unpleasant conclusion after considering the Patriots' ability to take anything they saw. "Uh, do you think Grandfather's Committee would take our house from Mr. Knapp?"

My parents' heads spun toward me and their mouths opened. I heard air going in, but no words came out. A second later, my father slammed the wall with his fist.

"By the living law! Shows how low those rebels will sink. They'll take this house, *his* house and the tannery. It's all one property. He'll lose *everything*, just for helping us. My God....and Ben Knapp is the finest man in this town, even if he is Tory." Father's voice sank as his expression dissolved from angry determination into the look of a man facing a fatal event.

That the cottage could be confiscated had been my idea, but I felt stunned to understand Father's version. Sarah could lose *her* house and her father would lose his leather business. Tories could not legally move from one town to another, so ....

At a meeting of the Committee of Inspection for the Town of Danbury, November 6, 1775:

Resolved, That it be recommended to the Selectmen of Danbury, not to allow any persons from abroad to take up their residence in the said Town, unless they produce a Certificate from the Committee of Inspection... that they are friends to the cause of American liberty.

SAMUEL TAYLOR, Com. Clerk.

Father dropped into a chair and put his hands over his face. Then they slipped down so that just his eyes showed. He appeared to be watching different visions of the future.

"I thought Reverend White spoke God's word when he fought against the Congregational Church's support of the war and founded his own church. But beliefs today count for nothing at all." His head sank again.

Mother and I watched him, as intent as if watching a dying person.

At last, Father straightened in his chair. "I'll have to go," he said in a childlike voice of wonder. "Just like when I was a boy, my father says to go and I have to do it." Father's fist slammed the tabletop. If it hurt, he no longer noticed. "At least *I'll* be the one paying the price, not a man with four children and a crippled wife."

"Do you have a pistol I don't know about? I'll fetch it," I asked, trying to be practical, although my whole body trembled from the wind currents of shock and anger coursing through the room.

"Lord above! Shooting a gun near that accursed stallion would be the last thing I'd need." Father pulled on his regular jacket with a vicious jerk, then drew a long riding coat over it. He selected his oldest hat and hurled it onto the table. He rifled through every cannikin and crock, shoving several dried plums and a piece of moldy cheese into his coat pocket. Two onions piled in on top of the fruit. In the hard winter past, Father had gnawed onions, saying it prevented scurvy, which made your teeth fall out.

I might prefer scurvy to year-old onions. Or the dried plums that had been next to those onions.

Mother clutched at the edge of the window frame, her knuckles white from her death grip on the wood. Her face turned white, too, from her death grip on herself.

A slow drumming vibrated the window glass. I shoved in next to Mother and she drew me closer, to let both of us see. It felt better that way, especially after our eyes evaluated the sad procession. The first Patriot horses were just visible under the arching elms, the new leaf buds swishing fitfully over their heads. The drumming ceased as the funereal parade approached. The cloud-weakened sun lit only ragged old clothes and ancient hats. No one wore his Sabbath best to war.

Father made no farewell, just put on his ragged old farmer's hat and headed for the door, motioning for me to follow. At the doorway, he turned to look at Mother. She turned back to the window. I don't think my father expected that.

He put a hand on my back. "Let's watch the deluded ones wander along toward their doom." His voice sounded unexpectedly quiet.

We walked out to the Barren Plain bridge and stood there, shoulder to shoulder.

The "Liberty or Death" flag marched next to the new flag of the Patriots. Too bad that no fifer was with them. A fifer like Private Gorton might have cheered things up.

Next in line, Colonel Huntington of the Continentals rode side by side with Colonel Cooke of the militia. Uncle Paul followed, surrounded by the Colonel Huntington's officers and sergeants, who rode Grandfather's horses, as did the militia lieutenants and sergeants. The other soldiers followed on foot. Only Colonel Huntington, Colonel Cooke and the militia captain wore full uniform. If the men had no gunpowder, their muskets counted as gun-shaped spears, the bayonets being the only functioning part. Not all of them had bayonets.

A question escaped before I could think better of it. "Father, did Colonel Cooke attend a college?"

"Yale, in New Haven."

"How about Colonel Huntington?"

"I believe he attended in Massachusetts — Har…Harvard, that's it."

"Why does college makes people become Patriots – I mean, rebels?"

"Rebellion passes through students like disease," Father pronounced, while looking displeased.

Captain Noble Benedict passed with the militia, flanked on each side by a lieutenant and followed by two sergeants. One of them carried the regimental white flag that said, "An Appeal to Heaven."

In the main militia regiment, almost half of the men had bayonets already fixed to the weapons slung over their shoulders, promising vicious hand-to-hand fighting. Sixty Danbury men passed, no one marching, just walking. They walked over the Barren Plain bridge and were gone from us.

Behind the militia, a dozen old veterans rode at Grandfather's side, heavily armed in a different way. Flasks hung from their saddles, as well as sundry cloth bags and coils of rope and leather. They resembled traveling salesmen. The gloomiest travelling salesmen imaginable.

Grandfather's glare scoured our side of the street before he reined his horse to a halt in front of us. Old Tom was shedding snarled gray clumps of hair. "They'll be entering South Street right now. I

could hear them coming a mile away. Go get your horse, son. Now."
He glanced back over his shoulder, as if the British could be visible any
minute.

Father reversed mood again, pivoting from incapable rage
to condescension. "Your colleague in catastrophe, Major Taylor, fled
town not long ago." Father portrayed eyebrow-arching innocence. "As
you have often mentioned, the cloth deposited with him for sale is not
mine, but *yours*. The town militia melts away like snow, leaving houses lying open for looting. Perhaps you need my help to retrieve your
cloth?"

Grandfather's companions exchanged wary glances. Baiting
Captain Hamilton seemed foolish in the extreme. They moved on, leaving the three of us alone in the street.

A ratlike suspicion surfaced on the Captain's stubbled face as he
studied Father's motives. "Is this your trick to evade going with me? An
excuse never to show up at all? Go saddle your useless nag. Your mad
beast would never let you carry a bolt of cloth. *I'll* get it!" A crack of
his riding whip sliced the morning air, and the Captain's old gray horse
exploded from a dead halt into a dead run, headed back to town.

"Grandfather looked like a fat ragbag," I said, as we headed to
the shed to saddle the stallion.

"This weather's brewing a storm. Your grandfather can sit in the
rain all night in his three coats, two waistcoats and three shirts. When
everyone else eats wind pudding, he'll pull corncakes and dried fruit
out of his pockets, just like eating at home. Pro'bly has three flasks, a
wad of bandages, two pocket pistols, a little bag of corn for his horse,
and thousands in those fake rebel dollar bills. Keeping troops going day
after day, year after year — that's his stock and trade." Bitterness oozed.

"Why doesn't he ever groom his horse?"

"It's part of his plan. People don't take a fat old man on a scruffy
horse seriously. They hold fire, and that gray nag could pop over a stone
wall or dive down a mountain. A thin thief on a filthy racehorse, that's
all he is. They could run all day, the two of them." In an unconscious
way, Father sounded jealous of the ancient horse and rider, united in
mind and task.

Father's horse practiced snapping its teeth while pieces of
equipment were fitted to him. The old leather bridle buckled under the
horse's muzzle and throat. Father tightened the woven saddle girth and
the breastplate that kept the saddle from sliding back when addressing
steep hills. The stallion stamped and threw its head, foam forming at

the corners of the iron bit as the beast registered its anxiety to join the militia horses he had heard trotting away.

"Where's the martingale?" I asked. The martingale goes from the bridle's noseband to the leather breastplate. It prevents rearing accidents.

"It snapped on Thursday when he fell. Forget it." Father pointed to our cottage. "Go in and ask your mother for all the money we have." He buttoned his coat and pulled on his gauntlets.

Mother put two shillings hard money and a few worthless Continental bills into my hand, whispering, "I don't want to do this, but it was his sister bought the chicks." Judging by Mother's face, our last money had disappeared.

"Was that all we had?" Father muttered when I put the assembled coins into his hand.

The shadow of some new fear crossed his face as he glanced back at the cottage.

Gathering his reins, ready to mount, Father bowed his head. His face crumpled like a wadded continental dollar. Ready to leave at last, he raised his head to the sky and wiped his face with his sleeve. "For three years, I have tried to keep this from happening. I am terribly sorry, Joe. God save us all." Leading his horse over to the stile, he attempted to mount with care. The result brought the stallion onto its hind legs, pawing the air.

"I can make a martingale strap out of rope," I yelled and darted into the shed.

It only took a second, but when I came back, Father had gone, passed over the bridge and into the day. Just like his father and his three brothers.

Chapter Sixteen

Saturday, April 26th, 1777
at Twelve o'Clock Noon

The instant Father's horse trotted out of town, I turned my face in the opposite direction. If Grandfather thought he could go downtown in safety, I could go, too – as long as nobody knew about it. I dreaded missing the British horse cavalry, the full glory of England on free display. If I could see the entire parade as it first entered Danbury, this one day would live with me forever. I looked back at the cottage and Mother was not to be seen, giving me free rein to disappear without a word. I might have gone back to Knapp's or into the shed, right?

I avoided the street and ran bent over behind the stone wall that ran down Town Street. No other people had been on the street since the militia had passed. Looking at British horses wasn't against the law, so I kept going, heart pounding from fear of missing the best part.

The fresh smells of onion ramps and new grass greeted me, but the usual friendly smells of wood smoke and cooking were missing. Many houses appeared abandoned, their winter-dirty windows blank and staring. The Inn stood as silent witness. Nothing remained but a shabby building with no cheer left to give. The King George was closed, too. The smell of bread lurked around Clark's tavern, but only closed doors and shutters greeted the vanished customers.

As I came closer to South Street, the air carried a far-away thunder – an unnatural trembling that might have stemmed from the earth itself. I sucked in deep breaths and ran, looking for the right spot to watch what the most powerful country on earth had to show.

When I reached Griswold's store on the corner of South Street, I sank to my knees behind the moldy stone mounting block and rested my chin on my arms, panting with relief. I had come just in time.

The sun came out, strong and bright, to illuminate the scene, I felt elevated into the world of dreams. I moaned with excitement as I watched a dream march into view.

The flag of the New York Loyalist Prince of Wales Division flapped in the rising breeze, next to the New York colony flag and the British Flag. Their colonel followed, his medals and his well-fed face all beaming satisfaction. The sun reflected off the silver metal trim on bridles and saddles, all as perfect as brand new. All faces expressed only curiosity and interest. The foot soldiers displayed the same dignified forest green uniforms with bright white collars and facings down the front.

Just as Mr. Knapp predicted, only a parade.

The next unit consisted of a dozen dragoons in blood-crimson coats, looking more fantastical than dragons. They hardly looked human, due to metal helmets with skulls on the front.

A unit of red coated British foot soldiers followed behind their mounted officers. The mood changed from pleased pride to suspicious glances. War-worn old sergeants appraised the surrounding houses with the eyes of experience — or with the eyes of thieves planning their evening work schedules.

The column halted in the intersection, bits and saddles jingling and creaking. The sudden stop produced several horse fights, beginning with stray squeals and whinnies, followed by the muted thud of hooves meeting flesh and curses of surprise – followed by stray squeals and whinnies. Officers' voices rang out, calling up the troop line for orders. Then silence.

Clouds cluttered the sky as the horizon behind the surrounding houses darkened. The sun still shone, but a deluge might come soon. First, I wondered where I would go if it rained. Then I wondered where our visitors would go. Beasts and men would find no shelter here. I looked down the endless column. Too many soldiers had entered too small a town.

A gnawing sensation of hazard overtook me as I considered the number of guns in view. Living where I was related to all the bigwigs, I had always felt safe from harm. Now harm had turned its face in my direction. I understood now my father's question. I understood completely how just one hidden sniper could turn Danbury into the first-ever Connecticut battlefield.

Just as a person slows eating when he has swallowed enough food, I had swallowed enough fear. I rose from my knees and began to sneak back the way I had come. A woodpile on the corner of West Street formed my new hideout. Satisfied, I settled in for a more relaxed view.

Two men in ordinary clothes trotted their horses to the front of the line. As they reached it, a hand pointed and a shout slashed through the overheated noon atmosphere.

A horse catapulted out of the street by the jail, plunging onto Town Street. The beast bolted toward me. I inhaled so hard that I ran out of room for air, while the rider fought to control a bolt of cloth tied to the saddle.

The rider was my grandfather.

Three British cavalrymen leaped from the formation, driving their long-limbed chestnut mounts after him. On his best day, the skinny old gray could never outpace these fine-boned racers. I felt like I was at a rabbit-hunt, as troopers yelled "Get 'im, get 'im!" and "C'mon, lads! Piece of cake!"

The three riders closed the gap, waving their sabers like whips, while extorting greater effort by raking the animals' sides with their spurs. The nags didn't need urging. The whites of their eyes showed, and their ears lay back flat against their heads. Foam dripped from their mouths as they slavered for the kill, as eager as their riders.

"Got you now, old daddy!" yelled the leader of the chase, a rail-thin officer not hampered by a musket. The rider's face simmered with joy as hunter and hunted raced directly toward the corner where I hid. His horse gained ground, its fiery eyes glowing with devilish determination. In a grand gesture, the rider drew his saber and pointed it at Grandfather.

I could see right now that a murder was about to happen.

Right in front of me, Grandfather slewed around the corner onto West Street at such an angle that his left stirrup bashed the rail fence. Grandfather glanced back at his pursuers. Feeling the balance change in the saddle, his horse slowed. The three troopers also lost ground, due to the unexpected turn. The lead rider caught up with ease. His companions struggled to reach him. Grandfather remained turned around, his eyes focused on his pursuers, instead of on escape.

He *must* go faster or death would be instant! Grandfather remained turned in his saddle, face raised to his enemy, hands still clutching the cloth.

Didn't he understand what was happening? I wanted to scream and pound the mounting block stones. *Turn around and ride faster!*

The lead trooper raised his blade to gauge his victim. The other troopers regained position, inches behind the first horse's tail. The sun flashed on steel as the deadly saber dropped with all possible force. Grandfather raised his head to follow the blade's arc, in acceptance of his fate.

A curtain of brilliant blood red flashed out, flying through the air, higher than the horses' heads, streaming like a solid scarlet sail. The British horses reared and plunged in every direction except forward. Arms clutched necks. A nose hit the mane. Reins slipped through fingers. One rider dropped his saber. The first officer recovered control of his beast and shouted to his companions. "After the old devil! Go!"

The roll of red flannel slammed the ground at every step, bouncing three feet high as it unfurled. The entire length flapped in the air, aided by the approaching storm. The end tied to Grandfather's saddle remained fast as the old man dropped onto his horse's neck like a jockey, applying his whip with a vengeance.

The redcoats collected their wits and tore after the gray horse, which now plunged forward, each stride opening a gap between him and his pursuers. The gray disappeared around the bend.

West Street became an empty space. My breaths came so fast that the world began fading to black before my eyes. I felt sick to my stomach from shock. I leaned over and put my hands on my knees, dropping my head as far as it would go, Mother's cure for faintness.

If they had wanted to kill Captain Silas Hamilton before, now his death would be even sweeter. I could imagine the end of the tale. British officers would not allow an American to humiliate them. Three against one....

As my vision cleared, my brain said to run, but I decided to wait for the soldiers' return, to see if they brought his — his body. Most likely tied head down across his saddle.

I guess I was about six when Grandfather bought old Tom. I wanted to ride to church behind him, but he said Tom was "too hot." When I was ten, I felt proud to ride on a cushion behind the saddle, holding onto Grandfather's old uniform coat, people greeting us as we trotted into town to church. I never understood a word of the sermons, but it didn't matter. I just looked forward to the ride home. As time passed, it became harder to remember those old times and easier to remember the bad things Father said. It felt disloyal to have any memories at all.

Several minutes later, a dozen troopers trotted toward me,

continuing out Town Street toward my house. Maybe they would block the road so I couldn't return home. I suffered a gnawing feeling of time passing and my chances of returning home passing with it.

At last the three Brits rode back into sight, all sabers safe in their scabbards. I scoured uniforms and horsehides for arterial blood clots, but the horses' coats revealed only sweat. The expressions on the soldiers' faces held as little answer as the clouds now filling in the sky.

I cried out as the crash of a musket shot echoed up the street, too close for comfort. Locating the source of the shot caused all British heads to whip around, searching for the snipers. Another shot came, followed by two more. One hothead had produced what Father considered the worst outcome possible.

The three returning troopers bounded into a canter, headed for the safety of the main column. A dozen other cavalrymen rushed out past them, on a direct course toward *me*.

I jumped to my feet, hunkered down to make a smaller target, and retreated with all speed toward the butcher shop. In the building's shadow, I stropped and leaned against the wall. I jumped back when the door creaked open and an old man's hairless head emerged, the sunken face grinning like a skull. A moment of horror before I realized he wasn't a ghost, but a regular old man I'd seen there before.

"Don't that beat all?" He hissed in an excited whisper. The gap-toothed mouth kept opening and closing. "He'll be gone now," the man confided. "Nobody can catch Cap'n Hamilton in open country. Fastest horse in New York when he bought him ten years ago. Said that horse was his life assurance policy, he did.

The noise of boots running up Town Street past us made the old man glance over my shoulder. He gargled a breath of saliva and gasped, "No!" The door slid shut before my dry tongue could beg for help.

I turned to see the sight he saw.

The flash of another musket shot had pinpointed the shooter's position. A Brit soldier roared, "Got 'em! The big house, on the left!" The soldiers deployed behind trees in front of Major Starr's house across the street. Why was Major Starr still here? A volley of shots followed a volley of shouts, and they charged the doors and smashed the house windows with bayonets. Then the screams began. Unearthly screams. The screams of grown men.

My mind exploded into full-blown fear, tempered by fear of what my parents would expect me to do. To verify what had happened to my grandfather, I would have to enter the maze of country lanes and tracks that lay out West Street. The end of my search might feature blood spouting and maybe Grandfather's head cut off. What good could come of following out there alone? I couldn't carry him.

I took off, running twice as fast as when I had come. I charged from wall to fence and fence to tree, desperate to escape the awful scene. Just as I came to the turn onto Barren Plain Road, I caught sight of the troops at the bridge by our house.

I took to the willows and cut the corner before they spotted me. Emerging from the weeds, I landed near our place. I staggered over to the wooden stile between our yard and the Knapps' and dropped to my hands and knees on the steps. I tried to slow my breathing and the pounding pulse in my throat. I felt so nauseated that I lay there until it went away and I could get up.

What had I done? My mother must never find out that I had run away like a scared rabbit.

I felt dirty, inside and out, but I brushed myself off, attempting to look respectable.

I looked at our front door, glad Mother wasn't looking out. I had to go in. I had to just walk up to the door and open it. Then I would have to lie like I had never lied before.

I couldn't see how anybody would believe the truth.

Chapter Seventeen

Saturday, April 26th, 1777
at One o'Clock of the Afternoon

Hands shaking as I pressed the latch, I opened the cottage door. Mother sat at the table, head resting on her crossed arms. Underneath, lay her Bible. "Joseph Hamilton, where have you been?" Dried tear lines stood out on her face.

I had to talk, and my words had to fall within the range of normal-for-today.

"British troopers are stationed by the bridge, but they're not doing anything." The truth always beat a lie. I just had to choose the right truth.

"Followed your father out the road, did you? You're a fine lad, Joseph." She sounded appreciative of the imagined effort, not angry, the way I had feared. I could tell her life had stopped for an hour.

"I went the direction Grandfather Hamilton did," I mumbled.

Driven down about as far as I could go, I had a disgusting taste in my mouth. Running with my mouth open had dried out my tongue and teeth. Cold coffee from this morning remained in the pan, so I poured a little. At least it took the dirt taste out of my mouth before installing a brand new unpleasant taste.

Strengthened by the awful brew, I resolved to learn the reasons for the horror I had seen. Danbury was coming apart.

"Lambert Lockwood told me that the British would hang the Captain as a traitor. Is that true?"

Hanging had become even more popular in Danbury on Monday, when General Parsons had condemned a spy.

Col Sam'l H. Parsons to Gen. Geo. Washington

April 22, 1777

Inclosd is a Sentence of a Court Martial against One Robert Thompson—He appears to be an artful intriguing Person, & may perhaps be made a very Useful Person to detect and discover the Masinations of our internal Enemies, if this should be th't of more Importance that the Good which may be derived from his Death.

"Of course it's true," Mother stated. "He's on that accursed Committee of Inspection that has ruined our lives."

"Grandfather Hamilton would be the only one they hung?"

Before Mother's composure dissolved, she looked accusing, as if I had asked the question only to hurt her.

"No, they'd hang my brothers, too. Tad and Tom are the real brains of the committee." She struggled to continue talking. "My whole family would meet the Hamiltons at the gallows."

I hardly ever saw my Benedict uncles. They were too important. Uncle Tom and Uncle Tad — town judge and town lawyer. Like the Hamiltons, the Benedict brothers ignored us. Only Josh and Jonah had ever remembered my name from month to month.

Now that I felt myself to be a coward, I decided to probe that word as related to my father. I had often thought about this. "Why does Father oppose the revolution when he believes we should be free of England? Did the last war turn him into a coward?"

"Joseph, for goodness' sake! Is that what you've been thinking?" Mother looked so horrified that I had my answer right there.

"And why does he want to get rid of me by sending me away?"

Mother gasped, "Good God in heaven! Get rid of you? The one thing your father wants is for you to be safer and happier than he was."

"Oh?" I asked. Maybe it came out wrong, because Mother took hold of both my wrists and pulled me closer to her. She looked up into my face and I knew I was going to get a lecture, but what she said turned me inside out.

One bad thing about the last two days was that things I knew, *I only knew part of.*

And what I did know meant different things from what I thought.

"You listen to me, Joe. Do you remember what happened the summer before we left the farm — when the militia went to war against

Canada?"

I tried to think back to being eleven. I shook my head. The militia came and went. Either my uncles were gone or they weren't. I might remember where they'd gone until they came back, no longer. My parents had too many relatives to keep track of. You knew you'd see them again.

"Joe, do you remember —" Her voice lowered to a whisper as she bent toward me. "…the children?"

I gave an involuntary cry, as that word brought the horror back to me. The horror I had not understood at the time it happened.

"The putrid fever came and they all died," I whispered back, staring at her marble-white face.

"That's right, Joe. Everyone in town thought the militia would die, to the last man. That we'd never see them again. But every single man came back from Canada, only to find that their children were dead. Seventy children died in one month."

At that time, I hadn't lived in town. I had not known any of those children well. They were in singing school, but I never went to their houses. They weren't who I sat by. My skin began to get goose flesh as I remembered my Grandmother Hamilton screaming whenever my grandfather came home with news. I didn't go to church for months or to the little Pembroke School where I had learned to read. Everyone in the family took turns teaching me, a kindness not explained in detail.

"Your father decided at that time that God opposed the revolution. It's why he tries to keep you from becoming involved in war." Mother's face never changed, but tears dripped steadily, wiped away each time with the sleeve of her bleached old black jacket.

I stood there, speechless. "The children." The enormity of what had happened and the effect this had on my parents gave me a lot to understand.

I had no answer to this, nor did Mother say anything more. We stared at each other, barren of words, barren of thought.

On this day, an interruption counted as a blessing.

Hurried hoof beats drew us to the window. The same lieutenant cantered up to the checkpoint at the bridge and motioned the British detachment back to town. The men stowed flasks, remounted, and formed a column. As they moved off, the lieutenant gave the Knapp's house a royal looking-over, craning his head and moving his horse to see barn, back house, and all.

But now they were gone. The bad stuff had ended. Mother looked around the room and blew out her cheeks with relief. She poured the last of the coffee into her mug, not stopping when grounds poured in, too.

"What should we do now?" I asked, since Mother looked ready to resume daily life. "We could start by killing the two old hens."

"I want to cook everything in this house, in case we have to flee," she answered with a determination unusual to her. Pulling out a sack of beans, she fetched the iron pot. I still hoped for chicken — as long as *she* killed them.

I went out to pee, and brought back wood for the cook fire. I watched Mother for a while, each of us thinking our own thoughts.

A crack followed by a tremendous thud, splintered the morning air. Easily identifiable as the ancient tree in front of the Knapp's house, the one that hung out over the road. Both of us whirled to the window, but we never reached it. A distant "schrumpf!" sounded like a building collapse, which was about the loudest thing I had ever heard.

The loud end of cannon fire is the safe end. The end where you hear wood splinter is not.

Mother and I flew out the front door, racing toward the Knapps' place to make sure it hadn't been hit. When another tree on the other side of the road suffered the same fate, followed by the same not-so-distant sound, we understood. Closer to the road was the last place we should go. Shattering windows and wood splinters would be more deadly than cannonballs.

"Get inside!" Mother pointed at the Knapp's sturdy barn. I jerked the door open and we dove in among the massed and milling sheep. Pony and Mr. Knapp's gelding stomped and neighed.

Another dull cannon-shot sounded, and Mother grabbed onto me as if I were about to vanish. Three more shots followed in slow cadence. After that, nothing.

In a trance of terror, Mother sank into a pile of rye straw. The lambs soon began to examine her. She stroked one with as little mind as a pendulum swings on a clock. Several tiny beasts folded their legs and sank down on the edges of her skirt, leaning half against her knees. The shorn ewes gathered to watch. Mother's eyes closed and her skin had gone as white as the sheep.

After a while, I got restless, frantic to know what the full damage was. All sound has ceased.

"Should I go out and see what the cannonballs hit? We can't stay in the barn all day."

"Go check the road. They might have seen militia coming. Soldiers might need help. Check on the poor Knapps, too." She answered, but she never opened her eyes.

Outside, the birds had been singing. Now, complete silence spread like a blanket. I dreaded going closer to the road, but I never got there, anyway. The Knapps' green paneled front door flew open just as I passed their house. Mr. Knapp stifled me in a quick embrace.

"Mother wants to know if they were aiming at the militia."

"I don't know what happened. I saw the officer issue orders to return to town, but no one seemed in too much of a hurry. If the militia had been coming into town this way, a skirmish would have started right here. Where's your mother?"

"In your barn, lying down in the hay." Looking flustered, he rushed away without another word.

I stood in the doorway, looking toward the road, the last place that I had seen my father. The only victims of the cannon fire had been two sycamore trees. Out of six shots, only the first two had hit trees.

If the Patriot troops returned, the cannon downtown had been aimed by an expert: dead center up the road.

Chapter Eighteen

Saturday, April 26th, 1777
at Four o'Clock of the Afternoon

The same detachment of scarlet-coated soldiers trotted back up Town Street. They drew rein at the Barren Plain bridge, just where they had been stationed before.

I eased over to behind the Knapp's woodpile, right on the corner of the road. My brown clothes looked like wood, I figured. Maybe I could overhear information if I got close enough. Information about Grandfather. Or the militia.

Two guards tied their horses on the north end of the bridge. With all soldiers busy, no one looked my way.

The other dismounted troopers hung their bridles on their saddles and tied their haltered riding horses to a picket rope strung between trees. Muskets were stacked, the long bayonets locking together at the top like teepee poles, holding the guns upright. The atmosphere relaxed as tobacco and flasks exited pockets. Two men detailed to water horses took them two by two down to the open ford in the Still River.

The soldiers looked prepared to stay, but surveyed the lowering clouds with worried expressions. Two troopers with sergeant's stripes strolled in my direction. Here was my chance to listen.

"That's the Knapp house over there," the leader explained. "Big barn, ain't it? Place belongs to a rich merchant — Benjamin Knapp. Old Dibble told the Colonel that Knapp wanted to cooperate any way he could. Lieutenant says this looked like a good place to house the generals. Says I should notify the man what to expect, 'case he don't know.'" He looked right over me as he assessed the property.

"How safe are we, here on the edge of town?" asked his associate sergeant. "Think the rebel forces might attack? Maybe stage a midnight raid?"

"If there are any rebel forces," returned his companion. Knowing smiles lit both tired faces.

"The three fools in that house we burned was probably all the 'forces' they had. Funny thing, how that slave come at us hammer and tongs, even after I ran him through with my bayonet. Hate to kill a man with that much courage. If England outlawed slavery, how can the colonies continue it? These people could use a good lesson."

Major Starr did not own any slaves that I knew about. His daughter Rebecca had been in the Academy, but had not been in school lately. Who *had* been in that house?

"All the same, good luck, landing in this Danbury town," said the other soldier. "Look at those nice fat hens scratching by the shed. I'll be the first to invite *that* crowd to dinner. I'm hungry enough to eat a boiled crow, ain't you, mate?"

The men turned away, but I had listened so hard that I never noticed Sarah had followed me. I gave out a yip of surprise when she dropped to her knees beside me, her white apron dragging in the dirt and wood chips.

If Patriot activities attracted British attention, a yip from a woodpile attracted even more. Pistol barrels were all I saw until the lead sergeant snorted, "'Tis but two young 'uns."

Sarah and I rose to our feet, ashamed of being caught. I wasn't sure whether to be afraid or not. The pistols dropped back into their holsters. The soldiers adopted the genial smiles of those seeking information.

"That's the Benjamin Knapp house over there, right? You the Knapps' servants' young ones?"

"I am Benjamin Knapp's daughter." Sarah's voice shook almost as much as her hands, which redeployed into twisting her apron.

"Your father get word that the generals will stay with him — uh, with you?"

"No one can come to our house, sir. My mother is unable to leave her bed," Sarah got out, with a bit more dignity than before.

"The leadin' Tories get the pleasure of the officers' company at dinner, whether they likes it or not. Five gentlemen plan to overnight here in this 'ere 'ouse."

.. un-
_e Amer-

_d his head-quar-
_s of a Loyalist nam-
_ the south end of the
d near the public stores.
Agnew and Erskine made
quarters in a house near
_t the upper end of the
_ow owned by Mr.
_e other houses in
_lled with British

HEAD-Q------RS OF AGNEW AND ERSKINE.*

*he ·

A feathery drizzle began to fall. The leather saddles and woolen uniforms would soon be dripping wet, and the spring nights still carried plenty of chill. The sergeant glanced at the threatening sky, using the watery mist as the silent explanation of all of his wants. "We need all them barn stalls, too. Our nags stood on them boats for two whole days of headwinds. We want the officers settled in before it pours. Go tell your pa, like a good girl. You the Knapp boy, then?" the sergeant added, attempting to sound pleasant.

I just said "Joe," not being too particular on the last name.

Sarah and I turned toward her house. I had to resist the urge to run, acutely aware that we only followed rude orders. After we choked out our news, mainly by pointing at the bridge and gasping, Mr. Knapp pronounced himself delighted to receive the generals. "One must uphold the dignity of the town, despite household concerns. We will welcome the generals as best we can," he announced, before slowly assuming the look of a man who has bitten off more than he can chew.

He turned to my mother, who looked to be in shock at the very idea of a houseful of British officers. With effort, he mumbled, "Yes, well, a few household concerns do exist."

"Concerns, such as no food," Sarah hissed, loud enough for everyone to hear.

"Mrs. Hamilton," began Mr. Knapp, his hands folded in unreligious prayer. "Your husband would want you to remain safe in my home tonight. I also need your help. Might I beg you to arrange a dinner table fit for noblemen? Silver and pewter aplenty stock the cupboard shelves, but their arrangement forms a mystery. I am not confident of food choices, either."

"Noblemen?" Mother looked at him with caution. "I admit to

curiosity about how noblemen look in real life. What kind of noblemen do you mean? Princes?"

"No, that would be royalty," explained Mr. Knapp. "I heard yesterday evening that Sir William Tryon leads this expedition. He advises the British army generals Sir William Erskine and General James Agnew." I could tell that Mr. Knapp loved saying those titles by how slowly the words dripped out. His confiding voice offered immediate entry into a social world previously unknown in Danbury.

"I suppose we needn't be ashamed of serving common fare," Mother said. "We must try to prevent any more unpleasant incidents associated with the British arrival. One incident with cannon fire is quite enough."

Normal coloring reemerged in Mother's ashen cheeks as she changed from a pathetic wraith into being my mother again. Her eyes assumed a calculating look as she entered the kitchen. By the time she returned, the look had turned accusing.

"I, ah, food — that's the problem." Mr. Knapp threw up his hands, indicating total submission. "I had not planned for this glorious occasion, I admit."

"What I have is at your disposal," Mother offered.

"I beg you, neighbor, for the sake of my poor wife, to make a meal as grand as she would have done, were she well in body." Mr. Knapp glanced at the bedroom door, where his wife could overhear every word.

"I'll make every effort to entertain your noblemen, if you promise they do no more damage," Mother held out her hand. They shook hands on the deal, and Mr. Knapp ducked into the next room to tell his wife the plan.

Mother motioned for Sarah and me to follow her. In the kitchen, she became all action – *my* action, as usual. "Joe, go to our house and fetch bread starter. It's in a crock on the top shelf. I saw plenty of fine wheat flour here, but preparing yeast bread takes three hours, at least. Who knows when these lords and knights will arrive?

"We missed the egg delivery to Griswold's today. Bring over what eggs we have in the house, as well as the sugar from last Christmas. Wash and smarten yourself before your return."

Mother sounded more secure now that she had a task. I felt more secure now that any focus had turned away from me, not to mention any secrets I carried with me.

A new hope had filtered into my mind. If officers came to the

Knapp house, and one of them revealed Grandfather's fate, my mother might never discover I had been a witness. Or almost a witness. A witness to *what* had become my biggest worry.

I would not ask questions. I felt confident that if I kept my ears open, the story would pour out like liquid overflowing the cup. Adults always bragged about everything, especially the bad things they've done.

A light rain dripped off the edge of the cottage roof as I plunged through our back door into the chill of emptiness. The emptiness included my stomach. Wheat bread for dinner would be special, as 'most everyone just made brown rye bread, except for wedding or funerals. Lucky that Mr. Knapp's new house had an oven built into the chimney. Most folks readied their dough at home and took it to the baker's huge oven, which was hot all year 'round.

Upstairs in my loft, I searched through my old church clothes. It had been almost a year since I'd worn them. I almost laughed when I tried on my old wool jacket. Nothing doing!

Then I searched through *other* people's old church clothes, castoffs given to me when we were still going to church. A second-hand dark blue coat and matching cocked hat were the only things that fit. Since they looked expensive, they probably came from Uncle Tad Benedict's son. Tad, Jr. Since he was now twenty-six, we might have had them a while.

The coat felt extra-warm and I wished we had a bigger looking glass. Lucky that my shirt sleeves could hide their worn edges under the rich wool. I found a pair of Mother's clean long stockings to fit over my too-short trouser legs, making them look like breeches. I would have to remember to keep my shoes out of sight.

I combed and re-tied my hair and washed my face with water from the rain barrel. My cocked hat made me look older, so on it went, despite the way cocked hats dump rain down your shoulders. Looking closer, maybe the rain had already soaked that hat on a number of occasions.

A cannikin of corn meal was almost full and I found the gray sugar loaf, still wrapped in its beautiful purple paper. A bench helped me to reach the dried herbs and a bag of walnuts that hung from hooks in the ceiling beams. The braid of onions came down, too. I fetched more dried plums from the cloth sack under the floor. A wooden bucket held dozens of eggs, at least three or four days' work for our hens.

The cloth sacks went under my jacket for the return trip, but I held the egg bucket out, figuring the rain could wash the eggs. I shut the chicken coop's door as I passed. The chickens had gone in out of the rain. No foxes wanted.

The overcast sky looked and felt more like night than late afternoon. Distant thunder predicted more evil weather on the way — or maybe I heard distant cannon fire. I wasn't sure how to tell the difference.

Chapter Nineteen

Saturday, April 26th, 1777
at Five o'Clock of the Evening

The rich and peaceful smell of bayberry candles welcomed me into the Knapps' warm drawing room, where glowing fires now lit every room. I recalled Christmas visits to Judge Tom Benedict once upon a different time.

Reflections off the gold-rimmed mirrors turned five candles into twenty, brightening the peaceful faces of our king and queen, who stared out from their gold frames on the dining room wall. Imported furniture gleamed under high ceilings. The tall clock added music as it chimed five o' clock.

Mercy busied herself arranging pewter platters, plates, and tankards on the dining table, humming all the while. This new Mercy wore a clean ruffled apron and cap, as well as chestnut hair that glowed from brushing. Excitement flickered in her eyes as she imagined the coming party. She twirled toward the windows for a look at her reflection. "Maybe a lord will ask to marry me and a general will marry Sarah!"

I looked at myself, too, but made as if I only wanted to look outside.

"Look, Joe! Isn't it beautiful?" Mercy pointed to the snowy damask board-cloth, each place set with a matching napkin, horn-handled knife, and spoon. Only eight forks showed themselves, but my family only had two.

Mr. Knapp's pale gray wig had a braided queue at the back and seemed right for meeting English nobles. Glittery cut steel buckles on his golden tan knee breeches matched the ones on his black shoes. A frothy white lace neck cloth added to the portrait of a gracious gentleman. One would never guess that he worked with smelly cowhides.

"This evening will be a grand experience for you children." His face radiated as much warmth as the fire. "A dignified and peaceful army progression through Connecticut will remind the people to praise our king for his reluctance to injure rebel citizens. This revolution is madness, like the infectious insanity of the witch business a hundred years ago in Massachusetts Colony."

Sympathizers with the government of the mother country abounded hereabouts. They were men who honestly believed that the colonies had no right to secede from the crown, and they defended their belief when they could, and cherished it at all times. They were jubilant now. The proper authorities were in possession, the rebel element was overcome, and the Tories believed that Danbury was forever redeemed from the pernicious sway of the rebellion.

A bowl of mixed nuts and dried apples attracted my fingers – until Mr. Knapp snatched the bowl to safety. A second later, he added, "Don't mean to insult members of your family, Joe. In Danbury, it's hard to escape this revolutionary fever. In your family, it would be impossible!"

Too much Tory talk sent me to the kitchen, where the warm glare of copper pots reflected the firelight. Two large iron pots sat in the fire, their feet nestled in coals. The corn puddings must be inside. The hiss of corn cakes frying in hot bacon grease lured me to the fireplace. Sarah had changed into a gold-colored silk dress that fell to her ankles, now covered by a long linen apron. A thread-thin gold chain hung around her neck, making her the only girl I had ever seen wearing jewelry. She concentrated on turning the cakes as they browned in melted butter, her pan sitting on a trivet over the coals. She broke a johnnycake and I was happy to help dispose of the evidence, wiping my buttery fingers on my old breeches under my coat, where no one would see.

Mother had moved on to mixing a plum duff. Her jerky movements revealed a cook who fears her dinner won't be ready on time.

Mother might have new energy, but she resembled a crack in a mirror. She looked so – so worn and unkempt. Her black mourning clothes had seen every-day use since her father's death last summer. Washing had degraded the fabric to an uneven earth tone, while her tear-stained face spoke of no washing since yesterday. Her white cap had come off and her hair straggled everywhere. Pieces of hay from the barn still clung to her skirt. Her cloth shoes had not done well in the sheep-filled barn.

I stared at my mother for long enough that Sarah noticed. She took off her apron and glanced down at her own dress of silk, the design plain, and the fabric as shiny as real metal. She disappeared into the hall. A few minutes passed before she returned with a lace-trimmed blue silk dress. The crisp fabric rustled like dry leaves. Mother's worried face slid into a charmed smile at the unexpected appearance of a ball-gown in the kitchen.

"What lovely silk! Perfect for you when you're older, Sarah!"

"No, it's my Mother's. It's for you," Sarah announced, proud at her quick solution to an embarrassing problem. "Mother says you can wear it tonight."

Mother shook her head, but spoke gently, "I do love the dress, but wearing mourning black lasts one full year. I'm paying respect to my father."

My mother's father, Judge Thomas Benedict, Senior. Imagine a Patriot so determined that he died on the Fourth of July, 1776. Mother had called it a sign from heaven. A bad sign.

Her attention returned to the plum duff batter, though her eyes strayed back to the dress, indicating her longing to wear clothes other than washed-out black.

Sarah motioned to me to follow her as she returned the dress to a pine chest in the hall and plopped herself down atop the chest. She kicked her feet out and admired her mother's high-heeled shoes. She seemed to want me to say something, but I didn't.

"My father won't say anything, but your mother owns good clothes, doesn't she? I mean, her *own* clothes?" Sarah rolled her eyes to the heavens.

"Maybe something could spill on her and she would be forced to change into her old church clothes," I offered.

"Many things already did spill on her," Sarah mumbled. She stared at the wall before murmuring, "Mother said once that no lady —" and finished in a rush. " I know what to use!" Excited, she rushed up the hall.

"Father," she called into the drawing room, "what will these officers drink?"

"Bring out all the bottles in the hiding place. On second thought, better leave a couple of bottles of wine down there, just in case."

Sarah and I raised a trapdoor in the hall floor and extracted a dozen bottles. We hauled them to a sideboard in the dining room, stifling smiles as our plans became solid.

"I'll get punished so hard for doing this," Sarah whispered as we removed the wires, corks and wax seals. "I'm supposed to be a young lady, not a stupid child."

One Knapp would cause any trouble she could, just for amusement. We invited Mercy into a corner.

"Mercy," I whispered, "my mother refuses to dress up to receive the generals. If someone spilled on her old clothes ...."

"You want me punished for your stupid tricks? I'm going to tell!" The girl gave exceedingly nasty looks for a girl ten years old.

"Go ahead and tell," Sarah threatened. "See if we care."

Mercy's face blossomed with joy at playing a first-class prank.

Sarah poured a full tankard of rum and headed for the kitchen, towing Mercy by her sleeve. I followed behind, in the role of the not-innocent witness.

"Mrs. Hamilton? A cup of cider? Mercy, take Father this rum."

"Whew! I'm exhausted. A cider would be a fine treat, my dear," answered Mother, now seated at the table where she picked out nutmeats after Noah cracked the walnuts.

The maneuvering resembled battle tactics, as Sarah pulled Mercy to her station. "Here, Mercy, hold this tankard."

"Why, Mercy, take care! You'll — Oh, Mrs. Hamilton! How dreadful!"

Mercy leaped away from the cascade of Jamaica's finest rum, as it rolled from Mother's cap and hair all the way down her back. The rum soaked into her clothing, spreading its rummy scent across the room.

"Spirits will dry quickly in the warmth of the fire," remarked Mother, gritting her teeth against the icy wet stream. She favored Sarah with a smile. "Not your fault, dear, was it? Poor little Mercy, such a sweet child."

Not willing to admit defeat, Sarah emitted loud sniffs, "Oh, Mrs. Hamilton, but you do smell like rum! I hope the gentlemen don't think ... well, I dare not say!" Which invited curiosity about just *what* she didn't dare say.

Mother's face changed to horror as the meaning hit her like a slap. English noblemen would think Judge Thomas Benedict's daughter had become a drunken servant woman. Leaping out of her chair as if bitten by a snake, Mother escaped out the back door.

Chapter Twenty

Saturday, April 26th, 1777
at Seven o'Clock of the Evening

Tryon's assistants, Generals Erskine and Agnew, accompanied by a body of mounted infantry, proceeded up Main Street to the junction of Barren Plain Road ... where Benjamin Knapp lived...

In front of the Knapps' house, a crowd of muddy horses and muddier lieutenants assisted and obstructed two British generals and one New York colonel as they dismounted. Six officers pressed into the hallway, filling every inch not occupied by the wide-eyed Knapps.

The house had smelled of hot candle wax and corn cakes, but the guests' arrival added a manly atmosphere of sweat and horse. Their scarlet jackets showed such adornment of gold braid and medals that little of the weather-faded red background still showed.

The two British generals were hearty, smiling men, faces reddened by sun and wind. Their voices reflected the confidence of knowing the King of England, although maybe not by his first name. Sarah and Mercy bent their knees and held their skirts up at the sides to demonstrate refined curtsies. Mr. Knapp almost curtsied by mistake, but ended by shaking hands.

The New York Colonel, dressed all in green and white as a contrast to his English companions, shook my hand, assuming I was a Knapp, too. My new blue coat was making an impression.

A lieutenant rivaling Lambert Lockwood in his refined and elegant appearance introduced himself, accidentally mentioning that the Earl of Falkland was his father. The lieutenant chatted quietly with the generals while two other soaking wet lieutenants led the horses to the barn. Easy to see how this nobility thing worked.

The gentlemen seated themselves on the drawing room chairs, passed little silver snuffboxes, and awaited refreshments. Their crossed legs showed black leather boots as soft as tent canvas. I searched their faces, wondering who had the best information about my grandfather.

At the door, a soldier asked Mr. Knapp if that pony could move from the barn into a field. Mr. Knapp turned to me. "Take the little beast to your shed, will you, Joe? Prefer all my animals remain indoors on a night like this."

"Yes, sir, right away," I agreed, glad to comply. The best information might come from the men in the barn. Asking generals might have a bad result. They might wonder why I wanted to know.

I hurried Pony through the gate and over to our shed. Almost nothing of last winter's hay remained, so I tied her to the wall in the empty space and hung a water bucket on a nearby nail. If Father came home in the middle of the night, the stallion's stall would be empty.

Pony whinnied once before nosing into her dry dinner. Gentle chewing soon joined the rain pattering down on the shake roof. Grateful, I hugged her solid, furry body before I started back through the rain to the Knapps' barn.

I watched and listened while soldiers curried and wiped down the officers' horses. Then a most familiar sound chilled my blood. The screams echoed those I had heard from the house where the sniper died. The British exchanged pleased glances.

"Do us another, then, Al!" called one, which his fellows repeated in high-pitched falsetto. Everyone laughed. I gathered my courage, and looked outside the rear barn door that faced the Still River. I should have known. A soldier butchered the lambs we had played with in the morning.

Just wait 'til Mr. Knapp found out! Another thing I didn't plan to admit that I had seen.

As I looked out into the night, two flashes showed on the other side of the river. The Still River wasn't wide, just a fast creek, and the nearness of gunfire alarmed everyone. Scattered shots began to arrive on a regular basis. On the other hand, no shots hit anything.

Besides that, the neighboring people, on that eventful afternoon, drew nearer to the town with their long-barrelled guns, and taking advantage of the heavy growth of alders along the stream, fired at a redcoat wherever he showed himself. There was a picket stationed at the main Street bridge, and this party was a special target. All this made Mr. Knapp very nervous …

"Pickets back to the road! Everyone else, take cover!" A sergeant shooed me along toward the house. To my horror, two troopers lifted the skinned lambs and followed me toward the open front door.

"Don't go in there!" I yelled. "Ladies present!"

I motioned them toward the kitchen door, and the pair followed obediently. Sarah had not returned, which was just as well. The troopers dumped their load on the wooden floor and examined the kitchen. Just as if they belonged here, the men lifted the lids of pots and raked the fire coals. They seemed more at home than I did, and picked up conversation, apparently best friends.

"I'll just commence with these here carcasses, Bill. Wish we coulda' done the butchering outdoors, but can't risk our lives over a meal, now can we? Umm, what have we here? Bread just laid in to bake. Don't think a woman would care for this meat scene, no sireee. Generals pro'ly prefer my cooking, anyways. You, there!" He gestured at me, as Bill sorted through kitchen utensils, coming up with a giant cleaver.

"Just tell them officers out there that we got this under control. I'm Gen'l Erskine's person'l cook. We'll cook up this lot fit for a king."

I opened the door into the hall, intending to warn Sarah about the lamb bodies, but the front door opened and Mother appeared, framed in the front doorway.

In no way did she resemble the woman who had fled beneath a cloud of rum fumes. Her face shone clean and alive from scrubbing. Her almost-new church clothes, long folded away, fit right in as evening wear. The blue skirt still looked bright, while the close-fitting red flannel jacket revealed a ruffled white blouse of sufficient gaiety for a party.

All the men rose as Mother entered. "Good evening, gentlemen," she said, as bold and confident as a member of the first society in town. Just as my new coat made me feel ready to meet generals, her dress clothes had changed her for the better. A natural smile reminded me of the days when she wore these same clothes to church, riding behind my father's saddle and shrieking every time he tried to trot.

"Who is this delightful feminine addition to our gathering?"

boomed one of the officers, all gold braid and fringe. Most surely a general, complete with sword and sword tassel.

"Madam, I am William Erskine. Do you live nearby? Are you related to these fine people, to Mr. Benjamin Knapp?"

"Indeed, general, we live next door." Mother stopped, just as if her last name were Knapp. Answering with the last name of a Committeeman might not be a good idea. How clever of her to tell the truth, but make it a lie.

"May I present General James Agnew, madam?" General Erskine continued introductions with the smooth manners of those accustomed to ruling the room.

"Good evening, madam. And what is your husband's profession — since everyone in America appears to have one?" General Agnew continued with a little laugh, as if a profession counted as a common misfortune, akin to bad teeth.

Mother's new confidence blurred into confusion.

"My father trains and sells horses," I put in, anxious to fill the gap. "He is away now, to sell a fine blooded stallion." Proud of my half-true and mostly-lie answer, I smiled up at the general.

"Indeed," said Mother, recovering herself. "Would you gentlemen care for a drop of drink to relieve the thirst of a trying day?" A deft example of subject changing, also useful for my education.

"Brandy all around, if you please, ma'am," answered the general.

Mr. Knapp poured brandy, while Sarah tilted the cider and ale pitchers over a tray of silver-mounted coconut shell cups. Most of the party accepted both drinks. I took a pewter cup of cider and dropped to the floor along the wall.

The company settled down for conversation. Settled, except for me, tortured by certain subject. The chase scene had begun to seem like a dream, already fading into the background. What had I really seen?

Mother looked at the kitchen door, but General Erskine stood and raised his glass to the company. "My staff is most grateful to be here, for this has been a long day, indeed." He smiled at each one of us in turn. Such kindly reassurance blessed everyone, and we all smiled back, just as if the general had become the host. He sat down and sipped, gesturing for Mother to sit also.

"Now, about horses," a captain began, addressing General Agnew. "I need a new mount. My best steeplechase horse is 'most ruined from racing that appalling scoundrel this afternoon. What a filthy old bearded sod that one was."

I turned away to conceal the violent recognition on my face. The lead rider of the three cavalrymen sat right opposite me! I shrank back against the wall, even though I knew he'd never seen me before.

"Missus, you would not believe this," the captain stated, pleading his case to Mother. "A horrid old crook tried the nasty tactic of releasing a bolt of red cloth, probably looted, into the faces of our horses. My valuable nag returned dead lame, honest beast that it is."

"Yes, the robber's old creature looked ready for the butcher, but it dragged that cloth for over a mile, our horses refusing to ride over it."

"My gr – uh, the scoundrel escaped?" I asked, just to make sure. "He got away?"

Glances ran from silent redcoat to silent redcoat in the pause that followed.

"I wouldn't say 'got away,'" the New York colonel declared, while slowly checking his shirt cuffs. "More like 'temporarily evaded authority.'"

The others nodded, relieved that someone else had answered.

What an escape: not Grandfather's — mine! I sighed and kept on doing it, because it felt so good. I peered at Mother, but "filthy old sod" did not describe my grandfather, so she did not appear to recognize the story's main character.

The colonel continued. "This particular criminal was a leader of the Committee of Inspection. Americans are a loyal and respectful populace if not incited to revolt by this rabble. These Committee snakes lie about British taxation. The American war against the French bankrupted England. I know it's been fifteen years, but the costs were incredible."

"Expeditions like today only add to the debt," complained General Agnew. "You must agree that allowing the rebels to stock weapons would lead to wholesale war. No one wants this lovely country destroyed." All heads nodded, including Mother's and Mr. Knapp's.

Sheets of rain now pounded down outside the windows. Concern about the Patriots faded. All the military men agreed that no one would stage an attack in the rain. The gunpowder would get wet.

If there was any powder.

Sarah still held her tray of drinks, standing as if in a trance, her eyes fixed on the noble lieutenant.

Rhythmic pounding from the kitchen made everyone turn toward the hall. Before I could stop her, Sarah turned to investigate. We heard the door open just before a resounding thud accompanied her full-length crash onto the uncarpeted hall floor. The silver tray clashed the cups against each other like bells before they hit the floor. Little trails of cider and beer traced their paths as the cups rolled their uneven way back toward us.

I reached the hall in one jump. Both hands flew to my mouth. Framed in the kitchen doorway behind Sarah's unconscious body, sat a pile of skinned lambs. The surrounding pool of blood slowly soaked into the wooden floor. A hand yanked the door shut from the inside and the ghastly scene disappeared before my mother could see it.

The captain, sitting near the hall, had seen in through open door. "The general's personal cook has taken charge of our dinner," was the officer's over-the-shoulder comment. "Fine man with the meat. Don't trouble yourself about the meal, ma'am. He and our Bill can serve the whole dinner."

> The generals made themselves fully at home. There was no stiffness about them. They killed Mr. Knapp's stock, and cut up the meat on his floor, and the dents thereof were visible as long as the building stood. Mr. Knapp's wife was a sorely afflicted invalid, but her inability to attend to domestic duties did not in any way embarrass the guests.

The captain scooped Sarah into his arms, while my mother rushed to open Mrs. Knapp's bedroom door. The officer carried the body into the bedroom, arms and legs dangling, limp as a dead fish. Having bodies lying about did not seem new to him.

He returned and sat down, signaling that all was under control. After a minute, Mother followed. For her, nothing had happened except an overexcited girl had fainted.

And a British nobleman stood to greet her return.

General Erskine raised his glass to toast her. "To a most refined lady, caught in difficult times!"

Mother responded with a gracious, "Let us hear of your adventures before arriving here, gentlemen." She gathered the blue skirt and sank onto a white brocade chair, tilting her head to listen.

"Please understand, dear people," General Agnew began, in an official voice, "we desire no unpleasantry such as plagued our arrival. The situation escaped our control somewhat." He showed unnecessary interest in his coconut shell beaker.

"Do explain. I have not been downtown this whole day." Mother smiled, open to hear whatever misfortune had plagued them.

"A bit of street action enlivened our entrance," said General Erskine. "Just a few shots, fired by rebel rogues. Criminals from other towns had invaded a house. Just robbers, no doubt about it, although the house belonged to a rebel officer, so the burning was justified, any way you look at it. Don't concern yourselves about your local citizens. No one was injured." General Erskine observed the amber contents of his glass with care.

"Burning? A rebel officer's home, you say?" Mother looked concerned and appeared to ponder whose house had burned. Dozens of men in Danbury were now in various militias or the Continental army. Officers from the War against the French still used their titles. Perhaps it had happened in one of the settlements on the way into town. A stranger would hardly know the difference. Still, the corners of her smiling mouth had migrated downward.

"Strong reaction proves that we mean business." General Agnew wagged a warning finger in time with his next words. "That beheading, though – not approved at all!" He leveled a stern look at the noble young lieutenant, who failed to notice.

Benjamin Knapp noticed, and his hands clutched the arms of his chair as if he were about to leap to his feet.

> In the meantime Benjamin Knapp, the erstwhile tanner and now unwilling host, was having his own particular trouble. It is very rarely that a resident of a humble village has two brigadier-generals come to spend Sunday with him, and the advent of Generals Agnew and Erskine should have been an unbounded delight to Mr. Knapp, but it is doubtful if it were.

"Yes, a citizen's servant is dead," continued the General in a disapproving way. "Plus several other felons. Slavery is illegal in England now. The one thing unclean about America is slavery. Perhaps we can accomplish that. General Erskine's frown suggested that eradicating American slavery justified any and all British actions.

The Earl's son rose and moved to select a handful of the nuts. Turning back to us, he smiled gently. "We burned the house of the occurrence as a courtesy. Your citizens wouldn't have to bother about bodies. Nicer sort of house, too." He shrugged at the sinful waste of a nice home.

Mother and Mr. Knapp had jerked to the edges of their seats at the mention of beheading and bodies. Mother clutched a handkerchief in a way sure to rip it. Mr. Knapp's jaw looked about to dislocate. At last it slid shut and remained so.

Mother's voice had gone amiss, but the words at last stuttered out. "W-wh-whose house was it, the one that burned – I mean, where was it located?"

"Houses here all look the same to me – just wood," General Agnew said, perhaps more accustomed to stone castles in England. "The house stood in town, a long way from here. Local people assured us that none of the owner's family was present. Only robbers, as I said." The last words carried a finality the meant no further response would be allowed.

Mother and Mr. Knapp exchanged questioning glances. Both assumed watchful and cautious new expressions. A little strange, that they avoided looking at each other.

So Major Starr had not been shot, the way I had imagined. Maybe only robbers had been in his house, after all.

The smell of roasting meat slowly overtook the room, matching the aroma of baking bread. The British sniffed and pleased smiles appeared instead of conversation.

Sarah, pale as a faraway star, opened her mother's bedroom door and gazed at us. Her father motioned for her to sit next to him on the ivory velvet camelback sofa. She leaned against Mr. Knapp, eyes closed. When she opened them, her gaze soon landed on the noble lieutenant again. And remained there.

"Today did feature genuine amusements, interesting to anyone," the New York colonel said, trying to lighten the dead air that had fallen.

"I'll tell what happened in Redding. That's suitable for ladies," the lieutenant suggested. He bowed to Mother and to Sarah. After a moment, Sarah slid over on the seat, coming to rest halfway between her father and the officer. She folded her hands to hear the story, casting a shy glance at her companion.

"On the march this morning in Redding village, our column halted for breakfast. Straightaway, a young man on a flashy chestnut mare flew downhill as if on a racecourse. Charged right into our formation! Never seen such daring. I wonder how he failed to see two thousand men." All of the British laughed. So did Mercy Knapp.

"What followed?" asked Mr. Knapp in an icy voice. "He ran through them or they ran him through?"

"No bayonets in this story, sir," the taleteller reproved. "Indeed, this fine officer here shot his bird on the wing." He bowed to the captain who had carried Sarah.

"And that was so amusing?" Mother drove a peculiar bite into her words.

"Haven't reached the amusing part yet, ma'am. There the rebel lad stands, bleeding away, and claims that the head of our expedition, General Tryon, is his 'friend.' None of us believed a word of it, but the fairy tale was true! The general insisted a neighbor woman wash out the lad's wound. Fine-looking sort of fella he was, for a rebel. Had fine clothes and saddlery fit for a lord. And I should know." The noble-looking lieutenant finished on a self-approving note.

I had already identified the star player in this scene. How had Lambert Lockwood landed in Redding? I had worried about my uncles, but not about Lambert, because he worked for the Commissary.

Now I had to sit still and pretend to know nothing. To keep from yelling aloud, I bit my lip hard enough that a salty blood taste flooded my mouth.

"That horse looked to be as grand a mare as I've ever seen. What a runner!" The colonel said. "Would not mind owning such a beast, not at all." His enthusiasm sparked other admiration.

"You're a bit heavy for so refined a type, sir. Besides, I want her, too," said the beheading lieutenant. "We should get our hands on that animal and auction it off among us. You know, just to be fair."

Fair? Who was he to talk about *fair*?

"What became of the rider? Did he die?" I managed to ask, earning a black look from Mother.

"I don't think so." General Agnew hesitated, looking around for information. "Sometimes one glances away from the wounded for a few seconds and they expire without warning." He shrugged at the incompetent wounded, who failed at survival.

The two generals looked at each other. "Did we leave that one in – what was the name of the place again?" asked General Erskine.

"Redding," answered the lordly lieutenant. "And no, he came with us on the racehorse, not in the ox-cart with the others. I b'lieve the scoundrel went direct to General Tryon's headquarters, near where we entered town, by the Anglican church. Fine big house, looks just like this one, anyway. S'pose that horse is still there?" He and the colonel exchanged glances of silent unity.

I knew what house he meant – Mr. Dibble's house on Triangle Street. A plan took form for me, too.

General Erskine addressed my mother and Mr. Knapp in a frustrated, pleading tone. "Once again, the person shot did not reside in Danbury. The incident happened in Redding. If people go galloping around, they get shot, that's all."

"We never miss," said the lieutenant, raising his glass to the sharpshooter.

My mother closed her eyes.

"I must excuse myself," I said, as I stood up and headed for the door.

Danbury, January 26th, 1778

Ebenezer White, of Danbury, of lawful age, testifies and says that on or about the 26th day of April,1777 at evening, there being a number of gentlemen at his house belonging to the British Army, among which was one whom he understood was the Earl of Falkland's son, who told him (the deponent) that he was the first that entered Major Starr's house, and found a number of men in the house, among whom were two negroes, all of whom they instantly killed, and set fire to the house; and gave this for a reason why they did so, that it was their constant practice where they found people shut up in a house and firing upon them, to kill them, and to burn the house and further saith the deponent saith, that the said young gentleman told him that one of the negroes, after he had run him through, rose up and attempted to shoot him, and that he, the said Earl of Falkland's son, cut his head off himself: which negro the deponent understood since was the property of Mr. Samuel Smith, of Reading: and further the deponent saith not.

The Rev. Mr. Ebenezer White, the deponent, personally appearing, made oath to the truth of the above written deposition.

Sworn to me, Thaddeus Benedict, Justice of the Peace.

Chapter Twenty-One

Saturday, April 26th, 1777
at Half Eight o'Clock of the Evening

Welcoming the dark, I hurried through the rain. I felt plenty scared, because all the Brits agreed on one thing — Lambert Lockwood had taken a bullet. My new brother. I could hardly breathe. I had to see him.

If he still lived.

As I ran past the house where Lambert stayed with his step-mother, I searched for the vague glow of a fire or candle. Nothing.

I felt like a criminal, walking in total darkness on the street. The Committee had declared that anyone out at night must carry a lantern. Theft was rampant. If someone spotted me, I had already committed a crime. A minor crime, but enough for an adult to collar me.

As I drew closer to the village, a row of bonfires down the middle of Town Street gave reason enough to smell smoke. But just past West Street, I slowed my steps. My stomach rebelled, as I smelled a slightly different smell from burning wood. Major Starr's whole house smoldered on the ground. Only the two stone chimneys remained, standing like church steeples for the Church of Hell. Had a living man been beheaded in that house? How unbelievable: a head chopped off in modern times, although a thoroughly modern general had admitted it was true.

Crowds of soldiers stood, sat and lay everywhere. British red coats mixed with the green coats of the New York regiment, but no peaceful scene of evening campfires took place here.

Officers yelled curses that should make a soldier salute for a week. Their men paid no attention; playing dice, swigging from liquor bottles. Three soldiers carrying huge cheese rounds dared an officer to shoot them for looting Griswold's store. The officer held his musket with the bayonet pointing out as he backed away. It came as a relief when no shots sounded behind me as I legged it around the corner onto South Street.

How to get inside the Dibble house formed the question. A man might invent a credible lie to enter a general's headquarters. A boy had fewer lies available. Of course, the guards might shoot an adult. The misty rain continued, and the vents in my shoes let in water and mud from the various yards of Benedict relatives as I went from shadow to shadow.

Deciding that I needed to study the house for a while, I passed it, and established a safe position in the graveyard of the Anglican Church. The next move required careful calculation. Climbing in a window and searching the house was out of bounds. I had already seen ten men enter the building. There could be a man in every room.

A huge soldier guarded the front door, but what comments went between him and the officers he let in and out? Maybe I could learn what I needed to know. A sycamore in front of Dibble's house looked big enough to hide me and close enough for my purposes. A creaky cart rolled past, and I rushed from the graveyard to the tree trunk. Hiding in its shadow, I was close enough to hear the door squeak as it opened.

After a few minutes of listening to commonplace greetings, I commenced to shiver. The new wool coat, once it got truly wet, weighed twice what it had originally, making me wet to the skin. My chattering teeth must have made a lot of noise.

"Say, bub, do you think that I don't see you there? Come out 'ere, I say. What are ya' on about, then, lad?" called the guard, not sounding angry enough to do me real harm. Coming out of hiding formed my only choice, but I needed a clue how to act.

Sticking my head out, I saw the guard's engaging grin. Here was a man I wanted to have on my side, especially considering the humorous look to his face. Bigger and heavier than my father, he was a man mountain, for sure.

The troops by our house had been nice enough when they imagined Sarah and I were the children of servants. Maybe I should try my luck at using that key to this door.

"Sir, is there a prisoner in there? One who's wounded?" My voice gave a squeak akin to Noah Knapp's babyish voice.

"Can't have lads as carry spy messages be runnin' in and out. Which side's you on, eh?"

Not a bad result, since the man waited for my answer instead of chasing me away. I had a chance to blend the truth with — well, with whatever I wanted.

"Please, sir," I begged, in as small a voice as I could manage, "My poor mother cooked for Mr. Benjamin Knapp's party of generals. When we learned my brother had been shot, my mother couldn't come here on account of her work." I wiped my eyes and hung my head to act tearful. "My brother may be a rebel, but he's still my brother, so I came by myself."

After a muffled sob, I wiped my eyes to hide that no tears brimmed there.

I had to get into this house.

"Let me get this story straight, lad — yer brother went bad and is a rebel?" The big trooper chuckled.

A chill shot through me, alerting me to my painful mistake. Admitting that my brother had committed treason might mean bad news for that brother.

"Not anymore," I chattered. "He vowed to give up warring and will never fight again. Maybe he rode to visit his grandparents – our grandparents. That's it! He rode to Wilton to check on our grandparents. Honest, he did not have a musket!" I never had seen Lambert with a musket, anyway.

"Now then, you are the little brother and the weeping mother sent you here because her son is sore wounded?" He had reduced my words to exactly what I wanted him to think.

I nodded, trying to look innocent while appearing stupid, too.

Still suspicious, the trooper probed further. "And just where is the father, might I ask? Pro'bly taught yer brother that rebel muck, didn't he?"

"For sure, he opposes war against Mother England." I put my hand to my heart and turned my eyes toward the heavens.

"Awww, go on in there, boy, but let your daddy know that he won't be safe if he comes hunting your brother here."

"My daddy's out of town selling a horse." The truth was easy enough. I wanted to relieve the guard of any worry my presence might cause.

"A fine excuse if he's gone with the rebel scum that fled this town today."

"Truly, he left long before your army came." About thirty minutes, I figured.

"And just when does yer old daddy return?" The trooper questioned in a calculating way. He bent to hear the answer and his pockmarked face approached closer to mine, his eyes bloodshot. He appeared to hold his breath while he awaited my answer.

"He might not sell that particular horse soon," I countered, bending over backward to avoid contact. "It's a stallion and not an easy horse to ride."

The trooper's smile widened in pleasure. "I catch the drift, 'deed I do! All us Irish folk are great ones for the horses. Yer father had to get far enough away that the nag's evil tricks remain secret! Where does he have his barn, your daddy?" He ended with a grin of connivance in the imaginary crooked sale.

"It's just a shed next door to where the generals came today." I hoped that proximity to generals would provide me with a shield. The soldier's face had reminded me of a hungry person watching meat cook.

"Go ahead inside, lad. Say Tommy Flynn let you in. Yer brother's through there. Satisfy yerself that he's alive and squirrel back out here, quick as you can." A clublike hand pointed through the open front door.

Stumbling over the doorsill into the hall's candlelight, I still had no clue where to find Lambert. The polished wooden floor planks of Dibble's hall showed streaks and chunks of mud, so I followed the trail down the center hall. In a drawing room, a dozen men in uniform stood and sat around a candle-lit desk. The large man at the desk must be General Tryon. I didn't look at him because I didn't want him to look at me. My sudden entrance drew the immediate attention I had hoped to avoid.

"What do you want here, boy?" snapped an officer as he spun me around by the shoulder. His medals flashed like flames, and the powerful fingers clenching my shoulder bones shot fire all the way down my arm. He held onto me while more sets of eyes gleamed in our direction.

"I search for my brother, the wounded prisoner," I mumbled, without looking higher than his belt buckle. Now I would be ejected like a child.

"Him? Right over there." The officer propelled me by a shove toward the far corner of the room. I looked where he pointed, but I saw no one. Shadows swirled as the room's other occupants shifted. Perhaps he meant a door in that dark corner. I walked blindly forward, into the shadows.

Coming closer, I noticed boots. A pair of soft brown leather riding boots rested on the floor below a pile of clothing stacked atop a chair.

I recognized the pile.

Lambert sat slumped to one side, eyes closed, arms sprawled. One arm had a sleeve cut open down the seam and a bandage showed beneath it. Lambert, a man of full height, appeared shrunken. White as a corpse, he almost looked dead. Whatever his condition, conscious he was not.

I tiptoed up to his elbow. When I touched his shoulder to wake him, Lambert jerked violently and yelped, "Don't touch me!" as his bloodshot eyes cracked open.

Instead of reassuring him that a friend had come, I had made it worse. "Lambert, what can I do – get you water?"

His head lolled sideways and he looked unable to sit up straight. He must need aid and need it fast.

"No, nothing to drink. I fear coming over sick and fouling my clothes in front of the enemy. All the same, good to see you here, brother." I think he tried to smile.

He fixed his gaze upon me, looking more childlike than adult. His eyes checked the room before he motioned me closer and whispered, "I need help, not for me, but for … for my little girl. Find Desire and move her back to your place before someone snatches her."

The urgency of our talk had filtered through to the same officer as before. "No whispering, you hear!" His face looked fierce as he reached us in three strides and towered over us like a giant.

"We only speak of where his, uhh, his little girl is to be located, now that …."

I gestured at my hero, now transformed into this wreck. Lambert looked bad indeed. His skin looked crusted with dried sweat, repeatedly renewed by pain and fear.

After the first suspicious look, the officer murmured, "A child … a child … of course." A true concern flooded his face before he resumed his previous bark. "Just say whatever is necessary."

The officer returned to the general's desk, his fierceness drained away and looking only tired. He glanced over at me in a worried way, making me wonder why mentioning a little girl had caused such a change.

Lambert fixed me with begging and frantic eyes. "Don't let anyone stop you. Desire is all I have," he whispered, lips barely moving.

That may well be true, since my father had blamed the mare for draining Lambert's inheritance funds. I could not picture how I could find his horse.

Still, I could not help myself when he asked, "Can you do this, Joe?"

I nodded.

Lambert shivered a time or two, before shrinking ever smaller inside his tailored coat, now boasting splashes of rusty dried blood all down the front. He began drifting away, sounding vague and mystified. "I'm not sure what's amiss with me. Loss of blood, I suppose, yet I did not lose much compared to other wounded I saw in New York. I feel no septic infection, just a terrible weakness."

"Now I think on it," Lambert added, "maybe I had poor judgment when I drank nothing last night or this whole day. I don't trust water from unfamiliar wells. I fear collapse just when I am about to be set free. It may be all night before he lets me go."

"Let you go? Are they going to let you go?" I said, louder than I should have. The first officer shot a look that remained glued to us, making me feel like a prisoner, too.

The man behind the desk looked up for a second, the intelligent face warmed by the soft candle flames. A flicker of warmth glowed in his eyes. Lambert's general-friend, beyond any doubt.

"Yes, the same General Tryon I told you about sits at the desk. He will do the right thing by me, I know it." A simple trust shone on Lambert's face— rather foolish, since he could have been set free already.

"I can return with food and drink after I secure … uh, your little girl. Am I not your brother? I'll be back soon, I promise."

Our British monitor sent his razor glance in our direction. "What's this, now?" he demanded, striding across the room.

"I only asked my brother to bring food and drink, lest I collapse." Lambert sounded as feeble as he looked.

The Brit now aimed a more serious look at Lambert, noticing for the first time that something was critically wrong.

"You look about to keel over. That would make you rather more of a bother than you are now. Three fingers of rum would put you right." This seemed to be an offer of help.

Lambert held up a hand of refusal. "No rum, sir. I fear sickening from spirits. My mouth is parched. Cider or ale might keep me among the living."

An engaging smile flowed across the officer's face as he discovered a way to benefit himself and friends.

"Right, mate, your order taken by the tapster of Tryon Tavern." A mock bow accompanied the joking retort.

Calling to his fellow officers, he said, "This one here is about dead. Anyone else for a noggin of rum, gentlemen?" Eager voices across the room seconded the thought. The officer moved away to take their orders.

Out from under those watching eyes, Lambert reached into his coat while whispering, "They might try to fine me. I want you to take this for safekeeping." Although slow and awkward in his attempts to retrieve a handful of rebel dollars, he nodded full satisfaction when I stuffed his pay inside my shirt before I slipped away.

I looked back from the doorway. Lambert had sunk back into his previous semi-conscious state, head dropped back and mouth open. I had to hurry.

Chapter Twenty-Two

Saturday, April 26th, 1777
at Eight o'Clock of the Evening

"Find yer lad, then?" asked the door guard as I left. "All on the up-and-up now, is it?" The words sounded so strange that I didn't know whether to say yes or no.

"Yer brother? What was his condition?" demanded the trooper.

"Not so good. He didn't drink anything since this morning. And today has turned into night."

"Wounded men need to eat and drink. The liquid replaces the blood, it does," he said. His smile warmed the rainy night.

Considering why they had come, it surprised me that British soldiers acted so friendly. Maybe I had absorbed some Patriot attitudes, after all.

I didn't want to say where I was going, so I just answered, "Clark's Tavern is near," although I had already noticed the building stood shuttered and locked.

A meaty hand on my shoulder stopped my exit.

"All them taverns is closed. No need to hurry. Let's talk a while."

I shook off the hand and certainly had no desire to do anything, except leave. I considered where hot cooked food might be found on this cold and troublesome night. The prompt answer was Benjamin Knapp's house, right where I needed to take Lambert's horse. The problem of finding the horse remained.

I stared the trooper square in the eye and told the biggest fib yet. "I must return my brother's nag to the generals at Mr. Knapp's. They want to buy her. I—I wonder where that horse is now?"

Tommy Flynn pointed behind the house. We had been standing

in the doorway, out of the rain. I quailed inside at leaving the well-lit house for the watery dark.

I don't know what I had expected, but it took a second before I understood that the guard would not walk out there with me. Finding the horse in the dark might be the next step, but the step was all mine. I took a deep breath and moved from the pale circle of lantern-light into the drizzly dark shadows.

While bonfires illuminated the front of the house, the back constituted a wet and murky hell where fires flickered not at all. I didn't feel ready for this.

Dozens of beasts stamped and shuffled in the mud behind Dibble's house. Their attachment to ropes strung between trees and fence posts enabled the rebellious ones just enough freedom to encourage bad behavior. Canvas nosebags and wads of stolen hay strewn on the ground told of feeding, but still-hungry horses jerked on their tie-ropes and pawed non-stop. Screaming horse-fights erupted and perhaps blood followed, invisible in the night.

I remained rooted to the ground at the edge of the eerie scene. What if I slipped and fell under a horse? Their natural reaction would be to kick me to death. And it wasn't just horses that scared me. Wandering soldiers threw me lascivious looks that made me want to run. Without intending to, I bolted back to the well-lit house. The house and Tommy Flynn had transformed into a smiling trap, luring me in.

Tommy smiled a bigger smile than necessary when he saw me. "Oh, it's you again. What's the plan?"

"My brother's horse. He has a red chestnut mare – at least he did..."

Tommy smiled a wolfish smile. "We must find the lad here his hay-burner, eh? What'll ya' give me for the info?" He took hold of my arm and I jerked it back.

I emphasized the holy name. "General Erskine wants this horse right away."

Tommy Flynn shrugged. "They stashed the nag behind the house, is all I know. That was eight hours ago." Tommy turned as two officers exited the door.

I stepped out into the dark, shaky and unsure, but I bit my tongue to make pain overcome fear. Then I plunged forward into the seething swamp of cavalry horses. If only I stood taller! A kick in the wrong place could crush a knee — or a chest. When I reached the middle of the pack, I stood stock-still in the middle of forty horses, lost.

In black of night, their coat colors distorted by the rain, the horses all looked the same.

A horse fight broke out over to the right, in the darkest spot. Violent kicking erupted, followed by a horse snarl to chill my vitals. I for sure would avoid going over there.

But what would they be fighting over, if not a strange mare? I worked my way to the last row. Some reared back against their halter ropes. If they jerked the picket rope loose and ran about the town, my only chance might disappear.

No one could miss the white stripe gleaming in the dark. "That's her, that's her!" I shouted, thrilled that one thing had worked out in my favor.

Untying Desire's halter rope with fumbling wet fingers, I backed her out of the line. A stallion snorted as I threaded a path behind his steel-shod hind hooves. I had feared that the frightened mare might jerk away, but she dragged her feet, stumbling as the toes caught in the mud. All her feisty spirit had evaporated in the misery of rain and confusion, not to mention the sixteen miles to Redding and back.

Horses suffered constant switching from one place to another as more wooden fence rails met the flames. Saddles and weapons lay everywhere, thrown down in mud or sitting pertly atop bushes. Under those bushes, soldiers sprawled, asleep in their uniforms.

Two half-barrels of water sat at the Town Street corner, so I stopped to let the mare drink. I took off my soaking wet jacket, and threw it over her civilian saddle, hoping to hide it from prying eyes.

Too late.

The intent stares and determined strides of two approaching troopers indicated no random check. As they arrived in my vicinity, their eyes crinkled in amused interest and they greeted me with smiles of honest pleasure.

"We know what 'orse that is, but what are you doing with it?" asked shining teeth in a leathery face. "She's beaut, she is!" The soldier reached out to stroke Desire and continued to do so, tracing behind her ears where a bridle might have rubbed. His eyes lit up with the joy of it.

"How do you know anything about this horse?" I acted righteous and testy, as if I were just a normal citizen leading his brother's horse.

"Aw, c'mon here, lad, we mean no harm to you. Just explain who you are, 'cause we know this ain't your 'orse."

"She's my brother's horse," I said, still hoping to get away clear.

"We gotta know you ain't coppin' a good thing, is all."

Total dread overtook me. No way that I could escape now. I offered no resistance as one took hold of my arm and drew me to their mounting block. They sat down again, facing me at eye level. I had feared that I would form their evening's amusement, but they proved eager to amuse me.

"Yer brother's horse, hey? Here's a story he won't be tellin' ya'! See, we know whose horse it is. This 'ere 'orse belongs to that rebel who got shot this morning. Swear to God, 'twas the funniest thing I seen in this long life!"

"You looks scared, lad, but we'll give you a laugh, I promise. We was ridin' through that Redding town this morning and stopped to rest the nags and relieve ourselves. We hear gallopin' hooves and this grand beast comes a'flyin' down that there Couch Hill. Flyin' like a derby winner, she was. The fool rebel don't notice he couldn't stop if he wanted to. The witch had run off with him and he hadn't figured it out yet. His mare run up to that New York colonel's stallion like a homing pigeon, both nags a-whinnying from true love!" The men slapped their thighs, as chuckles rolled on into laughter.

I did not join in. Father's prediction about the mare going out of control in battle had come true.

> ...suddenly and rather unexpectedly came upon the foe. He must have been riding at a smart speed or he would not have become so helplessly entangled as he turned out to be...

"So I don't think it's your brother's nag. What *are* you doin' with it? Nicking it?" Their admiring glances implied that stealing Desire made an admirable goal, while insinuating that they could do the job better than I could.

"She really is my brother's. He's still a prisoner, but he knows General Tryon. He said I could take her home." It wasn't a lie. I never said who "he" was, did I?

"We thought it was a fairytale, that the rebel knew the general. Then we seen 'em smilin' and talkin'. We don't want to get involved with generals. Make free and hoof the gravel out of here, if you want to. These rich rebels might lose other things this night and we'll cop our share of that. Only right for causin' us this bleedin' long trip." Both gave a peaceful wave of dismissal.

Leaving the British behind didn't make me feel any safer. Not by a longshot. The firelight had formed a safety zone of its own.

Leading an expensive horse down the dark public street gave opportunity for anyone to knock me down and snatch her. Anyone with a mind like Isaiah's, bent on stealing. My skin crawled when I sensed shapes hiding in the dark near the deserted houses. Shapes that moved.

Desire pricked her ears forward as we drew near the Barren Plain bridge, where the British horses stood at the checkpoint. I forced her head down and held her ear in my hand, praying she make no noise. If she did, I would twist that silken ear to silence her. "Whinnying for true love" would not happen on my shift.

The covering noises of rain and river kept the British horses from hearing our approach. So far, all British soldiers had acted willing to give me a break, but I longed for the safety of our own little shed.

I cut the corner and threaded my way through the dark willows until we reached our property. I tied the mare in the stallion's stall and tried to untack her. The saddle slipped through my hands and the soaking wet leather fell on me, wrenching my neck. My numb fingers had a hard time with the tiny bridle buckles, but I finished the job. The stallion hadn't eaten his morning hay, so I needed to do nothing more to make Desire comfortable and silent. Pony snuffled once and Desire snuffled back.

I could hardly believe what I had done! Now, if anyone in the British party set out to steal her, the last place they would look would be next door.

Chapter Twenty-Three

Saturday, April 26th, 1777
at Nine o'Clock of the Evening

The guard's campfire sputtered in front of the Knapp's horse barn. Two troopers sat on Mr. Knapp's bench, under the overhang of the barn roof, removing boots and massaging their feet. The random shooting had ceased. No head turned as I passed. I moved on tiptoe to the imposing front door.

The clouds closed down further, forcing the smell of roasting chicken right down to nose level. It occurred to me that no contented clucking had come from our chicken coop. Now the smell made me wonder if I knew my chicken dinner by name.

I slipped the door open with no noise at all. My coat might look wet from the rain, but I didn't think I looked dirty. Maybe no one had noticed I had been gone.

Fresh tallow candles flickered, and the tallcase clock ticked with the regularity of a heartbeat. My numb hands absorbed the warmth of the fireplaces as I passed down the hall and slipped into the busy, cheerful dining room.

The same British officers worked steadily on plates of fowl and browned lamb, the half-full platters lined up down the center of the table. Corn pudding with green flecks of ramps, baked winter squash with onions, and parsnip mash filled the empty spots between fresh bread and butter. The whole spread smelled licking-good, better than any tavern. The only words I heard were quiet requests for various dishes.

Piles of bones lay on the white board-cloth in front of the por-celain plates, grease sinking through to the wood below. Wine glasses were refilled, but the filling arm often stretched too far, resulting in inaccurate pouring. The white board-cloth was again the loser.

A solitary figure remained standing, both hands resting on the mantel as she stared into the fire. The captain announced, "Here's the young master you awaited, ma'am."

Mother snapped to attention. "Where have you been for two hours?" she demanded, whirling from the fire to clamp a hand onto my shoulder, nails digging in. "You keep disappearing! And you're soaked. No one gave you permission to run off again."

I glanced sideways to see the effect of these words on the company. I was surprised to find rescue.

"Probably went to see our horses, right lad?" the colonel reassured her, wiping his mouth on his handkerchief and winking at me. "Mine's the finest, isn't it? Take a plate, lad. Eat your fill. You look a bit peaked, I'd say. "

I nodded, because speaking might set Mother off again.

"May I assist you to a seat, ma'am?" General Erskine rose to encourage Mother toward the table. She perked up mightily under such noble attention.

"Indeed, Sir William, I am happy to partake now that my main botheration in life has returned. My stars, did you bring these fine chickens with you or did you buy them on the way?"

Apparently unaware of the chickens' origins, the general muttered that such matters were for his cooks to arrange.

"But of course, Sir William." Both Mr. Knapp and Mother called the generals "Sir William" and "Sir James," although I was standing by the New York colonel when Mr. Knapp let go a "Sir James." The colonel caught my eye and gave a tiny shake of the head. I understood that "Sir James" was no such thing.

I helped myself to parsnip mash and corn meal pudding, letting tales of London and New York flow around me. I wanted some chicken, but I felt embarrassed to ask a nobleman to pass the platter. I never did taste any chicken, after a whole day dreaming of it.

The conversation circled back to a possible rebel attack, again rejected due to weather. "Maybe this rain will cool down the hotheads," remarked General Agnew.

Sarah sat next to the noble lieutenant on the other side of the table. I saw him proffer a glass of red wine. Perhaps the wine's deep ruby color reminded her of recent disagreeable experience. I felt secret satisfaction as I saw her turn away.

As the company rose from the dinner table, I planned my second escape. This time, with food.

"Did the men in the barn eat?" I asked the colonel, since he seemed the most likely to answer me.

"Good thinking, lad. Those chaps have been diligent, without much reward. Take them anything left on the table and what remains in that cider pitcher." Suspicious, he gently sloshed the pitcher's contents.

I filled a flat maple slab with leftover chicken backs, wings, and a large chunk of bread. The colonel opened the door for me and presented the cider pitcher, then gave an approving wink and pat on the back. I decided that the men on the other side could be funny and nice. Then I wondered why I thought of our parent country as "the other side."

I had exited scot free and with Mother's nodded approval, but I found myself watched as closely outside as in.

A single guard now stood near the house, gun in hand, and frown on face.

"What's the matter?"

I could almost see the hairs on his head rise from fear.

"I hear things all 'round, out there in the willows along the river. There's folk out there. I don't see 'em, but I can feel 'em, I can." We moved under the barn roof overhang to escape the rain.

I said, "Probably just the horses stamping," which was all I heard. The soldier waved my words away like flies.

"Think old Alfie's the fool? It's them rebels. T'other guard run off to the bridge with that lot. I don't like bein' here without a mate. Don't have eyes on the back of that buildin' there, do I? The later it gets tonight, the more dangers that could come calling. I'd lock everything down, if I was you," said Alfie.

"Think I'll go and check that pony," I said, but Pony wasn't the animal that worried me.

"If a robber roamed abroad tonight, he'd 'ave a easy time of it. Give over that food ya' brought. Good fella you are, I says."

I shoved the cider and the wooden slab at him and headed for our shed. If Isaiah roamed abroad….

Only the regular pulse of breathing disturbed the dark. I felt along the wall for the horse leg wraps my father used for his stallion, to prevent lameness. I planned to do the complete opposite.

I wrapped little stones into the leg wraps and cranked them extra tight against the tendons of both her slender front legs. Anyone with thievish ways would discover that the beautiful animal could bare-ly limp. She'd be too secure to *walk*.

Before rejoining the rain, I put my arms around Desire. She put her head over my shoulder as if she hugged me back.

Singing from the night watch on the bridge drifted through the drizzle as I faded into the shadows and felt my way back to town, tree-to-tree and wall-to-wall.

Chapter Twenty-Four

Saturday, April 26th, 1777
at Ten o'Clock of the Evening

When I approached the Dibble house, Tommy Flynn still stood watch at the door.

Tommy bared his teeth into a smile when he saw me. "And what's your last name, lad? Flynn here." He held out his hand. I didn't hold out mine. I sensed something off kilter, something not straight about this man. His overeager interest I felt unnatural, but I must not alienate this person, no matter what he did. A new guard might not have let me in at all.

"Joe." I snapped out my name as quick as I could.

He paused, but passed it over. "And you live near where the generals are? Next door, was it?" He asked, cagey as ever.

"Same property." Closeness to generals ought to shut him up.

"This town is a wild place tonight. You *and* your mother will remain in that house?"

I assured him that both my mother and I would sleep within the same four walls as the British high command.

"No one will be at your house?" Sounded like a robbery plan to me, all right. Robbery was better than what my schoolmaster called "crime against persons."

"Right," I said.

"Who took the horse?" Tommy asked.

"I gave it to Alfie for the captain to try out tomorrow." If this was a test, I was going to pass.

"Good man." Tommy winked and opened the door. I had

enjoyed the Colonel's wink of conspiracy. Tommy's wink felt disgusting. He wanted something from me, I could tell.

Only two officers remained with Tryon when I entered the drawing room. A quick word from Tryon, and no one paid attention to me as I passed. Lambert sat in the same corner, awake and alert. Normal color had returned to his face. The candlelight's reflection glittered in the sapphire eyes.

"I begin to be alive, brother," Lambert murmured as I came closer. "They found a loaf of wheat bread and a chunk of fine cheese. I took in two tankards of apple cider. Did you find that red-haired girl?" His smile looked like old times as he pointed to the chair next to his.

"Desire occupies a stall at our place. What about your arm? Do you need a doctor? What should I do?"

"No issues with the bone, just the flesh. Stay here and pass the time with me. We await the general's attention."

I sat down. "It's still raining. Do you think the militia will attack the British tomorrow?"

"They won't risk the Commissary and the military hospital, not to mention the whole town. Fact is, no matter what we have, it isn't enough. Don't worry about your father or your grandfather. If they stick together, they'll be fine." Lambert yawned again, began to stifle it with his wounded arm, and gasped at the pain it caused.

"We can talk to pass the time," I said. "Why did you ride to Redding?"

"I carried a message to tell General Silliman to bring powder and flints from Norwalk."

"Why were *you* the one who went? You're not a soldier anymore."

"For such a mission, a fast horse is better than a slow horse." He added a smile of misplaced pride.

"Did the British ambush you?" I wanted to believe that the British had attacked him in a cowardly manner.

Lambert's mouth opened and shut several times.

"I heard that Desire ran away with you," I prodded. "Is that true?"

"Galloping downhill is dangerous. I watched for rocks," came his over-quick reply.

"General Silliman never got the message." I said it like a fact.

"No, no, he didn't." Lambert's voice caught in his throat and strangled into a whisper. We both stayed silent, following that thought to an end as yet unknown.

"Another thing I want to know — I never once saw you before two months ago, and yet you live in a big house on Town Street. Where did you come from?"

"My brother Gould and I lived in Wilton until our mother died. My father remarried and moved to Danbury. Gould and I didn't like that, so we moved in with our older half-brother in Norwalk, where I apprenticed in his hardware store. Remember? That's where I met General Tryon."

"Why did I never see your brother here, not even one time?" This question had plagued me for three days.

"Aren't things bad enough without trying to find worse?" That sharp defense told me that Father was right again.

I thought I was changing the subject when I said, "Here's another question that's a mystery to me: why do my parents get so upset if Jonah Benedict's name is mentioned?"

"You don't know?" Lambert asked quietly.

"Know what?" I asked. "Why do people always think I know things?"

"Better that I tell you the whole story right now. About my brother. About Jonah."

"Which one?" I asked.

"It's all the same story — the story of Fort Washington, the worst thing to happen to our new country — the loss of the City of New York. But first, I must explain what led to a very bad decision.

"I enlisted in the Norwalk militia in 1775 when I was seventeen. The weather was perfect as we rode flatboats up the Hudson River to conquer Canada. But five bullets was each man's total allowance. Eventually, the Continentals talked about handing out spears.

"First, we ran out of food. One night, we attacked our own scouting party. Then smallpox came. The day the militia's time officially ended, we walked out past a line of cursing Continentals.

> GENERAL WASHINGTON TO THE PRESIDENT OF CONGRESS
> Can any thing ... be more destructive to the recruiting service than giving ten dollars bounty for six weeks' service of the Militia, who come in, you cannot tell how, go, you cannot tell when, and act, you cannot tell where, consume your provisions, exhaust your stores, and leave you at last at a critical moment?

"In January of '76, I went out again, to shore up New York City defenses. We all returned safe and sound. To me, war counted as a noble adventure. I couldn't wait to share it.

"I had befriended men from Danbury and my father wanted me to change into their militia, where the officers were proven and cautious.

"By the August all-hands alarm, I had plotted for my brother to meet us on the road to New York. He concealed that he was only fifteen by using the last name of our stepbrother's mother."

"What happened when you got to New York?"

"We retreated through Manhattan, back toward the safety of our fort on the Hudson River, Fort Washington. Jonah and our captain had already reached Ft. Washington when Patriot officers we didn't know screamed, "Do what we tell you — don't look for your own officers, they're lost." They pointed sabers, driving us like cattle. We boarded ferryboats and crossed the Hudson River to Fort Lee, New Jersey.

"Officers had spy glasses and we watched the massacre at Fort Washington." Lambert looked as if he still saw death and destruction in a little, round eyepiece

"And Cousin Jonah and the other Danbury men went to prison," I said, trying to make him continue the story. "Did the British chase you to Fort Lee?"

"They could have. Before a shot was fired, the Continental Army faded into New Jersey. The rest of us started walking home."

"Then what?"

"All four Danbury sergeants escaped, along with the first lieutenant. They took charge of Colonel Bradley's sick and injured. They promised to make me a sergeant if I stayed. Gould and I would help carry those who couldn't walk. We tried to reach the army supply depot at Peekskill, New York to find food and shelter. They had neither.

GENERAL HEATH TO GENERAL WASHINGTON
Peek' s Kill, December 26th, 1776

The case of the regiments of General Lee and Sullivan's divisions … will be very difficult. The naked, convalescents, and sick, were left here. They constitute the greater part of the regiments, and cannot get home with out their wages, being destitute of money; and unless the Colonels who are with your Excellency, send the men' s wages to them, they will suffer.

"We kept moving. No one welcomed victims of camp fever. Farmers claimed that we would pollute their wells. They drove us away at gunpoint. The clothes we wore in November were the rags left from what we wore in August.

"We aimed for the nearest military hospital. Those twenty miles took us three weeks.

"Fishkill Hospital wanted to get rid of the sick, not take them in. Gould died on the second of January. No blankets for the living or the dead."

Lambert fixed his eyes on a candle flame. "Thank God both our parents had died. They never knew."

"Why doesn't my father like you?" I asked, at last landing on my real question.

"Some said I only stayed because I wanted the promotion." Tears came to his eyes. "After that, I couldn't stay in the militia. Any promotion would have felt poisoned."

"So why does everybody in the army call you lieutenant?" I asked.

"In war, everyone has to know who is entitled to give orders, that's how this classifying of civilians happened My commissary pay equals that of a Continental lieutenant, so that's what they call me. They call Dr. Wood 'Major,' but he isn't in the army, either."

Time to change the subject again.

"How long do you think the British will keep Cousin Jonah?"

"He's been here for two weeks. Jonah Benedict is here in Danbury." Lambert tented his fingers while looking me straight in the eye.

My parents had not said one word about Jonah's return after five months in prison! And both my parents had acted most strange and bothered for — exactly two weeks.

What had Jonah done that my parents had concealed his return?

"I'm glad he got away. I can't wait to see him," I managed to say.

"Jonah is dying," Lambert said. "He hasn't much longer on this earth. It took his father two weeks to get him here on a wheeled litter, pulled behind a led horse."

No wonder my mother was distraught. But why hadn't she gone to see him? Months of mourning; two weeks to rescue him — and then my mother ignores it? None of this made sense.

A furious commotion at the outer door, followed by Tommy Flynn's equally sharp, "Yes, sir!" drew my attention away from this strange revelation.

Three British officers slammed into the room, bringing the raw scent of horse manure with them. The three jammed together in front of General Tryon's desk, anger and rain dripping off every body part.

"General! We must stop what's happening out there. The men are out of control!"

"What's the problem, Captain? I hear no shooting," asked General Tryon, dispensing a professional smile.

"The problem is arson. Those drunken louts just ran off to burn another church. We need authority to shoot these fools. The guides know where the rebel leaders live and now a dozen homes are burning. No way the population will forgive this one!"

"And that cad of a butcher runs around telling people he's the Earl of Falkland's son — Major says there *ain't* no such Earl of Falkland anywhere in England. Now the locals 're sayin' British nobility is murderin' people!"

Lambert and I sat motionless, suddenly afraid of the freedom to leave. Homes burning? Whose homes? And who were these "guides?" The name of the spy, Enoch Crosby, came to mind.

"Hmmm…," said Tryon, and a slow smile spread across his face. "Not a bad idea. Yes, that's how to punish the bad element and protect the good citizens in this village. We'll just burn the homes of committeemen, those pox-ridden traitors to the King!"

"Um, why, yes, sir, but we weren't *supposed* to burn houses. That's what General Agnew said. Now he's not here, so we —" His frantic plea for help ended when General Tryon broke in.

"All right, I understand your issue, so here's a direct order from me. Burn all houses of rebel officers or committee men. Now, what was that about a church?"

"The devils asked a local where the Congregational minister was, 'cause the church backs the war. After they burn it, we find out this minister, this Reverend White, preached *against* rebellion! What do you think he'll preach now? What a mess we've got ourselves into!"

"That's all right, just pass down my command, exactly as I gave it. But the men must be aware that no supporters of our legal government can be harmed. I don't care how you do it, but you must protect our own. Harm anyone else you like!"

The three officers saluted and turned for the door, discussing how to obey the two-part command. Tryon blessed their backs with a benevolent smile.

Lambert and I sent frightened glances at each other and he reached out for my hand. I couldn't tell which of us felt more frightened.

Chapter Twenty-Five

Sunday, April 27th, 1777
at Half Past Midnight

In the sudden peace and quiet, the general's smile swerved back to Lambert. "You young scoundrel, forget anything you've heard and come on over here. The little lad, too." General Tryon motioned Lambert into the charmed circle of light shed by a dozen polished brass candleholders.

Lambert rose with care from his seat in the shadows. He carried his right wrist in his left hand as we approached and took seats. Closer inspection of the desk revealed a light coating of crumbs, plus a spilled glass of red wine, the spreading pool inching toward the general's papers, which carried spatters of candle wax.

As the distance between Lambert and General Tryon narrowed, their eyes locked onto each other, lost in the memory of a summer afternoon of rescue and roast beef.

"Time to send you home, young fellow. Three years ago, you assisted me out of a situation ready to escalate into gunshots. Today, you escalated your own misfortune by poor horsemanship, but you're a fine young man still. You promise not to join the rebel army a second time, correct?" The General smiled and tapped his quill pen on the blotter, awaiting an answer.

"I swear on my honor to stick by my new profession, assisting a medical man," Lambert said, flashing a smile and avoiding my eye.

Lambert had named no names, since Dr. John Wood belonged to both the Committee of Inspection and the Commissary.

The general dipped his pen in ink and made test marks. "This parole frees you from any restraint, now or in the future." He began to write, repeating aloud, "I, Major General William Tryon … representing the forces … of His Most Gracious Majesty, … King George III, do —"

Doors slammed, curses flew, boots raced up the stairs and down again. Sharp exclamations came as spurs connected with the wooden steps, tripping their wearers.

"General!" called a major as he entered the room, spurs jingling and fine boots muddy to the knees. "The damned rebels are upon us! That conceited fool Arnold and that blasted old Wooster are setting an ambush. Leave now – this minute, or we'll never get to the boats without a real battle. General Howe would be furious, and King George believes every word he says!" A dozen voices called different orders.

"Got the general's horse out there?"

"Right here! Get him mounted and let's go!"

"Hey, get them papers off the general's desk. Don't leave anything they can find."

General Tryon swore an oath as he rose from his armchair, pulling coat and belt straight.

"You'll be all right. It's your town," he said to Lambert. He drew on his gauntlets as he walked behind Lambert's chair, extending a gloved hand to pat him on the shoulder. When he noticed that the wounded arm rested closest to him, the hand withdrew unnoticed.

Then Tryon and his aides swept out in a gold and silver storm of inlaid swords and gold-fringed epaulettes. Sabers clanked and hit doorframes. Officers cursed at exchanging the warm house for the cold wet roads. The door slammed.

Hoofbeats swirled around the mounting block, and then accelerated away.

The flickering candle flames took hold and burned on without a waver.

Silence.

"Well, Brother Joe, I believe the safest thing is to remain right here." Lambert leaned back in his chair and smiled the smile of an escapee.

I looked around for the best chair for sleeping. This was the latest that I had ever stayed awake and I didn't even know how late it was.

Still, someone must remove the messes of war, must do his duty, must have his fun.

Two English sergeants stomped into the drawing room. Scruffy, with their black tricorn hats askew and saggy faces, they entered the space now under their command. The tying up of loose ends and removal of anything valuable or incriminating — that was their job. Especially if they could keep the valuable items.

"Well, well, what have we here? Did the general forget a few things? The prisoners, perhaps? Can't have that, can we? Want a little sugar to eat?" The soldier's artificial voice sang a song of treachery.

"Unnecessary," answered Lambert, dragging himself to his feet.

A cold chill arose within me. I sensed ill will and lots of it. Both soldiers looked accustomed to ruling their environment, by either fist or brass knuckles. The bigger sergeant fingered his pistol. He smiled as he saw me notice it.

"All rebels need sugar, 'tis a certainty," he continued, pointing at me while winking at his partner.

The second man shoved a flat thumb in my direction, and added a frown. "No sugar for him, right? Just a little boy, you know?"

"Little boys is the worst ones for spyin', di'n't you hear?"

"A pup? Oh for the love of —" The other man threw up his hands.

"Oh, all right, all right. Shove the rebel brat back under whatever rock he crawled out from under. Let's find that oxcart and chain this here traitor in with the other riffraff. Sugar House Prison, here he comes!"

The Sugar House Prison in New York! That was where Cousin Jonah had been. Now Lambert had to go there. They might keep him until he was dying, too.

The second sergeant yanked me through the hall, while informing me of my "lucky turn." He cast me out the unguarded front door like casting a stone into a pond. I staggered, caught my balance, and ducked around the side of the house into the shadowed gloom.

Hide. All I wanted to do was hide, and this night was made for it. The brightness of the fires and the smoky aura surrounding them made the dark spots seem that much darker. That we were next to the Anglican Church graveyard did not cheer the surroundings. The shadows leaped and fled like ghosts.

Keeping next to the house, I waited for the sergeants to bring Lambert outside. The cold chill of past-midnight slipped into my coat with me as the damp arrived once more at my skin, refreshed by occasional new drifts of rain.

I touched the crinkled paper dollars of Lambert's pay and wondered how I could use them. I knew what a bribe was, but I didn't know how far thirty dollars carried.

The Committee had confiscated Tory outbuildings for storage, and Mr. Dibble's barn was no exception. The British had dragged the stored grain bags outside to stoke a fire. The heaped bags only smoldered, producing a poisonous stench that spread over the town like butter. The drizzly mist reduced it to a choking layer about nose-high.

A familiar red-coated figure materialized out of the smoke, beckoning me, his oily smiles now departed. Habit sucked me into his presence once again. Without thinking, I followed Tommy Flynn. I shivered so hard that I didn't dare talk.

"You gotta listen sharp, boy. This is life-or-death-important. Our side is burning out the rebel leaders, but loyal citizens get a white X in limestone chalk marked on their houses. If one of us marks your family's place, *let them do* it! It ain't like the Bible, see?" He looked as desperate as if he were the one in danger.

"The Bible?" I mumbled, in a daze of exhaustion, disappointment and fear.

"King Herod in the Bible marked houses, then his soldiers killed the boys there. When *we* mark houses, it means they are *safe*. Don't let some fool say they're not!"

Wanting only to get away from this suspicious person, I replied, "Yes, sir."

> As soon as the men were aroused and in place, excepting those detailed for picket, the work of destruction began. This was about two o'clock. In the next hour, the buildings owned by Tories were marked with a cross, done with a chunk of lime. The work of burning was then commenced.

Then he took my shoulder and shook it gently. "Good lad. We'll see each other bye-and-bye. Don't forget old Tommy, now."

I dodged the hand when it moved to pat my back. Tommy Flynn could go to London or hell.

Chapter Twenty-Six

Sunday, April 27th, 1777
at Two o'Clock of the Morning

I shook from the midnight chill while I eased up just close enough to see in the windows of the house. Nothing. The front yard showed me only an open door. They had taken Lambert away while Tommy held my attention. In this firelit scene of activity, I still had to save myself.

I returned to the dark safety of the graveyard and its many headstones, while searching the street, crowded with ox-carts and wagons. Maybe I could still catch the colonel. The green uniform and superb horse would be hard to miss. The colonel would be the only man on the British side who might listen to me. I didn't see him.

I dropped down behind a tombstone while two New York sergeants walked past. I strained my ears for information.

"Those English are vicious types! Couple hours ago, I saw a gang of bloodthirsty Brits savaging two helpless folk they dragged out of a house. It's right up here a ways. Must be them committee members. Still, it ain't human to do that stuff without no battle. I felt afraid to stop them, though, afraid for my life. And me a sergeant, too …."

His comrade nodded. "It's what the rebels get for keeping brandy kegs in their medical stores. Peaceful operations ended right there."

"Never did find any guns on this wild goose chase," complained the other man. "The rebel army probably took them. Hear a couple of their pretend generals know a few tricks."

"What if they do?" asked his companion. "Just shoeless rag-amuffins to follow them. Times don't change. Come on, let's scare some of our own into doing their duty. Shoulder arms, mate!"

They moved on. Islands of sanity floating through the rain-misted night.

> The night was dark, with dashes of rain. The carousers tumbled down here and there as they advanced in the stages of drunkenness. Some few of the troops remained sober, and these performed the duties of the hour.

Deciding that I would have to move along, too, I climbed over the graveyard wall into the nearby yard of Jonah Benedict's abandoned house.

Chunks of glowing debris hung suspended in the air until they sank gracefully to the ground. I pulled my shirt over my nose and mouth so that I could breathe inside it. Currents of heat and smoke swept over me, making my eyes weep. Wiping them only added more dirt. I squinted until I could hardly see.

Jonah Benedict's barn stood right in front of me. Checking Jonah's barn would only take a second. Mother would praise anything I could salvage. If he was helpless, no one would have secured the valu-ables. Remembering Father's warning about looters, I paused to make an extra-careful look around.

Away from the street fires, cracking and rending noises grabbed me. The lowering clouds magnified sounds of shattering glass and col-lapsing beams twice as loud as real. Horrified, I saw that Jonah's house at the far end of the lot was past blazing, and well advanced into caving in.

Returning to my own salvation, I decided to sneak through Jonah's lot and come out on Town Street. Forget about the barn. I kept walking, sticking to the dark places.

As I closed in on the glowing house, a fearsome vision material-ized, wavering between shadow and flame. Some evil spirit had trans-formed into this devilish apparition. What I saw could never be real. It just couldn't be.

Tied upright and back-to-back around a sycamore tree stood Jonah Benedict and his father — dead.

> ... was taken prisoner at Fort Washington in 1776. Was confined in the prison ship Grosvenor, and afterward removed to the Sugar House and subjected to great hardships and cruelty. When released was considered to be at the point of death and was carried to Danbury, Connecticut , about two weeks before Danbury was burn by the British. He and his old Father Mathew, who was living in Jonah's house, were taken out of their beds before daylight on Monday (sic) morning, April 27th, 1777, and tied to a tree in his garden, while the British troops set fire to his house.

Jonah's ghostly white nightshirt hung over what looked like a skeleton. The head hung forward at an unnatural angle, mouth open. Rain ran down the sagging face, dropping off the nose and stubbled chin.

I considered running. I wanted no part of dead people that I couldn't help anyway. Before I did, I went to the other side of the tree to make sure that the unconscious figure really was my mother's uncle.

Great-uncle Mathew hung against his ropes, legs bent, eyes closed, his face concealed under his long white beard. His soaking wet clothes revealed the form of a spare elderly man at least three times the skeletal Jonah's size. Then I saw twitching.

I croaked a fearful, "Sir?" and the old man leaped to life faster than the Bible's Lazarus rose from the dead. The powerful old body twisted as his bound hands made wild clawing motions at the tree behind him. Blood dripped from his fingernails before washing away in the rain. The crazed expression on his face fully qualified him as insane. I backed up fast, not knowing what he might do if freed.

"Thank God, boy!" Uncle Mathew roared when his despairing eyes found my face. "My son, is he alive? Get these ropes off!" Maddened by rage and fear, his voice sounded inhuman.

I pawed at the knots, but the blood-covered rope had turned as hard as rock. My father used special knots for outdoor ropes, because they shrank like cloth after being wet.

"I can't open the knots. They're too tight."

"Cut them! Get a knife! The hoof knife's stuck in the doorframe, right inside the barn door. Quick! Jonah's dying!" Great-uncle Mathew's red eyes almost erupted from his face.

I didn't want to say the truth, that I thought Jonah was a goner already.

I ran to the barn, while searing smoke flowed straight into my nose and mouth. My lungs felt like the hooked end of a hoof knife had already jammed between my ribs, and been torn loose again. I felt around the doorframe until cold fingers found cold steel attached to a wooden handle.

Returning to the tree, I sawed the dull knife back and forth twenty times or more. Uncle Mathew twisted like a snake. You could hardly blame him, when his son hung unconscious and invisible, only a foot away. At last, the hemp rope parted. Uncle Mathew staggered and fell in an attempt to grab Jonah before the dead weight plunged face first onto the rain-soaked ground.

I leaped away, somehow believing that Jonah might shatter into bits and pieces when he hit the ground. I bent to help Uncle Mathew, but both figures disappeared as blowing smoke scorched my eyeballs.

I plastered both hands to my eyes. When I looked up, Uncle Mathew struggled to drag Jonah out of the mud. This emaciated man must weigh as little as a child for such an old man to handle him so easily. The look on his face as he observed the senseless being in his arms! I recalled Lambert's story, that Jonah's father had walked to New York and back to fetch him.

"Help me get him in the barn. Open both doors," the old man commanded.

I dragged the barn doors open, hoping to herd them in out of the rain, and then continue on my mission. Too much time had passed. Lambert might disappear forever if I didn't push on.

Uncle Mathew deposited Jonah atop a pile of hay. "I'll get help," he gasped. "You stay here."

Uncle Mathew made it out the door before I could protest. His own house was behind Jonah's, facing onto South Street. He should be right back.

The door blew closed, leaving Jonah alone with me in in the dark. A faint light came in through the window, made from glass bottles. His head sat crooked on his neck. I wondered about straightening it out, but maybe bones had broken in there.

Was he still alive? I had nothing except Uncle Mathew's say-so that the spark of life still burned inside the thread-like body. How would I know if he died? I didn't have a mirror to hold to his mouth, the way Mother said was the best way to tell.

I didn't want to sit down next to someone who might die any minute, so I stood by the door, anxious for a getaway.

A rasping whisper made me jump a foot. "You! Who are you?"

"I'm Joe Hamilton, Si Hamilton's son."

No sound came for perhaps two minutes.

"Your father out with the militia?" Jonah whispered.

"Yes, sir," was all I could say.

No more words came, which scared me even worse. I fretted there in the dark for a long time before Uncle Mathew rushed in, trailed by some man who appeared about as scared as I was, but who carried a lit lantern.

"The damned British set my house on fire! Mathew, Junior's, too, curse them. God help us. Where can I take Jonah now? We got to be somewhere better than a barn or Jonah's going to die."

Uncle Mathew Benedict could not have imagined that I had a useful answer, but I did.

"The Dibble House is wide open and warm. The British were there, but they left."

The two men picked Jonah up, one on each side. Jonah's feet dragged in the mud, following along as best they could.

After a few steps, Uncle Mathew remembered me. "Run home, now, you hear?" He gave no thanks and made no sign he had ever seen me before.

The column left Danbury through Wooster Street, taking the Miry Brook Road. It was lighted by the flames of the burning buildings. It was not quite daylight of Sunday morning, April 27th.

The British were on the move, carts and teams hustling to get in line and leave town. The fires burned on, lighting the street — and the glowing empty areas where houses used to be. Not much remained of Jonah's fine house except blackened spires of corner posts, cross-hatched with miscellaneous lumber. The smoke of Griswold's groceries billowed up and welded to the smoke of the Benedict houses.

Back on Town Street, I looked back at Griswold's. I almost swallowed my tongue. Captain Daniel Taylor's majestic house spewed flame twice as high as the roof. All of Captain Dan's possessions flew towards the heavens, transformed into ghostly gray smoke.

I passed John McLean's house, where the fires fed like wolves on a deer carcass. Flaming matter from the nearby courthouse roof leaped into overhanging tree branches. Dried by the heat of burning buildings, dead branches joined them in ascending to the clouds. If not for the rain, the inferno would have soared sideways through the treetops, engulfing the whole town.

Now I understood Mrs. McLean's "Before it's too late…."

It was too late now.

I saw a little flame inside Major Eli Mygatt's drug store. I was right in front of it. I wondered who was in there. I stopped and looked in the broken window, but the faint noises I heard from the back were enough to propel me toward home, double-time.

At last, I stood at the corner of Barren Plain Road. The picket station at the bridge lay silent and empty. I searched the darkness, but both the Knapp's house and our house appeared untouched by any hands. I hurried into the shed and tried to see through a crack between boards in the box stall.

No horse stood there.

I was struck motionless. The world stopped in that second.

Then I heard breathing and looked down. Desire stretched flat on her side in the deep straw, sound asleep. Safe. At least *something* remained safe on this awful night.

Sleepy snorts issued from the sows' pen as I passed. Lucky the sows hadn't met the same fate as the chickens.

Next, I spotted the white X on our cottage. It gave me a turn, but I understood why the cottage hadn't burned. The white X also stood on Knapp's house, two feet high on the blank end wall. I hadn't seen any X's on my way home, but here stood the sign that Tommy had warned about.

The Knapps' barn doors gaped wide open. I stuck my head around the doorpost. Stripped. Mr. Knapp's ancient horse, gone. So was the pile of last year's hay and the barrel of corncobs that had stood there yesterday.

The watch fire's flame had died into smoking orange embers. The flame of my plan to rescue Lambert had burnt out, too.

I looked out the road, where I had last seen my father. Even if no battle happened, he was riding that killer stallion through a rainy night, surrounded by the Patriots who had caused this disaster.

I had no idea what could happen next, but I knew I would hate it.

Chapter Twenty-Seven

Sunday, April 27th, 1777
at Three o'Clock of the Morning

Nobody answered the door at the Knapps. I shuffled my feet while hugging myself to repel the chill. I longed to be inside this warm and bright home again, where all fires remained where they belonged. I leaned against the doorframe and wondered why no one came to the door.

I was about to sit down on the step when the door creaked back about an inch and our once kindly neighbor shoved a pistol into my face. Then the door swung open and Mr. Knapp's other hand latched onto my coat collar.

Aided by a certain grip on my coat, I lurched through a wasteland. Empty tankards and turned-over bottles accompanied the dirty plates resting on most surfaces. Many of the candles had burned out, as had the drawing room fire. The open kitchen door revealed ax marks in the wood floor and dark stains from the pools of lamb blood, already stinking.

The dining room reeked of cold lamb fat and spilled stale beer. My mother sat at the dining table, head propped on her hands, as she stared into the only fire still burning. She didn't look as young and happy as she had appeared at the party.

Sarah had fallen asleep on the floor in front of the fire, her head on a cushion. The golden silk dress still shone, but her mother's high-heeled shoes had gone missing. She sat up and rubbed her eyes, plainly interested to hear what trouble I would get into.

Mother forgot about me as a new fear took over her face. When the source of the overwhelming smell of smoke was located, she leaped to her feet. "What have you been about — rolling in ashes? Where have you been?"

Her little hands balled into fists. For the first time in my life, I thought she would hit me. Maybe more than once. I thought I deserved sympathy, not punishment, for being out on this awful night.

It took a moment to understand that Mother had seen no fire that was not in the fireplace.

This time, I had to tell the truth, the whole truth.

"Um, I saw something," I ventured, looking down to avoid the awful reaction I knew would come. Bad news could cause madness in ladies.

"What?" Mother demanded. "What did you see?" The fists remained clenched.

"They burned Cousin Jonah's house," I said, as quietly as I could.

"God in Heaven! Tell me they got him out. Tell me Mathew got him out!" Mother raved on, "Joe, what happened? Is he still alive? Tell me!"

"Jonah was tied to a tree in the yard," I continued, trying to keep control of myself and everyone else, although I wanted to rush on with the whole story.

A scream erupted from right below Mother's throat and then cut off, as she looked at Mrs. Knapp's closed door.

"Tell me someone rescued him!" The last words ended in the scream she had stopped before.

Mrs. Knapp called out to know what was happening.

"Somebody died," Sarah shouted. Her words fell as flat as undisputed fact.

A despairing groan arose from my mother, who ripped her cap from her head and buried her fingers in her piled-up black hair, which then fell around her face like the curtain falling at the end of a play.

"No, nothing like that," I called out in a hurry. "I cut him and Uncle Mathew loose and they went to Mr. Dibble's house."

"He's alive? *And you* did that? Yourself?" Mother gripped my face in amazement.

"Wait! Why Dibble's?" cut in Mr. Knapp. "Mathew Benedict's own house stands directly behind Jonah's."

"It's all gone," I muttered, trying to be as low key as possible.

Mother looked at me, her face blank of understanding.

Mr. Knapp rose and tiptoed toward me, approaching with a

horrified curiosity. "*What's* gone? *What* isn't there?"

"Downtown. The houses aren't there anymore." I explained. "The houses of all the committee members are burning. Uncle Mathew's and Uncle Tad's, too. And the courthouse and Reverend White's house. And Griswold's and the drug store.

After a moment, I said, slowly and distinctly, "Zadock Benedict's house was on fire, too." Jonah's youngest brother lived on Town Street, near to our corner. I didn't mention the white chalk X's on the Knapp houses.

How had all of this begun? Lambert Lockwood had told me a story.

I turned on Mother, angry. "If Lambert Lockwood hadn't told me Jonah was back, I would never have stopped at his house. You *knew* Jonah was back, so why didn't you tell me?" Her secret had almost cost Jonah his life.

"Your father and I thought that you were too young to hear the awful truth. We thought you were just a child. And here it was you that saved him. You took heroic action, Joe. Bless you." She broke off to wipe her tears with her sleeve.

Praise was good, but I had been in no danger while cutting some ropes. No, in my own mind, I still had a long way to go, maybe years, before I found another chance to be a hero. Invasions didn't come along every day.

Mr. Knapp moved in between us. "We need to make sure no one burns *this* house — with us in it. We must each watch a side. The rebels will try and get revenge any way they can." He stood in front of Mother, making "get up" signs with his hands.

"If the British are gone…," she began. She looked too tired to move, almost melted into her chair.

"We have to worry about who's still here, our supposedly patriotic looters. We must stand watch this entire night, I tell you," commanded Mr. Knapp.

Sarah hauled herself up from the floor by means of different handholds on the table. She shook her hair out and looked to her father for instruction.

"There's something else," I insisted. "Lambert Lockwood was shot by the British and taken prisoner. I brought his horse here and put it in our shed. They put him in an ox-cart and took him away."

To me the news still sounded shocking, but Mr. Knapp's push directed me toward the side window looking onto Barren Plain Road.

To him, what would have happened to someone else was meaningless. We had enough to do to save ourselves.

Mr. Knapp picked up his pistol and moved to the window nearest to his tannery. Mother headed for front of the house, which faced Town Street. Sarah chose the barn side as her battle station. I wondered how long she'd stay awake. She resembled a wilting dandelion.

The night watch began, but sleep proved more powerful than fear. I began pinching myself to stay alert. This changed into biting my lips and the inside of my mouth to keep from nodding off. Then into pinching and twisting the soft part of my inner arm.

Maybe I truly stood watch, or did only *dream* that I watched?

I jerked to attention when an apparition floated across Barren Plain Road. Or was it only the shadow of an owl's flight passing over the road? Or a cloud shifting across the face of the moon? Or an Indian ghost carrying a pine knot torch toward the riverbank? All those thoughts floated across my sleepy mind.

A more solid ghostly figure hovered near Mr. Abel Gregory's cottage on the opposite side of Barren Plain. Mr. Gregory must be checking that all was well. It had to be Old Man Gregory, for soon a candle flickered inside the house. After that first reassuring sign, the little lamplight grew brighter every minute.

Soon we all clustered around the window, watching the cottage blaze.

Fears of Isaiah and his "big raid" now engulfed me.

"Could we put Pony and Lambert's mare in your barn?" I asked Mr. Knapp. "Robbers could be after Father's stallion and find Desire instead."

"Your little shed is safer by far," he answered shortly, bothered by my intrusion into his thoughts. "I'm a bigger target for theft."

I wondered why he thought that until Isaiah's hatred of Tories came to mind.

"The British marked Tory houses so they didn't get burned by mistake. Maybe we should get the white X off our houses now," I said.

Mr. Knapp drew in a sharp breath. "Lord above! We'll all get tarred and feathered! Patriots will be mad for revenge. Wet this cloth in the rain barrel. Quick!" He pushed a rag into my hand while shoving me out the door. I could hear him, right behind me.

The minute the door shut, we knew.

A flickering golden light illuminated the far side of the stile. Wild screams knifed through the sodden night air, the screams of a horse frantic from fear.

Fire.

I raced over the stile's steps into our yard, while Mr. Knapp vaulted the fence. In front of us, a clawing fingernail of fire reached up the shed wall, rising to include the boards in the roof overhang that sheltered the pigs.

Too much flame, too high to stop. The fire sounded liked dozens of sticks breaking. Up 'til now, the fires in town had been the adults' problem. Two of us rushed to rescue the two horses. I would have to go into the flaming shed, too.

The wooden shingles on the roof began to catch fire. Smoke, instead of rising, swirled to the ground like fog. Mr. Knapp gave me a sudden vicious shove away from the door, shouting, "Stay out here!" Then he went inside and I heard, "Whoa! Whoa!" and saw Pony hurl her five hundred pounds backwards against the tie-rope, wrenching the knot too tight for Mr. Knapp to untie.

Imprisoned in the box stall, Lambert's mare gave a screaming whinny and reared up on her hind legs. Her front hooves pawed at the heavy boards, while her muzzle reached ten feet in the air, dead center of the ever-increasing smoke.

That was it for me. It only took three steps to reach the stall. Two of my fingernails ripped as I heaved back the boards of the stall gate. I think I screamed.

When the mare crashed back down to earth, I reached for her halter. She reared again and struck out with flashing forefeet. The iron shoes nailed to her hooves splintered a board near my head. If I couldn't catch her, this would be the end of her life. And a tragedy for my new brother, wherever he was.

A voice blasted in my ear, "Your father would *die* if anything happened to you!" A hand grasped my coat and dragged me, kicking and fighting, out into the yard. I staggered and dropped to my knees on the rain-soaked ground. I pounded the ground in fury.

Benjamin Knapp, my father's best friend, turned to watch the burning building. He made no move to go back inside to save his pony. I could never escape this fast and agile man, who probably believed with all his heart that he had saved my life.

Desire's repeated screams of terror were echoed by Pony in her shrill little pony voice. Then I heard Sarah's own scream and saw her collapse on top of the stile, hands over her face, as she understood that both animals were as good as dead. I wondered if she had been asleep when the shed first displayed flame. She would blame herself.

That was it for me.

I staggered to my feet and dodged Mr. Knapp's grip as I charged back toward the shed. I stopped to look at the fiery hell above the door. Then I tried to make myself enter.

I couldn't do it.

I stood in the doorway, paralyzed by my own cowardice. Again. I wanted to shrivel up and disappear into the ground.

Why had I run here, only to turn back at the last minute?

A crash from within told me to leap out of the way. Pony blasted through the smoke, driving straight toward me.

Right behind her ran a roaring, cursing lunatic, wielding a knife in one hand while the other hand lashed at Pony's hindquarters with a scarlet coat. Then the little mare burst out into freedom, racing alone into the dawn fog.

I burst into tears of relief at the appearance of the last person I had ever wanted to see.

Tommy Flynn's normal face had disappeared into a tortured mask of dread and determination as he swung around into the burning building. I stepped into the doorway and watched the scene in the open box stall.

Pitching a rope around Desire's nose and over her ears to make a sort of bridle, Tommy jerked the mare toward the stall door. Smoke swirled down, filling one side of the shed. Then something above shifted and sparks followed the smoke, but disappeared before they hit the ground — or anything else.

But the terrified mare would not leave the stall.

"Wait, wait!" I yelled. Without thinking, I entered the stall, dropped to my knees and unfastened the wraps from the mare's legs. When the gravel chunks dropped into the straw, I wasn't sure if Desire could walk or not. Maybe my great plan to immobilize her would work all too well.

Then the beautiful beast, eyes white with terror, rose straight up in the air. Her shoulder hurled Tommy against the wall so hard that he dropped the rope. When Desire returned to earth, Tommy threw his red coat over her eyes, an old trick for leading frightened horses.

Tommy pulled and I slapped her rump as hard as I could. Once again, nothing doing. She would not walk a step. Furious curses lost themselves in Tommy's uncontrollable coughing.

The red jacket dropped into the straw. A shower of sparks fell onto the damp wool coat. If a spark hit the dry hay or straw, all would be over.

"Here now! Here, here!" shouted Mr. Knapp from outside. This was so unexpected that Tommy and I turned to see if help had come.

My father had proclaimed that horses ran back into burning barns, but I never believed it. Now, Pony's face poked through the door. I snatched the dragging end of the cut rope and pulled her into the shed while Mr. Knapp screamed, "No, you fool! Don't let her in there!"

Father had told me something else about horses and fire. How had these old memories come back, just when I needed them?

More glowing sparks dropped from the roof. Tiny shooting stars in a dark night of smoke. I slid out of my jacket, hoping to repeat Tommy's blindfold trick with an animal more my size. I covered Pony's eyes and held the sleeves together under her head.

Yanking the little beast into the stall, I spun her around to face the doorway.

"Let Desire sniff Pony and she might follow her outside!" I hollered to Tommy.

He forced the mare's nose down to touch Pony's back, then twisted Desire's ear to hold her head down.

"Go!" He shouted. "Now!" Praying, cursing or begging in Irish, Tommy Flynn convinced Lambert's mare to take her first steps, her nose jammed against Pony's back. Slowly, we moved in tiny steps to escape the fiery framework of the shed.

A ripping sound followed us outdoors as the flimsy shell of the roof crashed down in a hail of flaming splinters. Then the entire shed erupted into a wall of flame.

An awful thought overtook me. The pigs! Totally forgotten by all of us… now turned into roast pork. To save them would have been easy. Just break down the fence outside the shed.

But no one had done it.

Except for the crazed stallion, everything my family had owned was gone.

Chapter Twenty-Eight

Sunday, April 27th, 1777
at Six o'Clock of the Morning

Shock at the collapse of the shed left us mute, robbed of the ability to move in any direction. As the sun threatened to rise, we all awoke from our trance and looked around. Saturday had died and Sunday dawn was born.

The Day After.

A damp, gray daybreak had replaced the fire's golden light. The heavens had closed off the drizzle. Sarah sat on the top step of the stile, hands still over her face.

Tommy Flynn held Desire.

I held Pony.

Mr. Knapp held a gun.

"So you had big plans to burn and steal your way through America?" Benjamin Knapp, the nicest man in Danbury, sounded mean as a snake. "Going to start a new life, was it – of crime?" The gun hand held steady enough to instill fear, although the man behind the bullets was only half the size of the Irishman.

Tommy Flynn awakened to the fact that he was now a prisoner. "That's not the way of it at all," Tommy stood open-mouthed, stunned by the accusation. He trembled, one arm thrown around Desire's neck. A dirty gray look on the formerly ruddy face made me doubt that he could stand up without holding onto the animal.

"Swear to God, I meant no harm," Tommy said. 'Twas sleep or die. I hardly slept in four days. I lay in the hay back there and woke up when I heard someone foolin' with the horse. I just think it's the lad here. What if he did see me, anyways? Knows me, he does. So I dropped off again. Don't know how the fire started and I wasn't stealin' nothin', I swear it!"

"Who are you?" The gun remained focused on Tommy's heart, six feet away.

"Thomas Flynn of His Majesty's 27th Foot, the Inniskillings."

I sniffed the morning air while my mind reeled from one thing to another. I smelled the fire, but something I *didn't* smell screamed for attention.

"Tommy?" I figured my question ranked urgent enough to interrupt. "Were swine there when you came?" I pointed to the remains of the pigsty.

"Aye, I heard them snort when I came. Did the divils get away?"

I sniffed again. No smell of roasting ham improved the ashy air. A minute ago, I had counted the pigs as cremated.

The ever-practical Mr. Knapp sniffed, too. "Ha! Maybe the fence burned and they got out. Take a look, Joe." His own eyes remained glued to his unhappy target.

I approached the ruin of the sty, ready for whatever horror I might see. A pile of golden rye straw lay outside the circle of fire. That was new, for sure. Only moldy and damp gray hay that couldn't be given to horses had bedded the pigs.

The sty held nothing but wood ashes. The gate lay open.

Isaiah. He swore he would steal the horse and if he couldn't, he'd get the pigs.

Voices came from the road and four armed men crossed the bridge. Their loud chatter ceased as they looked across at us. No matter who saw Benjamin Knapp talking to a redcoat, bad results would follow — either for harboring a deserter or for consorting with the enemy.

Mr. Knapp herded us toward his barn, where we tied Pony and the mare in the manure-filled stalls.

Neighbor Knapp motioned with the gun barrel for our return to the house. Numb and silent, Tommy obeyed, walking in front of his tormentor. Sarah and I trailed behind.

How I wished that the sun had been going down instead of coming up. I felt so beat.

My mother had never come outside. One look at the Irishman entering the hall sent her running into Mrs. Knapp's room. The door slammed behind her.

Mr. Knapp led us to the dining room, where he dropped into General Erskine's place at the head of the table. I took a bench at the side. Tommy, still prisoner of the pistol, stood for interrogation, looking appalled that his brave deed had transformed into a felony.

"I could do with some coffee," announced our host.

Sarah measured coffee into a small pot and hung it over the fire to boil. She produced one cup for her father, then asked whether Tommy should receive coffee, too. Her father nodded.

"Would you have any tea, sir, by your kindness?" Tommy asked.

"An American would choose coffee," huffed Mr. Knapp. "Anyway, the only tea in this town now is raspberry leaves. The Patriots don't allow imported tea."

Cup in hand, Mr. Knapp settled deeper into his seat. "Now, sir, you have involved me in your desertion. Why did you invade this property, if not to commit crime?"

"Me chums, Harry and Bernard, talked about deserting and staying here in Danbury. Once I'd seen this rich town for meself, I wanted to live here, just like you. How to hide away, I didn't know. Then the lad here hangs around me, telling how the father is off somewheres, and the mother's stayin' somewheres else. The exact location was easy to find — a little house next to where the generals stayed. Goin' in a barn didn't seem so bad a crime. Maybe nobody would shoot me for that, if they did find me. The boy gave me the complete plan, he did – the whole scheme, offered to me like meat on a platter."

All eyes turned to me. I could not believe how fast an adult could twist a story.

The bedroom door flew open and out came my mother, lips compressed and eyes ablaze. Mother didn't look frightened any more. "Just where does my son come into the picture with – *him*?" Mother pointed at Tommy as if he were a criminal – which he was, no matter which side you were on.

Mother had left a Patriot family to become a Pacifist. Then she played hostess to the British. Mother's mind seemed like a bird in flight, a flight that would land somewhere unknown.

"Joe may not have encouraged this act," Mr. Knapp explained, "but he played some part in it. This, uh, *invader* did not worry at discovery, because Joe 'knew' him." Mr. Knapp shot me a glare that made me flinch. Sarah copied her father's expression, making it worse.

As a judge's daughter, Mother felt able to dissect the legal points regarding Tommy Flynn. Accepting a coffee cup, she commenced cross-examination like a real trial lawyer. "Being an army deserter is against British law," came the opening declaration in what might become my own trial.

"Making me guilty of harboring an offender," continued Mr. Knapp. "You, Mrs. Hamilton, are guilty of drinking coffee with him while knowing he deserted. What's the term — 'accessory after the fact'?"

Mother smacked her cup down on the table, as if it held lye. The resulting splash joined the rest of the mess.

"I didn't know a thing about it," I muttered, without looking up. I didn't want to be a traitor to someone who had rescued the horse and pony. On the other hand, I didn't plan to be hanging from a tree branch next to him.

I didn't know any more what was right or wrong. Was the redcoat in the room the cause of our misery or our savior? Had I done something wrong or not?

Mother stood up, looking more like a lawyer than ever. "Is this alleged crime punishable by the Continental Congress Mr. Knapp? There was that *alleged* word again, Father's favorite.

Mr. Knapp's face clouded over. "By Patriot law, this 'person' may be killed at any time. He's the enemy. Or he *was* the enemy…." Mr. Knapp paused to figure out Tommy's situation after changing sides, ending with, "Deciding what's legal goes according to who's deciding – at least, that's the rebel way."

"So this person's desertion will be legal *soon*," Mother declared, utilizing the sweeping hand gestures of a lawyer arguing a case before a full courtroom.

"Madam, what are you saying?" Mr. Knapp snapped out. Mother had edged closer to the Patriot side by assuming that they would win.

Further discussion did not look profitable for a Tory.

Mr. Knapp turned on his victim. "Have you any trade or skill?"

"I joined the army at sixteen," Tommy began, almost in a whisper, "feeling lucky that I spoke English, instead of just the Irish. Old King George's army brought me to that Boston town, but it featured smallpox and the coughing disease about as bad as Limerick or London. This Danbury looks fine to me. That is to say, it looked fine yesterday, it did."

"I'm sure it *did* look fine. Until *you* got here," Mother's acid voice added.

Sarah presented a plate of dry bread ends, taking the opportunity to slide the gun out of her father's reach. She followed by sliding the bread out of Tommy's reach. Feeding ourselves would be a problem. Feeding the huge Irishman would be a bigger one, unless....

Mr. Knapp's calculating eyes clung to his target. "Were you of farming stock?" he asked Tommy.

"More like slum stock. The main profession was begging," Tommy admitted, keeping a white-knuckled hold on his coffee cup.

"Your situation appears desperate, sir. You would not get far on Danbury streets today. You could suffer an accident, possibly gun-related." He bared his teeth to indicate a smile.

He let this news sink in before he added, "Now, I don't *pay* for tannery work, just food and a place to sleep."

"Anything at all would be due to your kindness, sir." Tommy nodded in quiet submission.

"Agreed, then. I will show you to the attic and give you a blanket for the pallet you'll find there. We're all in need of rest." Mr. Knapp pushed his chair back from the table.

Tommy was the only one who went to a real bed. The rest of us fell asleep around the dining room table, heads on our arms, amid the crumbs and bones.

The candle ends burned on unnoticed as the sun rose, extinguishing themselves one by one.

Chapter Twenty-Nine

Sunday, April 27th, 1777
at Eight o'Clock of the Morning

"Joe! Joe, wake up. We must go into town," Mother whispered. "People on the streets may know what happened to the militia." I sat up, but my eyelids stuck together and so did my teeth and tongue. I couldn't believe that I had slept at all. I certainly didn't feel better. I looked up, unwilling to move. Mother snatched my ripped shirtsleeve and pulled. How had my sleeve ripped? I couldn't even remember.

Mother acted so agitated that I followed her without eating or drinking a mouthful. So tired that I could hardly see, I misjudged the doorframe and smacked into it. Hand to my face, I staggered out the door, mostly dreading what I'd find.

The drizzle waited for us to be outside, then began again in a languid way. A torrent of walkers and riders poured into town to stare at the wreckage. Everyone wore rags for fear of befouling their clothing past any future wearing. Women riding horses wore rough canvas skirts over their real ones and ugly old rags over their hair instead of their usual caps. The smoke of human flesh was in the air and everyone knew it.

Homes mourned their fences, trampled bushes and chewed-up trees. The mud had churned into a combination of all things nauseous. Piles of horse manure lay everywhere. Several energetic slaves joined the town's free black family in patrolling with shovels and barn forks, in search of cleaning jobs. I would never walk barefoot in Danbury again.

Riders clashed stirrups as they rode closer to their companions, listening to tales of stolen cattle and oxen commandeered by the British.

Mother adjusted her shawl to cover her cap and half her face.

Her bright jacket from last night made her stand out from the crowd. Women she knew either glared or looked away. No one spoke to her.

I stopped a man coming into town on a rail-thin horse and asked about skirmishes. He reported militia blocking the road in Ridgefield. A British wagon train had moved in the distance, walking unhindered toward Norwalk, with scouting parties flanking both sides, all quiet and orderly. Had he seen prisoners in an ox-cart? He had not.

We pushed on toward town, examining the damages.

"Tell me again about Jonah's condition," Mother asked. "Uncle Mathew wouldn't let me see him. 'Not a sight for a lady,' he told your father. Said it was indecent for me to see Jonah the way he was. I can only blame myself for believing that, not understanding all the facts behind it."

"I was afraid of Jonah, of how he looked," I said. I hated to recall my meeting with a man where the line between living and dead had smudged.

"What did he *say*?" Mother pressed on. "Tell me again, every word he said."

"He whispered a little at first. I told him Father was out with the militia. He didn't say anything else. Uncle Mathew and some man dragged him away." I didn't like to think about what Jonah might look like now.

"Dragged him?" Mother yelped. She walked faster, breathing harder than I thought ladies ever breathed. "I failed in my duty to my family. I accepted what Uncle Mathew said, the same way I accepted everything. I'm changing that this very day. In fact, right *now*!" Her hands twisted her indigo-blue shawl as if she wanted to wring a chicken's neck. Or a human throat.

Mother stopped, both hands to her mouth, her choked voice exclaiming "Oh, no!" She had just seen the courthouse. Except that no courthouse remained.

As we walked along, Mother's eyes roved to the nearby houses of her relatives. The whole Town Street to South Street neighborhood had become easy to see, now populated mostly by chimneys. Hands covered her face as she looked through her Uncle Mathew's now transparent house frame to where Jonah's house had been.

I remembered the wonderful roast ox dinner when they built that house. And the oxtail soup the next day, with sliced tongue on bread for lunch. And everybody got berry shrub to drink. Now it was gone. And maybe Jonah was gone, too.

We cut through the lots, as I had done the night before. "Look, that's where I cut Jonah and his father loose from the tree." I pointed at the remains of the ropes, still circling the sycamore. The barn doors hung open. Bits of horse tack and little tools lay scattered in the mud outside the door. Looted after I left.

Financial Losses Paid by the State of Connecticut in 1793 to Persons Mentioned in the Story

John McLean $19,409.64 (Head of the Patriot Commissary)
Captain Daniel Taylor $4,932 (Patriarch of Danbury, first Danbury Militia leader)
Colonel Jos. P. Cooke $4,704.50 (Colonel of Danbury Militia, Town Mayor, married into Joe's family)
Major Eli Mygatt $580.80 (Continental Army officer, owner of drug store and Franklin Library)
Major Taylor $3,504 (Danbury Town Clerk; cloth fuller)
Rev. Ebenezer White $1,637.84 (Minister of New Danbury Church)
Thaddeus Benedict, Esq. $3,610 (Danbury Town Lawyer, brother of Joe's mother)
Dr. John Wood $4,970.80 (Commissary Official, Lambert's supervisor)
Mathew Benedict $,1079.10 (Joe's mother's uncle)
Jonah Benedict $1,547.80 (Joe's mother's cousin, former prisoner of war)
Mathew Benedict (Jr.) $1,025.00 (Jonah's brother)
Zadock Benedict $549.25 (Jonah's brother, lived on Town Street, near Ben Knapp)
Lt. James Clark $4112.62

When we reached the Dibble house, a fearsome duo approached from the direction of the Commissary — my mother's two older brothers, Judge Thomas Benedict and Danbury Town Lawyer Tad Benedict. Both wore official-looking dark dress coats and breeches, their expressions as black and deadly as funerals. Neither man gave any sign or greeting until they observed us turn toward Dibble's house.

"Look who's here ahead of us," Judge Tom drawled, "a leading member of the 'peaceful and legal solution' club." The sneer in his voice cut like a saw. My Benedict uncles counted as hard cases. I would have bet a shilling that neither one could tell my name. Not the first time they tried, anyway.

"Where is your oh-so-peaceful husband, Sister?" The judge tried to restrain himself, but the face above his white stock tie had turned dark red with rage.

"My husband is with the militia," Mother stated in a small voice, but the judge ignored her and pointed at the house. "Uncle Mathew in there?" Then both my uncles stalked past us without waiting for the answer.

Meek as sheep, we followed them into General Tryon's former office.

With a stifled shriek, Mother caught herself just in time. Her muddy foot had almost landed on Jonah's bare anklebone. He lay on the floor just inside the door, atop last night's blanket. His stick-like legs poked out from under his knee-length nightshirt, displaying a repulsive resemblance to a bird's scaly legs and clawed feet. The mouth hung open and the eyes remained closed. I could not tell if Jonah fared better than the night before, but the answer probably totaled worse, judging by the look on his father's face.

Uncle Mathew sat motionless, facing the door. His blank eyes stared at nothing, and no words issued when we came in. He looked like a man who had abandoned all hope of anything … anything at all.

Mother turned her face away at first sight of Jonah's bare legs, but Death dictated decency today. She dropped to her knees, the floorboards groaning as she and the blue church skirt landed on the mud-encrusted plank floor. She grasped one of Jonah's hands. Mother was not much for touching people, but she repeatedly stroked his hand and arm, as her upper body sank down, her face close to his.

Repeating his name drew no reaction.

I wished that I were somewhere else. Maybe in an ox-cart with Lambert. Yesterday morning, war had been a grand stage play that I had a free seat to watch. Now it just felt disgusting. I went to a corner and stood there, hoping to avoid looking at the scene.

The many footsteps that shook the wooden planks jarred Jonah into a sort of awareness. "I remember now, the fire," he whispered. "Tad? Tom? How did you get here?" Only Jonah's eyes moved, wavering from one pair of legs to another. Then they fluttered closed again.

When my mother looked up, her brown velvet eyes had filled with tears of true-life terror.

Jonah's eyes flickered open again and Mother pounced. "Have you had anything to eat?" she questioned in a sharp voice, repeated when Jonah didn't understand. Unable to focus, his eyes sank shut again. Then I understood – not only that Jonah might be dying, he might have already done so.

Mother turned on Uncle Mathew, shouting at him, trying to

force an answer. "Has he eaten? When?" She forged on, her voice rising ever higher when no response came. She had risen to her knees, shouting, when Uncle Tad got hold of her shoulder and gestured for her to be quiet.

At last, Uncle Mathew stirred, taking time in his own defense. "I tried him on cream, like Doc Wood told me. Hard to find cream these days. Maybe he got some down day before yesterday. All the docs left town yesterday." A strange noise issued from between Mother's clenched teeth, a sound like a dog snarling.

"Maybe he didn't get enough to drink, like water," I put in, remembering Lambert's quick recovery of the night before. It might not take a doctor. Even Tommy Flynn had known that liquid was the solution.

"So when did Jonah last drink *anything*? Water, ale?" Mother's clenched fists stretched in front of her.

Uncle Mathew's mind submerged into the last day and night, hunting for an answer. All the while, he continued staring at the ceiling. "I found myself a lick of cider when we came in here. But he shouldn't drink no cider. I don't dare try anything but cream and he won't take that in, when I *do* have it."

This summary caused the Judge to whisper a string of swear words.

Mother's fingers clutched at my jacket hem and pulled. "Joe, Joe, where, today of all days, where can you get anything he can—"

"I know where!" I called. I ran to the room where bottles had rattled last night. In Dibble's kitchen, sniffing one green bottle told of apple cider. I grabbed it, snatched a cup, and ran back to the drawing room. Judge Tom wasted no time in ripping them from my hands.

Uncle Tad raised Jonah and propped him against the wall. Then he held his head back and pinched Jonah's mouth open, the same way you open a horse's mouth for the bridle bit. Judge Tom let small dashes of cider pour into the half-open mouth while Mother begged for pauses to allow Jonah time to swallow. Half of the cider had disappeared before my uncles took a longer pause to see whether they were doing good or harm.

"Just where does your husband skulk now, Sister?" the judge asked Mother. Lawyers and judges could make anyone sound guilty.

"I told you already. He's with the militia," Mother murmured. Then she seemed to realize that this same scene had played out when we entered the house. She raised her haggard face and fired off a frigid and righteous stare. *"Did you hear me? He's with the militia!"* she shouted, so loud that Uncle Tad jerked as if she had hit him.

The judge looked away, but Uncle Tad riveted attention on us as if we were the ones dying. Stranger still, he looked guilty.

An unpleasant silence followed. Uncle Mathew shifted in his seat, trying to think of something to say. Perhaps blaming the wrong cause, he tried to break the bad mood that had descended. "Think you boys hit on something with the cider. Going by Jonah's previous life, if cream tasted like rum, it would have gone down him fast enough."

"Hmm! Rum could be a useful answer," Uncle Tad began, seeming surprised by his own idea. "Mix egg, milk, rum, sugar, and ground cinnamon bark. Egg and milk — both good for sick people. Rum and cinnamon cover the taste. Of course!"

"You sound like a tavern-keeper, sir." I hit on the first thing I thought of, only trying to make him stop looking at Mother and me as if we were plague victims.

"Tavern keeper? Just listen to that, will you! A tavern keeper, indeed." Judge Tom's condescending attitude filled the room.

"Now, don't get on Joe." Uncle Mathew spoke up, aware enough to defend me. "After what he did last night, Joe is a true hero to me and Jonah."

"Fine, so be a hero again, boy," Judge Tom interrupted. "Go up to Clark's Tavern and quick-march back here with that same drink. Tell the barmaid you want a rum flip." He jammed a quarter-penny into my hand, turned me around and shoved me toward the door.

"Is the tavern open?" I asked.

"Maybe just the bar," Uncle Tad said.

Clark's was always open Sundays for the church crowd. The water in our town was so bad that everyone drank ale. People died from drinking at the wrong well or stream. Every stream was open to animals. Every well lay near a backhouse.

Mother pushed me to the door, whispering, "Find out anything you can about the militia!"

A restless crowd milled in front of the tavern. An open door led into the bar, a line already formed. The door to the eating room remained closed. I walked around the building to the same back door where I had applied for work only three days ago.

"Oh, it's you, is it, Joe?" Accustomed to daily visits, my sudden appearance did not surprise old Mrs. Clark. "If you need food for the family, go to the front and wait. Ready at eleven."

Perspiring, she dabbed at her face. The pause grew longer before she added, "Or thereabouts...."

Bread loaves lay ready to serve, at least two dozen. A kettle of stew simmered on an iron hook over the coals, while bean pots warmed in the edges of the man-sized stone fireplace.

Six fowl lay, gutted and plucked, on the counter, while old Mrs. Clark threaded an iron rod up the centers of six more chickens. A place stood open for two spits to roast above the coals. Eleven o'clock? The tall case clock in the corner had dinged quarter past ten as I came in. Those chickens should have been cooking an hour ago.

Another flaw in the kitchen picture appeared. A whole pig hung on the iron spit in the walk-in fireplace, one side already an over-crisp dark brown, the other side a raw pork-fat white. No one had turned the spit. The fire had sunk into embers and no wood lay nearby.

The first spit of chickens clicked into the rack over the fading fire, but when old Mrs. Clark's glance hit the semi-raw pig, her determination dissolved. She removed her cap and pried her damp hair out of her eyes. A hundred people counted on her for a meal. A tear escaped, then two, dribbling down her cheeks to her chin. The back of her wrist rose to remove them.

"I'm at my wit's end, Joe. My daughter-in-law took the children and fled. Their house is gone up in flames. I don't know where they are. I stayed here all night, I just had to open. We'll have to build new, and this is the most money we'll make all year!

"The Stevens girls are here, but it takes one on the bar and one on the till. You searched for work – could you help me now? Double David's wages?" The words surged out of her mouth in a flood.

"I just came for a rum and milk flip for Mother's cousin, Jonah Benedict. He's mighty bad after last night. He might pass away. I have to do whatever my mother says."

"Can you find me some other boy? *Today*?" As she spoke, her fingers reached for wood, but found only splintered kindling. "Whatever that poor Mr. Jonah needs is on the house. Find me some help, Joe Hamilton!" Issuing orders strengthened the old woman enough to return to threading chickens onto the next spit.

Anger struck as I walked into the public room. How did choosing my trade end up so that I could *not* have the job that I had wanted? Turning spits wasn't even work. Hunger turned a knife inside me, yet I could think of nothing I desired to eat.

As I waited, I added up *whose* fault this was, not just for me, for the whole town. The Patriots dictated everything — Patriots, meaning the Committee of Inspection. Meaning Captain Silas Hamilton. My grandfather.

Anner Stevens took my order and presented the filled tin can, but my shredded fingernails hit the side of it and I came near to spilling it all. The searing pain increased my fury at refusing Mrs. Clark's offer.

Since the apprenticeship had already been my agreement with my parents, anything I said now would only make them angry. I was stuck, for sure!

As I walked back to Dibble's, carrying Jonah's drink, I wished that Mrs. Clark had offered me something to eat.

That changed into *why hadn't I asked*? Who else was supposed to fix my clothing, my school, my job, my life? Here I was, carrying a little tin pail, only a boy following orders, as usual. This had better change and change soon. *How* it was going to change formed the real question.

Passing under the Tory white X, I entered the Dibble drawing room to find Jonah, still on the floor, propped up against the wall. He absorbed a few swallows of the rum flip while we all watched. Two spoonfuls of apple conserve from the pantry passed the same test. Within a few minutes, Jonah's eyes began following the conversation around him. He occasionally moved his arms and legs, although he peered down to check whether they had in fact moved.

Mother remained crouched on her knees, but I saw her exchange a relieved look with Uncle Tad. When she held up her hands, he lifted her to her feet. To catch her balance, she had to hang on to him for a minute. A long look passed between them before brother and sister turned away from each other.

"Did you hear anything at the tavern?" Mother asked me, her eyes as alert as an eagle's.

"I overheard a man on the street say that the Patriots planned a big skirmish today. He also said it wouldn't disturb the British one bit."

"Let us pray that all Hamiltons and Benedicts return unharmed," Mother said, shaking off the floor's dried mud.

"All Hamiltons are great patriots," Jonah whispered, sounding like a frog's last croak.

"Humpf. Well, some are," The judge muttered, mostly to keep Jonah calm.

"Looks like Jonah's making progress," Uncle Tad said. "What are we going to do now? We can't go to the bar for every drink. I can get a nutmeg and a bottle of rum, but milk spoils. Got to have it fresh every day. Who has a milk cow?" He glanced around, awaiting an answer, and somehow his eyes stopped at me.

"I could bring Jonah milk from Knapp's cow," I volunteered. Mostly in hopes of instructions to go home right that minute. I had seen the cow in the tannery once and that was all I knew about it.

"Oh, Knapp has a *cow*, does he?" Uncle Tad's cheerful enthusiasm made me want to retract my foolish remark. To make him forget the cow, I reverted to the last subject I should have mentioned again.

"The tavern was packed with folk come to see the town. A good tavern would make a fortune, not just today, either. Think of all the people who have no homes to cook in." I pointed to the window, which gave a view of crowds and burnt commissary warehouses.

> There were three taverns here at the time, and the business they might have done, had they the liquid facilities, would have been immense.

Uncle Tad dropped the smile as he walked to the window and stared down the ruined street, littered with smashed barrels and axed wooden crates. "All this damage and no one to sue. Now the boy here thinks 'tavern keeper' is a grand job for the town lawyer. How did it all go this wrong?" His words, though not directed at anyone, sounded terminally sad.

It hadn't occurred to me that my rich lawyer uncle now had no office, because the courthouse had burned. His fine house had burned, too. Rebuilding lost houses would take years of cutting trees and sawing boards. Someone had told me that building boards had to dry for months before use. No matter how much money lay in his pockets, Uncle Tad would have to live with other people — the same exact way my family lived.

Uncle Mathew rose to his feet, exhaling a blast of air to indicate that our visit was over. He blessed everyone with a two-handed handshake, beginning with Mother and finishing with me.

As we prepared to leave, both my uncles embraced Mother. The judge pushed past me to the door, but Uncle Tad inspected me as if he had just met me for the first time. "Joseph, my boy, I was pleased to meet you. We may have a long friendship." Then he shook my hand. Only odd thing was, Uncle Tad had met me plenty of times before.

The sun of afternoon began to warm the day, which didn't

improve the day much. I shuddered when we passed the jail and the graveyard. Death's heads rode the tops of all the tombstones. Some men had stones with angels on them, but they only looked like death's heads with wings.

Colonel Huntington's Continentals might have ambushed the British wagon train where Lambert rode. I plodded along, but looked into the face of each passing man, trying to read any news he might have. They all looked about as glum as we did, but not much worse.

Mother swiped at stray tears, but eventually stood straighter and walked faster. We walked along for a bit and Mother sighed before saying. "Major Taylor's shop burned down, your Uncle Tad said. Major Taylor had all the town land records in there. Your uncle's going to have a hard time sorting out the law in town. Your father was right about that cloth. At least we still have that."

I said nothing. Mother had not yet understood the cloth's journey out West Street.

My mind returned to Grandfather. I had plenty of time to think about him as I stumbled along toward home.

All of Grandfather's recent deeds had one thing in common: doing the unexpected. When threatened with instant death, he had done the last thing the enemy could have imagined. When he threatened my father, he used someone else for the victim.

I needed to do something unexpected, too. Something to try to draw us out of the quicksand that would sink my parents and me. How could we go on living with nothing left to sell and Father going to jail?

Chapter Thirty

Sunday, April 27th, 1777
at High Noon

On our way home, Mother had assigned me to produce sufficient milk for Jonah. Sarah and I had trotted Pony down to the tannery last year, but the smell of the place kept us from ever going back. I didn't know whether Sarah had learned the gentle art of milking cows. If not, she might learn it today.

Sarah sat by the drawing room window, brushing her hair. I filled my hand with the ends and husks of leftover nuts and sat down across from her. "Sarah, do you know how to milk the cow that lives in the tannery? Mother's cousin was starved in prison and needs milk."

"The tannery apprentices milk her." Sarah gazed out the window toward the tannery. "I bet those nasty apprentices ran off yesterday and joined the rebels. I'll just bet they did. Maybe nobody fed her or gave her water. I like the cow, but I'm not going near that tannery alone. I do know how to milk, though. If you go with me, we could milk her right now. It's stopped looking so gloomy outside."

"Jonah needs more milk today, so let's go," I said.

"We could take the pony," Sarah offered, jumping to her feet and jamming on her cap, anxious to leave the house. Destination anywhere.

A slow but steady stream of Tory visitors kept Mr. Knapp at home. He agreed that someone needed to look at the animal and check the tannery buildings, insisting that Tommy accompany us to his new workplace. To Sarah's and my open-mouthed amazement, he entrusted Tommy with his gun. "Just in case."

The three of us strolled along the riverbank, away from the road and towards the tannery. Sarah swung an empty milk pail. We all felt grateful for the sun, hoping it might blot out the memories of last night. Tommy sang a mournful Irish tune as we crossed the first field, green with fresh grass, but minus its former sheep population. Violets bloomed under the trees, and witch hazel and pussy willows framed the river's edge.

Tommy asked about fishing, but his words ground to a halt as the warming spring breeze blew the scent of cow cadaver into our faces. The wildflowers closer to the tannery must smell the same, I thought. Tommy's steps dragged as he closed in on his future home.

"Don't know a thing about tanning hides, only that it stinks somethin' awful. Does it *always* smell like this?" His eyes reflected growing dread.

Sarah just looked at him. "It's a tannery. Dead cow skins stink," was her flat explanation.

Piles of tanbark from the hide softening process sat along the riverbank near wooden pools of the lye used to remove the hair from the leather. The river in April promised a truly evil stench in July.

A long minute passed before he began walking again. He did not look as pleased with America as he had been a few hours ago.

No one had fed or watered the cow, leading to much excitement when she saw us coming. "At least she's still here," Sarah said, but no one paused to help the beast.

The first task was to check on whether the night of burning and looting had reached the abandoned property. Sarah stuck to Tommy's shadow while she looked around.

Made bold by having a bodyguard, she pointed to the ground in front of a shed with a chimney. "Look, fresh prints in the mud. The apprentices *are* here. Let's try to catch them playing dice or sleeping!" Holding a finger to her lips for silence, she threw open the door, but then fell back with a scream, grabbing onto me for dear life.

Tommy, not considering the sight unusual, said only, "Didn't see to watering the beast, eh?"

Not likely. Sitting at a rickety table, his bloody face resting on crossed arms, sat Isaiah.

"So, the little Tory boy found his way here, complete with his redcoat friend," Isaiah snarled. He levered his body by his elbows to force himself upright. His old clothes looked more torn than usual. Under some dried blood around his nose, his face bore an even coat of dirt or ash. A stout stick leaned against the wall, last night's weapon-of-choice.

The whole picture said *thief*.

"Were you at our barn last night?" I tried to sound mean.

"What if I was?" The snarled answer did sound mean, no effort needed.

"You said you'd steal our pigs and our pigs were stolen,"

"See any pigs? Hear any snorts?" He pretended to look into corners of the room, furnished only with the table, two homemade chairs, and two rag-covered bunks.

"The whole school heard you threaten to steal our horse or our pigs. *Someone* stole our pigs and here *you* are, right next door. Know anything about that?"

"No horse nor pigs is here and I don't know where your pigs *is*, swear to God."

This oath wore a halo of truth, but I knew Isaiah.

How handy that Tommy qualified as the large and violent type. When his shadow fell across Isaiah, it became a magic potion. Fear flew across Isaiah's face and he flinched, putting up a hand to ward off blows. "Honest, I started to, but I didn't," he wailed.

"So you stole the pigs and burned the barn, leaving the horse and pony to die inside?" I shouted, remembering the early morning of this day all too well.

"You mean that pony was in there?" Furious with himself, Isaiah realized that the truth had poured out. "I did *not* take the horse, on account of it was lame, and I did *not* burn the barn. If I'd a' knowed about the pony, I would have nicked *that* before those stinkin' pigs."

"So you took the pigs after swearing an oath that you didn't?" Sarah thrust her finger right in his face, almost putting out an eye.

"I swore that I don't have the pigs *now*. I was drivin' the pigs over to the road when two men come up. One chased me and the other took the pigs and run off. That's how I got the way I am."

"What do you mean?" I asked.

"Like this." Isaiah pointed at himself in explanation.

"Like *what*? Speak plain!"

"Two men jumped me in the dark."

"Just tell the story the way it happened." I knew Isaiah would boast about anything done under the cover of patriotism.

Sarah sat down on a bunk, but I chose the seat across the table from Isaiah, planning to grill him the way Mr. Knapp had grilled Tommy.

"Well, last night sure turned into a bust," moaned Isaiah. "My daddy an' me wanted to nick stuff and burn Tory places. We chased off the Tories as was burning the Inn's benches, then we torched Old Man Gregory's. Got me a real fine shirt out of there. Don't know where it is now." Isaiah looked around sadly.

"Where did you go from Gregory's?" No houses lay on Barren Plain, except the Knapp properties

"When the dawn light showed, I looked in Knapp's barn, but nothin' was left. I went in your shed, but I seen that red horse's legs all bandaged up and figured she was lame. Them pigs was 'bout the last thing I could grab 'fore anyone saw me. I started down Barren Plain and don't think nothin' of footsteps. Think it's my daddy. First I knows, the one of 'em knocks me down and kicks me about twenty times. Must of broke some ribs."

I imagined broken ribs heaped up inside him like the broken bones after a chicken dinner, sharp ends and all.

"Why did you come to the tannery?" Sarah demanded. "Did your daddy follow you here? Did he take any hides?"

"You think if I could walk, a little Tory girl could question me about my daddy? I crawled in here to get out of sight. I ain't bettin' I could walk home. Now I can't enlist or nothin', even if I had a horse. Hurts like to die."

"Let's go back to where you stole the pigs and set our shed on fire," I said.

"I never done it. Guess my daddy lit your shed up. Maybe somebody was comin' an' he ran before he seen the pony. He's a real Patriot, my daddy is," Isaiah announced. He leaned back against the chair in an experimental way. The result did not satisfy, judging by his exhaled moan.

"Say, could I get me somethin' to drink? I can't hardly move." Isaiah looked more miserable than ever.

"We'll think about it," I said, motioning Sarah and Tommy outside for a conference.

"Seems like that lad's tellin' the truth about what happened. At least, now you know," Tommy said.

An unusual feeling of power flooded over me. If only the whole school could see me lord it over Isaiah!

But how could I *use* that power?

Tommy fetched a bucket of water from the rain barrel and we watched the cow guzzle it down.

"Do you think the apprentices will come back?" I asked Sarah.

Sarah's response failed to consider who heard it. "I hope I never see them again. Apprentices are all disgusting, even *before* they work here."

She held her nose and made a face as she dropped onto a tiny stool and began milking. "The only ones work here are boys who can't go anywhere else. And can't go anywhere *after* they work here, due to the smell!"

Tommy stifled an oath. Her vivid description now included him. He turned to stare at the Still River. He had nowhere else to go, either. He now resided in the prison of Freedom.

A sad decision came upon me. I had used Tommy to get to Lambert. Tommy had used me to find a hiding place. Still, he had risked his life to save Desire and Pony. He made me enter the shed when I was afraid, so I got rid of the title of coward.

I owed him, but I only had one thing to give.

"Tommy, would you rather work in a tavern?" The words flew out of my mouth, almost against my will.

"A tavern? I would downright love it!" Tommy whirled around, his face shining as eager as a child's. "How? Where?"

"Old Mrs. Clark needs help in the kitchen of the only tavern left open."

"I would be out of sight?" Tommy frowned as he gestured at his uniform breeches and boots.

"Joe! If Tommy leaves, there's nobody to work here." Sarah's exasperation played into my new plan.

I pointed toward the cabin where Isaiah sat. The spark of mirth in her eyes looked more like the girl I knew in the days when we singed old ladies' shawls as we cantered past.

When we went back inside, I mentioned the position of apprentice tanner, but Isaiah didn't miss the fact that he was the last choice in the entire world.

Tears commenced leaking out of his eyes.

"I'm a Patriot! Working for a Tory will kill me for sure!" A murderous look accompanied the whine. He sank lower in his chair.

"We're leaving now," I said, thinking this would be the only good thing in Isaiah's day so far. I smiled and waved good-bye to make him feel worse.

As we walked back, Tommy broke into full song, but a feeling of helplessness hung over me like the smoky smell that surrounded the town.

My disappointment surged into a driving desire to challenge my grandfather for bringing all this misery down on his own family. Why did Patriots think everyone wanted to be like them? I wasn't in the least bit like my grandfather and didn't want to be, either.

I knew that for sure.

Chapter Thirty-One

Sunday, April 27th, 1777
at Two o' Clock of the Afternoon

When we returned to the house, Tommy confessed his change of heart. Mr. Knapp couldn't force him to work by any law, Tory or Patriot. The judge would have laughed all day — *after* imprisoning both Mr. Knapp and his British guest.

None of us had the courage to tell Sarah's father about his new worker down in the tannery. The one who was unable to work.

Tommy and I decided to make our getaway into town. I hauled the tin can of milk for Jonah, while Tommy carried his scarlet coat rolled up under his arm. His boots and breeches told their own story.

A red coat was not street wear in this town, for sure. Buying new clothes would be impossible. Old hats and boots deserved mention in wills. Last fall a Committee on the seacoast sent five Tory prisoners to the Danbury Committee. A copy of this letter stood posted on a board downtown.

JOHN McLEAN TO GOVERNOUR TRUMBULL
Danbury, December 24th, 1776.
This is to acquaint your Honour that there is five prisoners here, sent from the State of New-York, viz: one Commissary for the Engineers, one Lieutenant of the Sixteenth Regiment, one Captain of Transport, one of their wives, and one child, which is in utmost want of necessary clothing, and have made application to the Authority, Selectmen, and Committee as nothing of that kind could be procured here... We therefore would acquaint your Honour that they really are in great want of articles of clothing ... am, sir, for myself and the rest of the Authority, Selectmen, and Committee, your Honour's most obedient, humble servant,

We passed the remains of Major Starr's house. Reverend Ebenezer White stood in the ruins. A litter for human remains sat on the ground in front of him, but only two skulls rested there.

Hard-driving hoof beats from behind us aimed so close that we barely escaped before the lathered horse rode over us. The stricken look of despair on my grandfather's gray face quenched any greeting. The staring eyes, the open mouth…. Wholesale slaughter seemed likely.

"Looks serious as death, he does." Tommy whispered, so awed that he made the sign of the cross. "Who on earth was that, ridin' so hard?"

"My grandfather." I hurried on, more anxious than ever to reach Clark's Tavern.

Introducing the Irishman to his new workplace proved easy. Amid the clash of spoons and pewter chargers, Tommy radiated good will. With no effort, a slab of ham and egg pie found its way to one hand while his free hand turned the spit. He commenced to whistle.

Danbury gained three citizens, and, so far as we can learn, they were good citizens, in the persons of three deserters from the British Army. One of these was a fifer, whose name was Harry Brocton. The others were privates. Thomas Flynn was the name of one of the latter. …Flynn also married here. He settled on South Street.

All news migrated to taverns before anywhere else. We hadn't been there for five minutes before one of the Stevens girls ran in from the bar and whispered to Mrs. Clark.

"Dying?" Mrs. Clark groaned as she said it. Then she repeated, "Oh, dear Lord!" and "God save us!" to every whispered sentence. At least, no one sent meaningful looks toward me.

"Is there news? A lot of wounded? " I asked Mrs. Clark.

"Just one man," she said. "General Wooster took forty British prisoners near Ridgefield before the red devils shot him!" She began to skewer chickens again. Extra hard.

"Can't General Arnold lead the militia instead?" The Patriot boys at school favored Benedict Arnold of New Haven, who paid for his militia's guns and uniforms.

"General Wooster had common sense. That Benedict Arnold is mad," she declared, with a conviction that made me wonder just what Lt. Clark had told his family.

The Tory boys always sneered that General Arnold killed his troops on the way *to* battles, having run into the accidental bad luck of poor planning.

I started for Dibble's with the can of milk, but a growing feeling of disaster, fueled by no sleep, drove my desire to pursue the man responsible for every bad thing in my life.

"My" life? When was *I* going to take control of it? This was the second time today that I had left without asking for food. I wanted to kick myself for being afraid to speak up.

My progress stopped when I caught sight of a ramshackle carriage and two mismatched horses standing in front of the house. A crowd clustered nearby, some women crying, but some men crying, too. Perhaps Jonah had died. I began running, holding the milk can out in front of me.

The open front door showed only the black void of the hall. I peeked in before entering. My grandfather stood at the foot of the stairs. Tears leaked into the lengthening gray beard stubble. What had happened to Jonah? Where was Uncle Mathew?

Upstairs, voices called instructions, followed promptly by an unearthly scream. Not liking the awful sound, I walked closer to Grandfather, who put an arm across my shoulders, without looking at me. His bulky rainproof outerwear was gone, revealing a stick-straight military figure under a faded uniform coat that showed twenty years' of brushing with too harsh a brush.

"Is that Cousin Jonah Benedict up there?" I asked, trying not to put my hands over my ears to cancel the dreadful groans.

"His father took him away somewhere. Dr. Turner and Dr. Foster put General Wooster here. He is surely dying. Our best general... gone."

It seemed that old Mr. Dibble and his son had vanished, but the house continued on its own, under whatever master chose to occupy it.

I chose to hit on Grandfather's favorite subject before I dared question him about Father. "Where are my uncles?"

"Went with Arnold and Silliman to herd the British back to their boats. It's more herding than chasing. If the redcoats turn to fight, it won't go well for our side," came the dull answer, his attention still focused on the stairs. "Norwalk's got militia. We'll see what they can do."

I was right. Grandfather had known all along that the Patriots had no chance whatever.

The ancient Captain Daniel Taylor barged in the door. Tears coursed down his sagging face. Not saying a word, he dragged himself upstairs by means of the railing. The first leader of the Danbury Militia now assumed the position of chief mourner. Grandfather was free to leave.

With his arm still enfolding my shoulders, he said, "Long time since we talked together, isn't it, Joe? I'll take you home on my way to the farm. Last time you rode behind me, you were just a little lad. A lot of things changed since then, didn't they, little lad?"

I put the milk can down on the hall table and followed at his heels, biting my lip. Always the "little lad" in his mind. I had played the child yesterday to get into Dibble's house. Not today.

My turn had come, my turn to get straight answers.

When we reached him, old Tom's head was hanging. "This old horse is too tired to trot with both of us, so it might be a slower ride than you're used to, my boy. Been riding this horse for two solid days and nights. Five more miles to home."

The old man maneuvered himself from mounting block to saddle, then motioned to me. I jumped, then clutched Grandfather's coat to pull myself into position on the horse. Now Grandfather couldn't just walk away from me. Unless he threw me off the horse, he would have to listen.

"Did you see my father after the skirmish?"

"No, Joseph, I know nothing of where your father is. Heard there were deserters. He could have been one of them, for all I know." Grandfather's usual outlook: Father had to be up to no good.

"Your mother all right, Joe?"

"Yes, but somebody stole our pigs and burned the shed. Not the British. Some robber."

"Sorry 'bout that, Joe. Gives all the scum of the area free rein, doesn't it?

Since Grandfather never objected to patriotic crime, I offered, "Lambert Lockwood was arrested and he's on his way to prison in New York. The British had his mare, but I stole her."

He twisted his head around, trying to see me. "Joe, lad! What a brave act! Only thirteen and you confiscated your first horse!"

Pleased amazement described his reaction, which felt better than I had thought. Just like this morning, when Uncle Tad admitted that I was alive. Maybe these were signs that I was growing up, not just in real life, but in their minds.

"So Lambert could end up in prison and you wouldn't care, although he's a Patriot, just like you?" I asked.

"Lockwood? If you dumped him into the ocean, he'd swim

right to the surface. I'll bet Lockwood's swilling brandy with top British officers right now."

Wanting to correct the idea of possible drunkenness, I said, "No, sir. When a British officer offered him rum, he ordered cider instead."

"He *ordered*...?" Grandfather let go a guffaw. He still lived in some 1760 war-atrocity world where being captured and in jail counted as normal.

People we passed gave Captain Hamilton respectful salutes and ladies made mournful nods. Unfortunately, the slow pace allowed Grandfather to form questions of his own.

"Heard you rode a Tory pony over to the artificer camp, boy. Nice pony, I hear," he said in the tone of a prospective buyer. "Going to join the Patriots, are you, boy?"

Here it was again. The Old Trickster, as my father called him. If I said yes, Pony would be mine. And Sarah would think evil of me for the rest of her life.

"I'm only thirteen, too young for the army," I said, as if that had to be the only reason to refuse.

A sign on the King George Tavern said "Moved to Beaver Brook" in big charcoal letters, now smeared by the night's rain.

Grandfather pulled up his horse to inspect situation. Or so he said.

"Your father's little trip may start soon," came out in a casual way.

I could have bitten right through a stick. Grandfather spoke to me as if I was six years old. As if I didn't know where the "trip" would end.

"You said father had to enlist or go to jail," I burst out, pushing blame in the direction I wanted it to go.

"Lad, it's the new Connecticut *law* that your father must register for the draft," came the patient voice. "The Sons of Liberty will act on their own, if I *don't* put him in jail. A tar and feather uniform is the fashion now, a midnight black suit to blister the skin off his body."

"Father said that the Sons of Liberty are robber gangs from New York."

"The Sons over in New York do, uh, 'small activities' for me. Just business, you know." Grandfather shifted in his saddle.

"Do you *want* my father to go to jail?" I asked straight out. I was ready for a showdown. Maybe too ready.

"You don't get it, boy," Grandfather barked. "Your father will be *safe* in jail. The Sons could string somebody up, if they were provoked. Hang him! Those cow-boys get violent. The sheriff don't live here, you know."

I couldn't believe it. To Grandfather, jail meant safe storage of his own son.

"It's shameful to be in jail. He'd go out of his mind," I tried to explain, but I could tell that it was useless.

I had a plan. Now was the time for this snake to strike, just like the snake on the rebel flag.

Father had told me not to get mixed up in rebel business. He never said anything about not getting *him* mixed up in it.

"Could Father hire a substitute?" I asked.

"He owes me eight pounds for a horse that belonged to *me*. Does he think I'll pay for him to shirk his duty? He can have his choice of prisons: debtor's or regular!"

"What if Father joined the commissary?" I asked.

"He'd never do it. Thinks John McLean got rich off it. But John McLean's money forms the backbone of the Commissary."

"Why can't Father weave cloth for tents or uniforms?" I begged. No need for Father to leave our own four walls or even *talk* to Patriots.

"Only tents any good are French ones, like the hundreds of tents that disappeared last night. And uniforms? You sound no different than the Connecticut General Assembly, ordering thousands of uniforms when we can't get ten blankets."

Grandfather sounded angry now, but I wasn't sure that his anger was aimed at me. Blankets had been part of Lambert's story about this brother's death.

It was directed, (under a recommendation of Congress,) to purchase a quantity of homemade cloth, (or other cloth if that could not be obtained,) of a brown color, for 3,000 coats and 3,000 waistcoats, and as many blankets as could be obtained in the colony; 3,000 felt hats, check flannel or linen for 6,000 shirts, 6,000 pairs of shoes, to be collected and deposited in the proper stores in the several counties, proportioned to each county.

"Blankets! He could weave blankets!" I shouted in desperation. Rather unfortunate that I shouted it into Grandfather's back, not his face.

He stopped the horse again, this time in front of the Inn, shut up tight.

Turning in his saddle, he craned his neck to look me in the eye. "All persons must conform to the laws of Connecticut, son. Failure of total support is responsible for our present situation."

This was the last straw.

"Responsible?" I shouted, lifting my face into clear air right below Grandfather's ear. "It's *you! You* and your awful committee are responsible for everything!" I turned and swung my arm past the abandoned taverns and the lane revealing the charred remains of the Sandemanian church.

A hand reached back, took hold of my jacket, and assisted me to dismount. Staggering as my feet hit solid ground, I did a sit-down in the dirt.

I jumped up as Grandfather issued a cold and condemning stare. I presented a clear target, as I stood stranded in the middle of the Town Street and Elm Street crossroads.

"If our fight for freedom fails, your father could end up in India, fighting for the British and dying of fever! Did that ever occur to you?"

Passersby smiled at my humiliation. A girl from church hid her mouth. The stifled laugh hung in the air, only vanishing when her awful mother added, "Poor little boy!"

I longed for lightning to strike them both, right where they stood.

Redirecting his reluctant horse, Grandfather turned back toward town, nudging Tom into a sluggish trot. I may have shaken my fist at him.

The sun said it was only midafternoon, but I wished it were midnight to hide my tears of humiliation. After wiping them off on my new blue jacket, I decided that my dirty hands had made a mess of my face the same way I had made a mess of everything else.

My big chance to change my family's future had failed.

Chapter Thirty-Two

Sunday, April 27th, 1777
at Four o'Clock of the Afternoon

After a foot-dragging walk back to the Knapps' house, I didn't dare tell a word to anyone about anything. Reporting about General Wooster would cause worry about Father's safety. Reporting my meeting with Grandfather would cause worry about my *own* safety.

I washed my face and hands at the rain barrel and then slipped through the Knapp's back door, as silent as a spider. No one looked up or said a word when I entered the drawing room. I found a bench with a cushion, and sank down next to it, leaning my head on its seat. Mother had passed the point of caring who came in or left.

I closed my eyes, pretended to sleep, and listened.

Mother mended Noah's clothes and drew in her breath each time she stuck her finger with the needle. Mr. Knapp walked from window to window, talking to himself. The door to Mrs. Knapp's room stood open while she murmured the Sunday Bible lesson to Mercy and Noah. Sarah rocked the baby's cradle with her foot, although the baby had been asleep when I came in. After a few minutes, the noise irritated Mr. Knapp and he sent the two of us outdoors.

Sarah and I led Pony and Desire out to the new grass that grew close to the bridge. As they dropped their heads to eat, strangers riding home from town felt free to look us over and comment to each other.

"Isaiah's father is still out there," Sarah said. "He could be watching us now. He might steal Desire and Pony, then burn *our* barn. Can't you take her somewhere? Please?"

I had no business keeping Desire. I knew that. "I give up," I said. "Desire won't be a problem here anymore. I'm taking her to Mrs. Lockwood's house." Sarah followed me to the barn and helped me saddle the red mare and put an old halter on her. I was afraid to ride her, but her saddle and bridle had to return home.

My last link to Lambert would be broken, which made me too sad to talk.

As I led Desire toward the road, a sigh that was half a sob came from Sarah. "When I was younger, I could go anyplace and ride there, too."

Struck by this strange reversal of what usually happened to girls, I said, "You wouldn't recognize the town since it burned. Come on."

Sarah brightened as she took the bridle to carry for me. "Maybe I could have gone to the Academy, too. I wish I had." After a pause, she added, "On our way home, we should hunt for greens and wild asparagus. Hardly anything's left to eat."

"I don't think a penny's worth of food remains in our house, either. Maybe a sardine," I said. I brightened, too, mostly at the thought of the search.

We walked on with the horse's haltered head between us. Sarah checked the open spaces between houses, usually a source of greens. Nothing showed except three women and two children, making the same search for free food.

When we got to Mrs. Lockwood's, we walked behind the shuttered house to the barn. Pomp emerged from a shed. I usually said "Good Day!" to slaves, trying to be polite, but now I shook Pomp's hand while he grinned. When I introduced Sarah, Pomp bowed at the waist. She started to curtsey, but then shook his hand, too.

Desire took advantage of our politeness to yank the rope out of my hand. She brushed past Pomp and walked into her own stall. She was home. Pomp removed her saddle. I steeled myself to recite the story of Lambert's imprisonment.

"Is Lambert's stepmother here?" I asked, thinking she should know first.

"Not here. She flee!" His eyes danced, as if fleeing was a dirty activity performed mainly by white people.

"The British took Lambert prisoner," I said.

"No, Lambert here last night. Here." My head snapped up in time to see Pomp point to his shed. "Late night, Lambert come. Stay with me and Peg. Not go in big house. Afraid it burn."

"But I *saw* it. The British took him," I said, louder. A lot louder.

"No, Lambert sleep in shed. All safe." Pomp's grin widened. He looked so proud.

"How did he get away?" I shouted, so loud that Sarah put her hands over her ears.

"He say, enemy man give him cider and make him free."

The officer who had questioned us knew that Tryon planned to free Lambert. I wondered if a certain "little girl" had caused such mercy.

"Where is Lambert?" I swiveled my head toward the house.

"Lambert meet commissary mans. Not here."

Disappointed, I wanted to leave, but I felt that I had to check something first. "Do you belong to the Lockwoods, Pomp, or are you free?"

"Belong Lambert's father. He die. Now belong wife, Miss Hannah."

> I give and bequeath to my beloved wife Hannah the use of my Negro man named Jeda on this condition only, that she doth not take the Negroes Pomp and Peg, which she once owned, which I give to her over and above the fulfilment of the Jointer (sic) agreement I entered into with her before Marriage, otherwise I give him his Time if he can support himself.

"I'm sorry," I felt obliged to say.

Pomp shook his head. "No be sorry. Friend Roger, *he* free. Last night, British take Roger ox. Now, no master loan money for new ox." Pomp paused to give Desire her hay.

"Did you know that if you enlist as a soldier, you would get twenty pounds and could buy yourself after the war? Then you'd be free."

Pomp mimed being shot in the head. "Free to get dead? That be *too* free!"

Sarah laughed and we said good-by, turning toward home.

Two nervous-looking militiamen trotted their boney horses past us. Their refusal to make eye contact verified Grandfather's suspicion of deserters sneaking home.

"Sirs?" I called to them, "Where are you from? Did you see the militia? Do you know any of the Hamiltons?"

"Yeah, boy, heading home to New Milford. We know ol' Cap Hamilton. He left before the skirmish at Ridgefield got started," called a very young soldier. "Left when the general got shot."

"Say, here's some news for you," added the other man from under his graying beard, "maybe not about your own folks, but some man lived on this street had his horse fall over backwards when he went to mount this morning. He's dead. Good-looking man, too, God help him. Pro'ly had a wife and young 'uns."

The blood rushed to my face and I began to shake. I felt sick to my stomach. "We live on this street. My father is the Captain's oldest son, Si, Junior. Was it him?" I searched their guilty faces and saw both sets of eyes widen in horror as my question registered.

"Terrible!" Exclaimed the first man, face twisting in remembered panic. "An awful scene. Blood all over and the horse falling on him like that! I thought them officers would never get him loose." His older friend alternated nodding in agreement and shaking his head at the horror of the gory scene.

"Did the horse rear up when he got on?" I asked as fast as I could. The answer would confirm that it was the stallion.

"Yes, that black devil reared up. How that man can ride, though! Just drove that crazy beast forward toward Norwalk." He broke off as sudden movement drew his attention.

The county sheriff from Fairfield approached at a brisk trot, followed by two determined-looking deputies whose hands already rested on pistol grips. Both deserters whirled their horses and headed out West Street, transitioning within a few yards to a dead run. The sheriff and his men flew after them, spurring hard.

Sarah and I could only look at each other with no words. The vivid picture of a bloody man, trapped under a fallen horse while others fought to save him had to be true. It had been tragically real to the men who told us.

Or was it? *Somebody* had died under a fallen horse. But somebody had "gone on toward Norwalk." Had two stories mixed into one? Or had one story split into two? The only thing clear was that the story involved my father, for it had been his name alone that had drawn such violent emotion from the deserters.

We slowed our steps to a crawl as we tried to recall the exact words, then mixed them up ourselves. Once again, I knew things, but not one solid fact. I warned Sarah to leak no word that my mother could overhear.

I wondered if some ancient farmer from Ridgefield would appear, driving a cart containing what was left of Father. Dead or alive.

Or, like Jonah, mostly dead … but not quite.

Chapter Thirty-Three

Sunday, April 27th, 1777
at Five o' Clock of the Afternoon

When we returned to the Knapp's, Sarah and I pulled up some grass for Pony and we took turns sitting on her back in the Knapp's barn. We hardly said a word. I felt convinced that my father was dead. My imagination dropped a dark cloud over life. But it wasn't imagination. Those deserters had been as real as death. I had no doubt whatever that "…some man lived on this street had his horse fall over backwards," and that the person in question was dead. That was God's own truth, for sure.

What about the second story, that related to Father's name. Had there been an accident "with blood all over," but not a *fatal* accident? Had he simply remounted? A broken nose could provide a lot of blood, indeed.

As shadows lengthened, we at last went indoors. No one asked where we had been for so long. Mother and the Knapps sat in the drawing room. Mr. Knapp had carried his wife to a chair, where she held the baby. Mercy and Noah played a game of their own in the window seat. Sarah unraveled old silk socks and wound the thread for later re-use. Mother still sewed repairs on Noah's britches, reduced to giving little shrieks each time she speared her finger on the needle.

No one had the strength of a cat after being awake all night. Sarah slumped down next to her mother. I collapsed next to mine, holding my awful secret tight. I already had one escape from bad news and I figured that was all the escapes I was allowed. Other boys' fathers died, why not mine? I doubted that we would remain in the cottage. Mother would become some kind of cook or washerwoman at Judge Tom's. At least he still had a house, which Uncle Tad did not.

I wished that I had one more chance with Father. Since I had remembered about the children who died, I felt that maybe I could have acted more grateful or said I understood why he had fears for me. Instead of "acting" grateful, maybe I could have said that out loud.

Had it hurt him to leave the life on the farm? I remembered when my uncles were younger and they all broke horses, shoed horses and cut hay together. They did *everything* together then. Were his father and brothers angry that he was shirking the work of managing all the horses and their equipment? I had never thought of that until I saw my uncles and grandfather leading all the horses to the blacksmith. Yes, the changes for the worse all seemed directed against me and Mother, but who else got hurt by Father's refusal to fight?

Mother asked if anyone wanted corn cakes and no one bothered to answer. I wasn't hungry any more, having fallen into a sort of trance. Mr. Knapp shook his head without a word. Sarah didn't wake up.

Then Noah called from his window seat, "Someone's here with a horse. He went into our barn without asking."

"The horse looked like a real raggedy horse," Mercy stated, ever critical.

Raggedy horses indicated raggedy people, maybe begging money. Maybe robbing.

Mr. Knapp and I went outside to identify the unwelcome visitor who had entered the barn. From the doorway we spotted the tangled and burr-filled tail of a down-at-heel beast.

There, removing his old saddle, stood my father. He crushed me against him so tight that a button on his coat almost took out my eye.

"I didn't know it was you! What happened to your horse?" I gasped. I had to step back and identify him again. How had he risen from what I had assumed was the dead? But it was him, all right. Putting an arm around me again, he embraced Mr. Knapp with his other arm. I hugged hard, just to make sure there was a body inside those clothes.

"It's over for me, Ben, but pray for the poor devils still out there. Joe, Joe, I came back! I can hardly believe I'm home. I pinched this old nag out of a pasture. I must go to the backhouse, then eat and drink. I'll tell what happened after that. Can you water the old thing and give it some hay?" And off he went, his arm around Mr. Knapp.

I dipped a bucket of water for the new nag while sorting out the evidence. My father's own broken-framed saddle and bridle sat atop the waist-high stall wall. The sheepskin had disappeared. Probably covered with blood. The deserters' tale had to be true. The stallion must have broken a leg or its neck. My family now had nothing. No cloth, no pigs, no horse.

I took a better look at the new one, although this scabby rack of bones barely qualified as a horse. It appeared doubtful about its right to eat hay. Looking at a saddle sore, I saw maggots crawling. (It might not mean anything, since doctors put maggots on people's sores.) This new beast's hooves had cracks from top to bottom. It could be lame any minute, if it wasn't already.

Poor old thing shied away when I tried to pat its head. At the doorway, I turned back to look at it again. The horse had swiveled its neck around to watch me.

When I went inside, Mother mixed corncakes as fast as she could, while Sarah fed the kitchen fire, warming the room to a cheerful level. Father stood with his face buried in a steaming wet towel. His blurred voice stated pleasure at feeling only half-dead.

That reminded me of the deserters' story. *Someone* had fallen beneath his horse. *Someone* on our street had died. But who could it have been? I was afraid to ask.

Mr. Knapp led us into the dining room, where Mercy produced the last wine bottles from the hiding place. Father sank into the New York Colonel's chair, groaning as both shaking hands accepted a pewter tankard from Mr. Knapp. We watched him take several long gulps before he looked around, ready to rejoin our world.

"I see where my shed went under the torch. My sows in your barn, Ben?"

Mr. Knapp shook his head without a word.

"So that's the way of it, then," Father looked resigned. "The cloth from Major Taylor's shop — did The Captain leave it in our place?" He glanced from Mr. Knapp to Mother, who filled the corncake platter, ready to serve the table.

"Uhhh," began Mr. Knapp, pausing to draw in a long breath.

Then Mother laid the hot platter of fresh corncakes down in front of him.

"Let us say grace," Mr. Knapp said. We all bowed our heads, but no one had the wits left to remember the words to the grace prayer. Father's question disappeared in the shuffle of grabbing hands and the passing of a dusty jar of plum preserves.

"What happened to your own horse, Si?" began Mr. Knapp as

he slathered plum preserves onto his corncakes. Seeing how much he took, Father took the rest. Mercy started to say something and Sarah slapped her just hard enough to make her shut up without making her cry.

A screaming whinny sliced through the walls, and a voice with the power of heavy artillery bellowed, "Knapp! You in there?"

Here begins the bad part, I thought.

Mother dropped her corncake, and the Knapp baby began to wail. Mr. Knapp stood up and reached for his gun.

Motioning him away, Father approached the window from the side, careful not to show himself. "Well, well, home for half an hour and he appears. How fast does a horse trot?" were his sarcastic remarks before ordering, "Joe, take the Captain's horse to the barn before he gallops in through the front door."

I shuddered. Now my awful crying scene with my grandfather would be public information. Just how my punishment would come, I didn't know. All I knew was that I would pay big.

Mr. Knapp stood in front of the door, barring the way. "That man is not entering my house," he said. "The town fathers and their trumped-up committee have caused more damage than anyone else."

Mother's new sharp voice shot back, "It's different times after yesterday, Mr. Knapp. The sheriff will go back to Fairfield tonight. Who else can keep order against looting except the Committee? What if home invasions begin?"

Father stopped and stared at her. "Have things gone that bad?"

Father beckoned us to follow him outside. When he paused to signal Sarah and Mercy, I recognized what he was doing. Collecting witnesses.

A chill evening breeze rose again as the afternoon declined into sunset, but that was not the only chill in the air. Captain Silas Hamilton had come to call, but he had no intention of dismounting. He remained in the saddle, solid as a rock, facing the front door and waiting.

My father and Mr. Knapp stopped, side by side. Mother's hands gripped my shoulders, and she moved behind me, turning me into a human shield against the wind. I could feel her shiver, but I wasn't sure it arose from the weather.

Sarah and Mercy stopped behind us. They held onto each other the same way that Mother clutched me. Their loose hair blew sideways in a breeze that carried no fresh air.

Grandfather observed us in silence, his expressionless gaze

sliding from face to face.

"You had something to say, did you, Captain Hamilton?" asked Mr. Knapp, crisp and decisive. Our kindly neighbor sounded not so pleasant now. The party was over.

Grandfather's face focused into a forbidding scowl at Benjamin Knapp. Folded papers appeared from an overcoat pocket. He cleared his throat, the presiding judge forcing silence on the already-silent court.

He read, "Anyone not complying with the directives contained herein will leave Danbury tomorrow by order of the Danbury Committee of Inspection." He read more paragraphs, finishing with:

> ...or have aided or assisted in ... measures against America, such county Court within the County where such estate lieth, are hereby ... empowered to issue a warrant to attach such estate.

This was the authorization to seize the home of anyone who disagreed with the Patriots. The only one here who owned a home was Mr. Knapp.

A noose cinched tighter. A noose our neighbor hadn't recognized.

My father's face had a hard and final look to it. "The British are gone, so what is your exact difficulty?"

"The difficulty is not mine, but yours, son, yours and Neighbor Knapp's. Vengeance for the atrocities committed last night will be quick. You and Neighbor Knapp must save your own hides. You, Knapp, gave aid and comfort to the enemy. The penalty for treason is hanging."

Only last Monday, General Parsons had sentenced Robert Thompson to hang for the same offence.

Grandfather began to dissect the dinner party as if he'd been there. "Two British generals established headquarters in your home. Fed by whom? You, Knapp!"

"But ... all I did was ... the British just visited this house for a few hours," Mr. Knapp croaked, all his former confidence flown with the wind.

Invisible threat surged through the air. Sarah's grip on Mercy tightened until the girl screamed and twisted away.

Collecting his wits, Mr. Knapp added, "You know perfectly well that I can't enlist because I have four children and my wife can't even walk to another room."

"Benjamin Knapp, your family difficulties put you onto a safer, if more expensive, path. Four Patriots financed the Danbury relief funds for the afflicted — until yesterday."

We have appointed Captain Daniel Starr, Messrs. John McLean, Zadock Benedict, and Andrew Comstock a committee to receive such donations and transmit same...

"Today, John McLean is fled. Mr. Benedict deals with his burnt home and his brother Jonah. Mr. Comstock labors with the burnt Commissary buildings. Major Daniel Starr is dead. His horse fell on him this morning.

An indescribable sound issued from my mother.

I understood the deserters' puzzling story, at least the first part of it. Major Starr would never know that his fine home was now cinders, or anyone was beheaded inside it.

"Brother Knapp, you will avoid harm ... harm such as, say, *eviction* from your residence, if you sign the oath of allegiance and undertake war relief for the afflicted of the town." Under order of the Committee, you will leave ten pounds with Reverend Ebenezer White by tomorrow at noon. Then all Patriots will be proud to trade with you, including the Commissary."

Grandfather paused, waiting for Mr. Knapp to nod, but shrewd Mr. Knapp looked outraged and helpless. Ten pounds formed a sizable sum, not easy to produce by noon tomorrow, even for the rich. He turned to father, who muttered something and turned away again.

Grandfather motioned for Mother to come forward. She pushed me to the side and walked toward him, holding herself as straight as a soldier. The expression on her face recalled The Last Judgement.

"Regarding treason — who functioned as hostess to this traitorous evening party? My own daughter-in-law!" Grandfather stabbed a finger at my mother, who reacted as if her true role in the party had never occurred to her.

She glanced down at the garments that had charmed the nobility. Her face revealed an opinion that her clothing transformation had occurred through witchcraft. Her shoulders hunched as her fingers moved to cover the ruffles at her neck.

"Each Monday at noon, you will meet Reverend White and take one pound to the First Congregational Church. Reverend

White will assist in identifying which of your sister citizens needs help in this sad situation. Do you agree, daughter?" Grandfather's pale blue eyes drilled into her.

"Yes, Father Hamilton, I will," she said, in a clear, quiet voice. Head up, she continued to look at him, her face reflecting nothing but quiet acceptance.

How could my mother have agreed to represent the Danbury Committee of Inspection in public?

"Also, your brother, Lawyer Benedict, requires your help in opening his new place of business. You will receive wages."

How my mother could help in a law office, I didn't know. She could read, but not Latin.

"Joseph! To the front!" the Captain's voice rang like a field officer selecting volunteers for heroic missions. The old trickster would have invented cruel and unusual punishment for me, I knew.

"Joe, your cousin Jonah Benedict requires care. You will go each day to his brother's home around the corner. There you will assist your cousin to eat, dress, and walk."

I shuddered. My whole summer would disappear that way. At least, it would be in Danbury. I had wanted to hear war and prison stories, but maybe not every day

"Helping Jonah will occupy but two or three hours of your day. You will also assist your mother at Lawyer Benedict's new establishment."

I nodded, afraid to do anything else. What a bore that would be, copying the same law document ten times. Uncle Tad's last look at me had displayed the over-friendly attitude of a man who spots free labor. The new handshake, for example. If I knew Uncle Tad, he wanted to hire my mother the same way you hire a carpenter: the tools come for free.

I became conscious of a powerful silence hanging in the air, soon becoming unbearable. With such care had Grandfather stripped away all support from Father. He had forced the rest of us to accept the Patriot plan by making us responsible for others.

Now, two strong wills faced each other, lit by the last rays of sun and each believing that God stood behind him.

With unexpected speed, Grandfather stuck out his hand toward Father, palm up. "Hand over the eight pounds that you owe me for my rental horse that you stole." This cold statement hung in the air like a bugle call.

Father had only a few shillings, when he left home. I was willing to bet he didn't have them now.

Father slipped a hand deep into his jacket pocket and withdrew a fistful of coins. He stepped to Grandfather's side, where the ceremony of counting eight pounds into the extended palm lasted as long as possible. The coins disappeared into Grandfather's pocket, but he looked no more satisfied than before.

"Think you're smart, don't you?" drawled the Captain. "You saved yourself from being in prison, which would have removed you from the Sons' view. As it is, you might get tarred and feathered — *boiling* tar being the only way it comes. You know perfectly well that the old jailhouse couldn't keep a mob at bay. They could break in there with one iron pry bar. You must enlist."

"What if I don't?" Father spat out the same cutting words as yesterday. But today, hot sweat gleamed on his face and his mouth hung open, as if he couldn't get his breath. His hands hung at his side, fists clenching and unclenching. He did not look directly at Grandfather, the way my mother had. A greenish white circle surrounded his mouth. He looked like a hunted animal, ready to turn on the pursuing hound.

Now Grandfather began a sinister chain of sentences. "Plans are afoot regarding that other traitor, Mr. Dibble. I do not want you included in that amusement.

"What nonsense do you speak now?" asked Mr. Knapp.

Father looked up. What new trick was afoot?

"Mr. Dibble may go swimming," Grandfather uttered in low, but sharply defined words. "Maybe he'll live and maybe he *won't*." The evil whisper made the two choices sound about equal.

"How do *you* know that anything will happen to Joseph Dibble?" Mr. Knapp demanded.

"Because I already arranged it!" The shout carried the power of a bayonet driven into any belief that the Committee would play fair with Loyalists.. Primitive. Hardened. Brutal.

Mr. Knapp stepped back, blown by the force of the words, all resistance gone.

"A new choice presents itself, son," stated Grandfather, his voice slipping into that of a salesman of doubtful medicine. "Our *Joe* mentioned that you might weave blankets. A state contract would exempt you from enlistment, while providing income."

March 19, 1777
The blankets that had been ordered by the General Assembly, to be provided by the towns …, were ordered by the Governor and Council, to be delivered for the use of the continental soldiers of the towns, to the commanding officers of said troops, in this State ; and all the fire arms, blankets, &c., belonging to the towns or the public, within said towns, that had been delivered to the soldiers on short marches or tours of duty, to collect and repair, and when repaired, delivered to such commanding officers or colonels, as had the charge of troops in this State.

"Now, Joe," directed the Captain, "step around in front of your father and ask him to accept the blanket-weaving contract." He pointed to where I should stand.

I had thought to welcome the final act of the play that I had designed. But a deep pit now faced me, as the original idea circled back to me with blame attached.

Attached to *me*, because I had thought of it. *This* was Grandfather's revenge.

Maybe forcing Father to weave for the Patriots would be as hurtful to him as jail. I knew he hated weaving in our dark back room. Maybe Father would hate me for the rest of his life.

I began almost in a whisper, "Sir, would you weave —"

"Look up! Talk like a man now, Joe," came more stage directions.

"Sir, would you weave blankets to keep soldiers from freezing? You wouldn't have to worry about selling them." I managed to finish the sentence, but I could not have said another word, even to end this crazy scene. I swallowed about six times.

"You thought of this on your own? No one suggested it to you?" Father asked in a dull half-whisper, looking into my eyes and then away again.

I shook my head yes and then no, but I wanted to die right there. Just die. No heaven needed.

Mr. Knapp moved to Mother's side, while Sarah and Mercy stood frozen, understanding only that the scene revolved around me.

What were we all waiting for Father to do?

Sell out to the Patriots, the same way Enoch Crosby sold out to the British? I had just watched my mother and Mr. Knapp sell out their beliefs and go over to Grandfather's side. But was it wrong or right? They did it to help people, but….

"You don't have to *do* it," I yelped in panic. I wanted to leave Father a way out, even if his beliefs had cost us our home, our family, and friends. Part of that, he had done for me. Signing with the Patriots would equal his total defeat.

Hot tears came to my eyes.

Father cleared his throat. "I tried to prevent this war, but I will join my wife in preventing human suffering. I'll sign."

Nobody said anything as Father walked back to Mr. Knapp, dug in his pocket and produced another wad of money, giving him almost all of it.

Mr. Knapp stared at Father for a second, then put an arm around him. The two of them turned toward his house, the girls scurrying behind like frightened mice.

"Lest I forget, Mr. Knapp," called Grandfather in a cordial voice, "kindly mention to your brother that one pair of shoes is due to the commissary each fortnight. Any common size. I'll be around to collect. Good evening, sir."

Mother stood motionless, relief written all over her face. A call from Mr. Knapp requested her to join the parade back to the green-paneled door. She caught up and took Father's arm. Halfway to the house, he turned to see where I was. Then he turned back, and continued on.

I already belonged to the other side.

Chapter Thirty-Four

Sunday, April 27th, 1777 at Dusk

Grandfather and I remained alone in the gathering gloom of the yard. Why I stayed, I don't know. I said nothing as he dismounted. He staggered when his feet hit the ground. Then his head lifted and he stroked the gray horse's face. Which one looked more tired was hard to say.

The game of wits had ended and I had won. My parents had paying jobs and Mr. Knapp would remain in his business. No one had to fight and no one would be hung or go to jail.

Instead of feeling proud, I felt like the victim. My own reward totaled part time unpaid personal care. This would not buy a new pair of shoes. As for being a scribe in Uncle Tad's law office — not the apprenticeship I wanted, for sure. The only "for sure" would be "unpaid, for sure."

Grandfather put his arm around my shoulders and said, "You'll have to come visit Bear Mountain again, boy." I felt too depressed and exhausted to wriggle out of his grasp.

"It's too far to walk to the farm and work, too," I mumbled.

"I expect that's true, little lad," Grandfather said, giving a hug before letting go. The "little lad" fired me with renewed rage, but if I was going to get anything out of this, I could not sound as vengeful as I felt.

"I could ride out to the mountain if you had an old horse to spare," I suggested, trying to keep my voice even.

"No, lad. Our old horses have to earn their keep. Horses are more valuable than ever."

My anger faded into exhaustion, but curiosity regarding one particular horse caused me to ask, "What happened to Father's stallion? Did it die? Where did that money come from?"

"The sheriff repeated the story to me," Grandfather answered, with a purse-lipped shake of the head. "General Arnold's horse took nine bullets and fell dead on top of him. The officers rescued him, but not one man offered up his own horse. General Arnold ran into the woods to escape. When the skirmish ended, your Uncle Paul fetched your father and his beast. Your father demanded twenty pounds, swearing the creature could jump a five-foot fence. A lie, if I ever heard one, but the preposterous amount of money changed hands."

"Could General Arnold ride the stallion? What happened when he got on?" I asked.

"Beast reared right straight up. General Arnold galloped away, but believe an old horse dealer, son: no man can ride that horse in battle and live. Your father will have killed our best fighting general…."

Grandfather ground the palms of his hands into his eye sockets, giving a moan as he did so. Tears leaked out of his eyes when he took his hands away. Exhaustion had crept up on him. He leaned his arms on his saddle and put his head down.

"Not one man offered up his own horse," he repeated, shaking his head. "And all the officers knew that stallion was a killer."

"Guess Uncle Paul knew it. Maybe those officers don't like General Arnold much," I suggested, thinking of Mrs. Clark's opinion.

Grandfather raised his head. A sharp look came my way as he connected Uncle Paul to the sale of the horse. His eyes closed again in serious concentration. He remained deep in thought while the river of his mind flowed on behind closed eyelids.

His awareness of the outside world dimmed even more. "Arnold acts like a petty tyrant, anyway," he mumbled sleepily. "Got to ask Crosby. Crosby can find out anything."

The last words riveted my attention. Grandfather never truly comprehended when I murmured, "Did Enoch Crosby lead the British to Danbury?" I stopped breathing while I waited for the answer, which flowed out in the same unconscious way that he had spoken before.

"No, no, some fool like my son Paul would shoot our best spy."

Grandfather jerked back to reality, his bloodshot eyes matching his guilt-stricken horror. His mouth flew open and stayed that way. Captain Silas Hamilton, the Old Indian Fighter, who had survived seven years in the last war, looked terrified. Only then did I know for sure.

"Oh," I chirped, "I knew all the time that Crosby was spying for the Patriots!"

Grandfather's hand shot to my coat collar so fast that I lurched forward as a violent shake almost disjointed my neck. I uttered a cry, only to receive another shake of the same concussive force.

"You ignorant boy! You'll get him killed! Who told you this?" The eyes had frozen wide open in the mask of his face, revealing the furthest depths of soul-freezing fear, the fear of causing the death of the friend he loved.

I couldn't speak without touching my bruised windpipe, but then I croaked, "I figured it out myself. How could some cobbler fool you? So Enoch Crosby only pretends to be a traitor to George Washington?"

In control of himself again, Grandfather had to deal with reality. "In a word, yes. Nobody, but *nobody*, must ever know of this, Joe. It's top secret. Only one committee member in each town knows, so that he won't be killed."

"Lambert said the Patriots arrested Crosby. Everybody at those places must know the secret, since they set him free."

"Crosby was *not* set free. The spy ring *broke* him out of confinement, while trumpeting escapes. Big rewards made him appear even more legitimate to the British."

"I wish I could tell Lambert," I said. "Then he wouldn't hate him so much."

Grandfather's face shot to about a foot from mine, his sour breath blasting right at me.

"You wish you could *tell*, do you?" The lungpower issuing from one old man could have blown leaves from the trees. "You should be under lock and key, so that you never tell *anyone* a single word!"

"I won't say anything, I promise, if...if...." I stuttered, not knowing how to go on.

His snarled, "If what?" sounded like my removal to jail might detour to the whipping post.

After discovering this goldmine of information, I had ended up the same as before — with nothing.

The idea of public punishment gave me a clue. "You can't do *anything* to me without all of Danbury learning why." I tried to sound sure of myself.

"I — I suppose that's true." A new fake smile tried to resemble genuine. "Just promise your old granddad never to mention this again."

A friendly hand attempted to land where a violent hand had landed only a minute ago. I ducked.

"Well, I might if, if…." I stalled, trying to think what might gain me *something. Anything.*

"Say what you want, boy. A new shirt? Your grandmother can sew one right smart."

Grandfather acted way too happy to settle all charges. How could he think that I would trade treason for a shirt?

"I need a beast of my own," I said, louder than I should have said it. Then I decided that I liked the way it had sounded just fine. So I said it again. "I need a horse."

"No, and that's final." The riding whip cracked against his boot sounded a lot more final than his words.

"Then I'll tell," I said, repeating Mercy's recent threat.

"You can't tell anything *like* that!" The Captain shouted. He looked around as several riders clattered over the bridge. The crowds were drifting home as shadows grew. Dropping back into a more reasonable voice, he said, "Truly, you must not tell *anyone*. Stop this foolishness, boy."

"I want a *horse*," I insisted, louder than ever. The heads on the bridge snapped toward us. "Then I will never tell another soul, as long as I live."

I meant it. All I wanted was a plain, friendly horse, like Pony.

Just my luck: the Captain's eyes lit on Knapp's barn. A wrinkled smile flickered on his face. "We can solve this problem right now. How about I confiscate that pony mare? Even after you grow big, she'd get you some fine foals to sell."

"Not *Pony*," I said. "Mr. Knapp can't run his business without a beast to pull the cart. You took his team and the British took his old horse."

"'Spose that's fair enough, now that he's coming through for our side. That team was a prime catch." Grandfather sounded proud of knowing the best places to confiscate. He cast around for another answer.

Interest sparked as he pointed to the snarled and tattered tail that showed in the barn doorway.

"That old nag your father confiscated managed the eight miles here from Ridgefield, didn't it? It's still alive, anyway." He dropped Tom's reins on the ground and put an arm around me, drawing me into the barn for a closer look. This time, I let him do it.

"Nice safe mount for you, lad!"

Possibly true. Falling off a horse that feeble-looking would be difficult. Grandfather smacked its behind to move it over, but then he examined his hand and sleeve after observing some lice jump away.

"But it *belongs* to somebody," I said. "Father borrowed it in an emergency. He didn't confiscate it."

"If it belongs to a Patriot, a claim will go to the Committee in Ridgefield. The state will pay. If it's a Tory horse, I'm confiscating it right now. He's all yours, Joe!"

Grandfather checked the new horse's teeth and legs, while the horse snuffled my face. When I rubbed its ears, it arched its neck as if nobody had patted it in a long time. I did feel sorry for the pathetic thing, but I brushed my sleeve and shook it in case a louse had jumped aboard.

"It ain't that old," Grandfather announced. "Just gone ten, maybe. You'd have to get the shoes reset six or eight times to fix those cracks. Buy tobacco to treat the worms. Kill the lice with cider vinegar. Could be, this nag's a bargain!" Grandfather produced a sly smile at finding a bargain of his usual variety — no actual payment involved.

After considering the no-payment-to-me problem, I stepped closer to the edge of caution.

I stared Grandfather right in the eye and said, "Where do I get the money to pay for those horse shoes and that tobacco? I don't get money for taking care of Jonah, do I?"

An unpleasant frown at me moved on to the jagged hooves, followed by a sigh of agreement.

Grandfather groped his pockets. Out came a pistol, a corncob, an onion, and some Spanish coins before he said, "Here's five shillings, but that's all you get, you hear?" A new frown indicated the final offer.

I nodded, thrilled. Five shillings was a lot.

Grandfather grinned an old-time grin. "Joe, you sure know how to play your cards right. Just like your old Grandad! You're all right, boy, you know that? You're a lot like me."

The tired face came alive with a warm pride. Hard to believe that I smiled at him so soon after the shaking incident, but I couldn't help it.

"Now, Joe, your Uncle Paul's going to be a captain soon. He'll need a cagey lad like you to ride along with him. Think he has an old saddle back at the farm. Maybe he'll give you his old musket." He hugged me tighter as he said each phrase.

I recognized this for the old attempt to lure me into rebel stuff, but I had gone about as far as I could go.

The Captain kept his arm around me until he picked up the reins of his own sleepy animal and prepared to mount. "Are we on the same page of the good book, then, you and I?"

My smile faded as I examined the plan for tomorrow. Morning would be Jonah and the afternoon would be Uncle Tad's new law office, wherever that was

I had a genuine question about that location and maybe I should have kept my mouth shut, but I recognized my last chance to make a deal.

"Except just one thing — I don't want to be Uncle Tad's law clerk." Uncle Tad had acted nice today, but how long would that last after he learned the truth about my Latin?

Grandfather snorted. "You, a law clerk? You're thirteen! I suggested Lawyer Benedict buy the King George Tavern. He'll re-open as soon as he gets a state tavern license. You can work in the kitchen with your mother."

"The tavern?" I screeched. "Uncle Tad bought *a tavern*? And I get to work there?"

In the record of the General Assembly, May session, 1777…Thaddeus Benedict, of Danbury, representing to the Assembly that the British troops, when in Danbury, burned his dwelling-house and several other houses kept for public entertainment; and stated that he had provided a convenient house in the centre of said town, and asked for a license to keep a public house, which was granted by said Assembly.

"Then we have a deal?" Grandfather asked. He reached down and we shook hands. Grandfather beamed at me, as if we had always been on the same side and never had a hard word. He gathered his reins and adjusted his set of horse pistols.

Then the smile dropped. "Just do one more little favor for your old grandad. Just one more. You go in that house right now and tell your father that your grandmother longs to see him before she dies. Just exactly those words."

"G-g-grandmother Elizabeth is *dying*?" I managed to say. I waited for him to explain what had happened to her.

"Got some nice colts out at the farm, too," he continued. "Your father might find one to his liking. And my sheep need shearing. Your uncles won't be home to help. War is coming fast."

Grandmother Elizabeth lay dying and getting replacement labor at the farm formed his main thought? Why did he not tell my father before?

"I — I'm sorry about Grandmother." I stuttered in disbelief.

"Pay attention, boy! I said to tell your father. I didn't say it was true, now did I? I trust you to get your father out to Bear Mountain any way you can, understand? You do that and your grandmother will do the rest. I trust you. You just say whatever is necessary to get it done."

I looked down, trying to decide what to say. Then I saw four gray horse legs walk away.

"Getting the family together"– just what my mother and my uncles had talked about this morning. Josh had talked about it. Maybe Uncle Tad's plan for his new tavern formed his way of keeping the Benedict family together, my mother and me included.

Grandfather walked Tom out to the street and turned right, toward Bear Mountain. As they crossed the bridge, he stopped the horse and turned to face me. With a slow dignity that matched the ancient uniform, he produced a formal salute.

After a minute, I realized what I was supposed to do. I saluted back.

Then Tom commenced a slow jog trot, headed north. After a few strides, Grandfather began to post up and down. The sound of hoof beats sank away and the blue uniform faded into the gray of dusk. The evening breeze continued to blow, carrying the promise of a late April frost.

Grandfather's mention of horse, saddle, and rifle — the plot had gone just the way Father said it would. My mouth would open, but someone else's voice would come out.

Refusal was impossible. One word from Grandfather and my new horse and the job at the tavern would disappear.

I was on my own. No one would direct where I should stand or how to talk. It was left to me to straighten my shoulders, rehearse my script, and go on in.

I looked up at where the doorknocker used to be. Then I watched my hand press the brass lever of the lock.

Trusted.

THE END

The History Behind
1777—Danbury on Fire!

After the War

Joe Hamilton was an imaginary character, as were David Weed and Isaiah. All others were real persons.

You'll never find a Hamilton in the pension application file, because pensioners were all virtually bankrupt. The Captain had religiously purchased land every year. If he didn't have the money, he bought with a friend. His many land deeds still survive in the Connecticut State Library in Hartford.

The Captain continued as usual until both his wife and a son-in-law died. At that time, he moved into his daughter Elizabeth Barnum's house on Town Street. The cabin at Bear Mountain was visible until about 1835. Now the old farm is part of Bear Mountain recreation area, north of Danbury. Silas Hamilton, Jr. ('Joe's' father) sectioned off land from The Captain's farm. Paul and John Hamilton married Lt. Ezra Stevens' two daughters, Anne and Anner. James Hamilton died young in 1778, of unknown causes.

Enoch Crosby only spied for two years before the British caught him, beat him and left him for dead. He became a judge in New York and lived a long and pleasant life, never discussing his past. James Fennimore Cooper wrote The Spy, based on Enoch Crosby. Crosby's handler was John Jay, who knew Cooper.

Benjamin Knapp continued into old age. Noah shared the family property. Sarah, Mercy, and Urana all married and became delightful ladies about Danbury.

Benedict Arnold would not have worried long about the stallion's behavior, as below:

Arnold then prepared his force to attack the British, but a well-timed bayonet charge by Erskine's men broke the formation in spite of determined action by Lamb's artillery and Arnold's attempts to rally the troops. During the skirmish, Arnold had a second horse shot out under him, and Lamb was injured. The British successfully embarked and sailed for New York.

Lambert Lockwood followed Dr. John Wood as Deputy Assistant Commissary General. Later, Lambert moved to Newfield/Bridgeport CT, where he ran a grocery/dry goods/ printing business and library on the waterfront and became a most energetic and civic-minded town father. Lambert bought a hundred copies of *The Spy* for resale and the circulating library in his store. Lambert's belief in fun for young folk caused him to finance two of his sons in selling the first commercial toys and board games in America.

Lambert Lockwood probably met all the dignitaries of the time. Lambert's sister and her husband owned a tavern near where the Count de Rochambeau kept his troops for a summer. She enjoyed their society so much that she named a child after the Duc de Lauzun. One supposes that Lambert, living not far away, met his fill of French nobility, which relates to the last big scene of his life.

On the night of August 20, 1824, General Lafayette and suite, while on a journey from New York to Boston, stopped in Bridgeport ... At five in the morning, the bells began ringing and the cannons firing. Lafayette had arrived and slept securely through the night at Knapp's (Hotel). A few minutes later the street in front of the hotel was thronged with men, and the walk before the brick stored was filled with ladies. Lafayette and his suite made their appearance on the balcony, between Mr. Hubbell and Mr. Lockwood.

We leave him there on the balcony, lit by the rising sun, and warmed by the cheers of the crowd.

A RETURN OF COLONEL DAVID WATERBURY, JR.'S REGIMENT.

DAVID WATERBURY, Jr., *Colonel.*
PHILIP BURR BRADLEY, *Lieutenant Colonel.*
DAVID DIMON, *Major.*
SAMUEL SQUIRE, *Commissary.*

CAPTAIN MATTHEW MEAD'S COMPANY.

Lieutenants: JAMES BETTS, GAMALIEL TAYLOR, DANIEL ST. JOHN.
First Sergeant, 18 AZOR BETTS.
Sergeants: 19 JOSHUA ADAMS, 16 THOMAS BETTS, 19 JONATH. RAYMOND.
Clerk, 16 HEZ. ROGERS.
Corporals: 16 ALVAN HYAT, 19 GILES MALLERY, 19 PHINEAS HANFORD, 18 JOS. ROCKWELL.
Drummer, 28 DANL. HYAT.
Fifers: 19 MATTHEW HANFORD AND 17 SAM. DEFORESST. ?

PRIVATES.

16 Akin, Thomas	18 Hayt, Ezekiel	19 Marthers,? Noyes
16 Brown, Danl.	18 Hawley, Elijah	18 Nash, Bela
17 Brown, Jonath.	18 Hawley, Ebenezer	17 Nichols, Samuel
16 Burrell, Samuel	17 Hayt, Daniel	19 Olmsted, Isaac
19 Betts, Mose.	20 Hurlbut, Gideon	20 Olmsted, Nathan
20 Comp,? Josiah	20 Johnson, Nathaniel	17 Persons, Barth. ?
18 Duning,'Thaddeus	20 Johnson, William	16 Raymond, Jonathan
17 Dunning, Jr.,David	18 Jezup, Joseph	17 Starling, Nathanl.
17 Darrow,? James	18 Keeler, Justus	18 Silleck, Deodate
17 Gregory, Uriah.	18 Keeler, Aaron	19 Smith, Samuel
17 Gregory, Jr., Matth.	18 Keeler, Isaiah	18 Smith, William
17 Gilbert, Moses.	16 Kellogg, Elijah	17 St. John, Ezekiel
17 Grumman, Aaron ?	17 Lockwood, Lambert	19 Trowbridge, Joseph
18 Gilbert, Eben.	18 Lockwood, Stephen	19 Taylor, Josiah
16 Hyat, Jessee	19 Lyon, Peletiah	19 Turrell, Nathaniel
17 Hubbal, Salmon	16 Lockwood, Jesse	19 Tuttle, Peter
17 Hubbell, Zadock	17 Mead, Elias	18 Whitney, Hezekiah
18 Higgins, William	18 Middlebrook, Jonat.	17 Wescutt, David, Jr.

NOTE—No change has been made in the spelling of a name, even when obviously in error. When the spelling cannot be deciphered, aided by comparison, an interrogation mark (?) has been added. The numbers appearing at left of names are the days of the month of January 1776, when enlistments were made. Dates are not given in all cases as they do not appear in original record.

CAPTAIN BENEDICT'S COMPANY.

Names and Rank.	Enlistment.	Discharge.	Remarks.
Jonah Benedict, Serj.,	Aug. 12	Taken Nov. 16	At Ft. Washington.
David Olmsted, "	" 22	Dis. Jan. 11	
Tallmadge Hall, "	" 15	Dis. Dec. 27	
Jesse Foster,	" 25	App⁴ Serj. Sept. 21 Dis. Dec. 28	
Lambert Lockwood,	" 13	Dis. Jany 12	
Jesse Munsel, Corpl.,	" 14	Taken Nov. 16	" "
Jesse Peek, "	" 26	Dis. Dec. 25	
Abijah Benedict, "	" 13	Dis. Jan. 11	
Daniel Stevens, "	" 13	Dis. Dec. 25	
John Comstock, Drum'r,	" 21	Taken Nov. 16	" "
Nathaniel Peek, Fifer,	" 21	Taken Nov. 16	" "
David Bishop,	" 12	Dis. Dec. 25	
John Brooks,	" 14	Taken Nov. 16	" "
Justus Barnum,	" 11	Dis. Dec. 27	
Noah Barnum,	" 21	Taken Nov. 16	" "
John Bostwick,	" 24	Dis. Dec. 25	
John Barnum,	" 21	Dis. Jan. 11	
John Boughton,	" 22	Taken Nov. 16	" "
Robin Benedict,	" 30	Taken Nov. 16	" "
Philemon Baldwin,	" 22	Dis. Jan. 11	
Stephen Bump,	" 26	Taken Nov. 16	" "
Eleazer Benedict,	Aug. 24	Dis. Dec. 25	At Ft. Washington.
Thadd⁰ Brunson,	" 21	Dis. Dec. 25	
Daniel Boughton,	" 22	Dis. Jan. 11	
Simeon Barnum,	June 26	Taken Nov. 16	" "
Samuel Cook,	" 13	Dis. Jan. 11	
David Chittexler,	" 14	Dis. Jan. 11	
Ezra Coley,	" 22	Died Dec. 30	
Cornelius Dikeman,	" 24	Dis. Jan. 11	
Wakefield Dibble,	" 21	Dis. Dec. 25	
Elijah Deane,	" 22	Dis. Jan. 11	
Samuel Foster,	" 24	Dis. Jan. 11	
Thadd⁰ Gayre,	" 14	Dis. Dec. 25	
Gershom Griffin,	July 2	Taken Nov. 16	" "
Henry Grigg,	" 10	Dis. Dec. 25	
Noah Hoyt,	June 21	Dis. Jan. 11	
Eleazer Hewsted,	" 21	Taken Nov. 16	" "
Jonathan Hayse,	" 26	Dis. Jan. 11	
Daniel Hoyt,	" 21	Dis. Jan. 11	
John Hambleton,	" 21	Deserted Oct. 2	

NAMES AND RANK.	Enlistment.		Discharge.	Remarks.	
Gilead Hubbel,	"	15	Taken Nov. 16	"	"
Goold Hawley,	"	22	Died Jan. 4		
Samuel Knap,	"	21	Taken Nov. 16	"	"
John Keeler,	July	1	Dis. Dec. 25		
Nathan Fairchild Kellogg,	June	22	Dis. Dec. 27		
John Fairchild Lacy,	"	16	Dis. Jan. 11		
Sylvanus Nelson,	"	12	Taken Nov. 16	"	"
Joel Northrup,	"	24	Dis. Jan. 11		
Ezra Nash,	"	25	Dis. Dec. 25		
Stephen Peck,	"	21	Dis. Dec. 25		
Jesse Peck,	"	21	Dis. Dec. 26		
Eliphelet Peck.	"	24	Taken Nov. 16	"	"
Dowes Porter,	"	26	Taken Nov. 16	"	"
John Storr,	"	21	Taken Nov. 16	"	"
Daniel Stone,	"	21	Taken Nov. 16	"	"
Levi Stewart,	"	21	Taken Nov. 16	"	"
Luke Smith,	"	15	Died Dec. 1		
Hill Sturges,	"	25	Taken Nov. 16	"	"
Nehemiah Smith.	"	22	Taken Nov. 16	"	"
Jacob Finch,	"	21	Dis. Dec. 25		
Eleazer Taylor,	"	22	Dis. Dec. 28		
Ezra Taylor,	"	15	Taken Nov. 16	"	"
Daniel Trowbridge,	"	16	Dis. Dec. 25		
John Trusdell,	"	25	Taken Nov. 16	"	"
Zalmon Taylor,	"	25	Dis. Jan. 11		
Ezra Wood,	"	21	Taken Nov. 16	"	"
John Wildman,	"	28	Dis. Dec. 25		
Major Warring,	"	26	Dis. Dec. 25		
Benjamin Warring,	"	14	Dis. Dec. 25		
Jeddediah Limestone,	"	27	Dis. Dec. 25		
Ebenezer Jackson,	"	22	Dis. Dec. 25		
Nimrod Benedict,	"	12	Dis. Dec. 25		
Elkanah Peck,	Aug.	12	Dis. Dec. 25		
Joseph Monrow,	"	12	Dis. Dec. 25		
Josiah Nichols,	"	12	Dis. Dec. 25		
Miles Hoyt,	"	12	Taken Nov. 16	"	"
Abijah Vining,	"	12	Dis. Dec. 25		
James Wilks,	"	12	Taken Nov. 16	"	"
Prince Cornwell,	"	12	Dis. Dec. 25		
Elisha Linkins,	"	12	Taken Nov. 16	"	"
Moses Dickinson,	Sept.	5	Dis. Jan. 11		
Eleazer Hoyt,	"	5	Dis. Dec. 25		

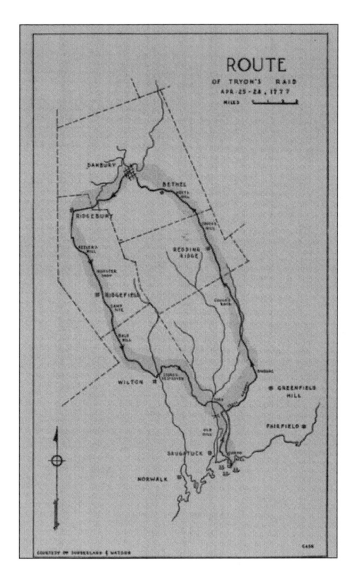

From James Royal Case

African American Revolutionary War Soldiers in Danbury

The numbers for Jehu and Robin Starr indicated their pension filings. Jehu Grant's master, Isaac Grant (R4195) was on a prison ship, as was real-life Jonah Benedict. Jehu's number and his master's are separated by only one number, indicating that they may have continued contact after the war.

Robin Starr and Roger were classified sufferers because both suffered loss of property in the raid. Many masters acknowledged that slaves owned personal property, such as tools, animals, saddlery, or clothing. Some accumulated tools/harness/animals in preparation for future freedom. (The Civil War era book Children of Pride is composed of family letters that religiously track the ownership of one man's ax and another's horse and cart.)

Slaves enlisting were supposedly manumitted, but some preferred slavery to the army. One Rowland hated the army so much that he was happy to have his master purchase a substitute and returned to slavery via a five year indenture. He had tried enlisting under the last name of 'Sanford,' the name he had used at home, but the captain (his former master's brother) would not allow it, and so he chose the last name of another former owner. Some masters did not allow a black soldier joining the same regiment to use the same last name.

Danbury
AMOS, African American ("Negro"), Danbury
ANTHONY/ANTONY, JACK, African American, Danbury
BOSTON, TOBY/TOBE, African American, Danbury
CAESAR, African American ("Negro"), slave of John Edwards, Danbury
GRANT, JEHU, African American ("Negro"), waiter, wagon master, R4197, Danbury
JACK, African American ("Negro") Woodstock
JUBE, African American ("Negro"), Danbury
LOGIN, CATO, African American, Danbury
ROBEN/ROBIN, African American ("Negro"), , ("Conn. Sufferer"), Danbury
ROBIN, African American ("Negro"), Danbury
ROGER, African American ("Negro"), Danbury
ROGER, African American, Patriotic Service (sufferer), Danbury
STARR, ROBIN, African American, S36810, [died April 3, 1832; Abel C. Starr only child; "left no widow"], Danbury
URIAH/VARIAH, African American ("Negro"), Danbury
WHITE, FORTUNE/FORTIN, African American, Danbury
WILLIAM, African American ("Negro"), Danbury

Chart from: www.libertyfunddc.org

At a legal Meeting of the Inhabitants of the Town of *Danbury*, in *Connecticut, December* 12, 1774,

Captain THOMAS STEVENS, *Moderator*:

The Town took into consideration the present alarming situation of the *American* Colonies, from several late unconstitutional and oppressive Acts of the *British* Parliament, and feeling deeply impressed with a sense of our common danger, we should have earlier manifested our sense of the natural and constitutional rights we are, or ought to be possessed of, and of the wanton infringements made upon them by the oppressive plan of policy now prosecuting by the *British* Ministry, were it not that we thought there was the greatest propriety in waiting till they were stated by a General Congress; lest, by every Town's attempting particularly to state them, there might be a disagreement in their claims, which might occasion disunion among ourselves, and give cause of triumph to our enemies. But our rights, and the infringements of them, having been particularly stated by the late *American* Congress in their Resolutions or Bill of Rights, which, from the best knowledge and information we are able to obtain, we apprehend to be accurately and judiciously done: We do therefore,

1. Declare our full concurrence with said Resolutions, as truly stating the rights and privileges we mean to defend; and the oppressive infringements we mean to oppose to the extent of those abilities which *God* and nature has furnished us with.

2 We do heartily approve of the Association containing a Non-Importation, Non-Exportation, and Non-Consumption Agreement, entered into by the General Congress, as the most salutary, wise, and probable measure for obtaining redress of the grievances we labour under, and will use our utmost endeavours to render the same effectual, by a full compliance therewith ourselves, and by treating with deserved neglect any one who shall dare, in opposition to the voice of *America*, by counteracting this Agreement, to seek his own emolument, to the endangering the liberties of his country. And that **such as break through this Agreement, and refuse to be reclaimed by gentler means, may be held up to publick view as objects to be shunned and avoided by every friend to liberty and lover of his country,** we have appointed the following gentlemen a Committee for the purpose specified in the eleventh Article of said Association, viz: **Doctor *John Wood, Thaddeus Benedict,* and *Daniel Taylor*, Esquires, Lieutenant *Noble Benedict*, Colonel *Joseph Platt Cook*, Captain *Silas Hamilton*,** *Samuel Taylor*, Esq., Messrs.

Andrew Comstock, James Siely, Daniel Benedict, and *Richard Shute,* Captain *Thomas Stevens,* and Mr. *Joseph Bebee.*

3. We think it expedient there should be a meeting of Deputies from the several Towns in the County of *Fairfield,* to choose a County Committee, agreeable to the advice of the Congress, and to agree upon measures to be taken with any Town in the County (if any such there should be) who should refuse to concur with the Association agreed upon by the General Congress; and we desire the Committee of the County Town to notify the several Towns in the County of the time and place for said meeting.

4. It is with singular pleasure we notice the second Article of the Association, in which it is agreed to import no more Negro Slaves, as we cannot but think it a palpable absurdity so loudly to complain of attempts to enslave us, while we are actually enslaving others; and that we have great reason to apprehend the enslaving the *Africans* is one of the crying sins of our land, for which Heaven is now chastising us. We notice, also, with pleasure, the late Act of our General Assembly, imposing a fine of one hundred Pounds on any one who shall import a Negro Slave into this Colony. We could also wish that something further might be done for the relief of such as are now in a state of slavery in the Colonies, and such as may hereafter be born of parents in that unhappy condition.

5. As we look upon the Town of *Boston* to be suffering in the common cause of *American* liberty, we would manifest our hearty sympathy with them, in their present calamitous state, and readiness to administer to the relief of their suffering poor, according to our abilities; and do accordingly recommend to the several inhabitants of this Town to contribute liberally of money or provisions. For this purpose we have appointed **Captain *Daniel Starr,* Messrs. *John M' Lean, Zadock Benedict,* and *Andrew Comstock,*** a Committee to receive such donations, and transmit the same to the Committee appointed to receive them in the Town of *Boston.* Our being so late in contributing to their relief hath not arisen from our having been unconcerned spectators of their distressed situation; but hearing of the laudable zeal of others we were ready to conclude there was a sufficient present supply, and that our donations would be more needed and more acceptable in some future time.

Voted by a large majority,

MAJOR TAYLOR, *Town Clerk.*

Danbury, Connecticut, February 6, 1775.

On the 29th day of *November* last, was held in *Danbury*, a Town Meeting, to know the minds of the Town, respecting the doings of the late Continental Congress, when the Town adopted said, doings, appointed a Committee of Inspection, &c., which I have seen published in Mr. *Halt's* Paper. I could not then believe that if it had been a full meeting, the Town would have voted in the form as they then did; for there was but a thin meeting, and those who were friends to Government were fearful of discovering their sentiments, as the honour and credit of the Congress appeared to be great, in the adjoining Towns, and no one dared open his mouth against what they had done; but since then many have not been afraid of disputing the doings of that sacred body; which has emboldened many to shew their firm attachment to their gracious King and their present happy Constitution; so that, in a very full Town Meeting, held in this Town, this day, the following votes were passed.

Captain THOMAS STEPHENS, *Moderator:*

At the said meeting, the question was put, whether the Town of *Danbury* would do any thing respecting appointing a Committee to meet at a County Congress, to be held at *Fairfield*, on *Tuesday*, the 14th day of this instant, *February*; which question passed in the negative, one hundred and six, to eighty-six, to which sixty persons entered their protest in open meeting.

Also, the question, whether this meeting would disannul the vote passed in *Danbury*, the 29th day of *November*, 1774, appointing a Committee of Inspection; which passed in the affirmative.

JOHN WOOD, *Town Clerk.*

Committees of Safety and Inspection

Committees of Safety formed in 1774 to keep watch on the distrusted royal government. By 1775 they had become the operating government of all the colonies, as the royal officials were expelled. Massachusetts took the lead in the appointment of a committee of safety as early as the autumn of 1774, of which John Hancock was chairman. It was given power to call out mandatory militia, with penalties for failing to respond to a call-up, and provide means of defense. It provided many of the duties of a provisional government. Other colonies appointed committees of safety. … the New York state legislature replaced all committees with "Commissioners of Conspiracy."

… the demand for independence came from local grassroots Committees of Safety. The First Continental Congress had urged their creation in 1774. **By 1775, they had become counter-governments that gradually replaced royal authority and took control of local governments. They regulated the economy, politics, morality, and militia of their individual communities.** After December 1776 they came under the control of a more powerful central authority, the Council of Safety.

These Committees of Safety were in constant communication with committees of correspondence, which disseminated information among the militia units and provided a clearinghouse of information and intelligence on enemy activities.

From Wikipedia — The Free Encyclopedia

Bibliography

Author's Note: In general, one can take a quote from the text and enter it into a search engine and the result will come up on the correct page of the publication from which it came. Here are the books I consulted, many of which are online.

History of Fairfield County Connecticut, D. Hamilton Hurd, Vol. 1, 1881

The Pictorial Field-Book of the Revolution, Benson J. Lossing, Vol. 1, 1850

History of Old Danbury, James Montgomery Bailey, Susan Benedict Hill, 1896

The Commemorative Biographical History of Fairfield County, Higginson Book Company, 1899

A History of the Old Town of Stratford and the City of Bridgeport, Vol. I, Reverend Samuel Orcutt, Fairfield County Historical Society, 1886

The Standard's History of Bridgeport, George Waldo, 1897

An Account of Tryon's Raid on Danbury in April, 1777, James Royal Case, 1927

An Unknown Patriot, Frank S. Child, 1899

Tar and Feathers in Revolutionary America, Benjamin H. Irvin, Brandeis University, no date, but referencing: *A Century of Population Growth*, pp. 166-169 (Connecticut State Library) which cited:

- *Forgotten Patriots, African American and American Indian Patriots of the Revolutionary War*, National Society Daughters of the American Revolution, 2008

- *Connecticut's Black Soldiers 1775-1783*, David O. White, Chester, 1973

- Robert Ewell Greene, *Black Courage 1775-1783*, Washington, 1984

A Walloon Family in America, Emily Johnston De Forest, Jesse De Forest, Houghton Mifflin, 1914

Medical Men in the American Revolution, 1775-1783, Louis Duncan, The Army Medical Bulletin Number 25. Medical Field Service School, Carlisle Barracks, Pennsylvania. 1931

Congressional Series of United States Public Documents, Volume 912 ; 34th Congress, 3rd Session, Report 21

McCarthy, D. "*Map of the boroughs of Danbury and Bethell* [sic], Fairfield County, Conn. surveyed and published by D. McCarthy, C.E., lith. of Friend & Aub." Danbury Miscellanea Collection, MS 38. WCSU Archives.

Genealogy of the Stevens Family, Frederick S. Stevens, 1891

Recollections of a Lifetime, Samuel Griswold Goodrich, 1859

A Historical Collection from Official Records, Files, Etc., of the Part Sustained by Connecticut During the War of the Revolution, Royal R. *A Student's Guide to Danbury, Connecticut @ Danbury Historical Society;* Royal Hinman, 1842

American Archives; Documents of the American Revolutionary Period, 1774-1776 Produced by Northern Illinois University Libraries. Digital Collections and Collaborative Project

Wikipedia -- The Free Encyclopedia

Hamilton Genealogy

Joseph Hamilton   *Ruth*
1692 Kingston, RI - 1777 Danbury   1700 Danbury, CT - Danbury, CT after 1777

Capt. Silas Hamilton   *Elizabeth Knapp*
1724 Danbury, CT - 1790   1728 Stamford, CT - 1785 Danbury, CT

John Hamilton   *Anner Stevens*
1748 Danbury, CT - unk. Monticello, NY   1765 Danbury, CT - unk. Danbury, CT

Capt. Stephen Hamilton   *Lorena Hammond*
1788 Danbury, CT - 1858 Monticello, NY   1790 Roxbury, CT - 1868 Monticello, NY

George Bronson Hamilton   *Indamora Trowbridge*
1820 Monticello, NY - 1885 Dubuque, IA   1834 -1911 Dubuque, IA

Minerva Hamilton   *Fred Bell*
1867 Dubuque, IA - 1953 Cedar Rapids, IA   1863 Dubuque, IA - 1942 Dubuque, IA

Capt. John Hamilton Bell   *Louise Whelihan*
1890 Dubuque, IA -   1900 Cedar Rapids, IA -
1976 Cedar Rapids, IA   1981 Cedar Rapids, IA

Millicent Haight Bell
1942 Cedar Rapids, IA -

Acknowledgements

I didn't know one thing about writing until I joined the Society of Children's Book Writers International.

I didn't know much when I joined Pennwriters.

Anything I do know came from Round Hill Writers in Round Hill VA.

Thanks to everybody who managed a seminar I attended or who helped along the way: Bobbi Carducci and Ellen Braaf, in particular.

Ellen Braaf recommended my first real editor, Linda Wirkner. After Linda's death, I did the royal tour of editors: Thalia Newland, Ann Westrick, Ramona Long.

Then Bobbi Carducci suggested Valerie Muller Egger, who provided the right help at just the right time.

The Danbury Museum and Historical Society was most helpful, especially Diane Hassan. Brigid Guertin also encouraged me to finish faster than might have been the case.

Olivia Scully at the C.H. Booth Library in Newtown CT provided Hamilton material. While not new information, old verification is valuable, especially when many genealogy sources are not correct.

I will never forget holding Silas Hamilton's land deeds, signed by the Captain and certified by Thaddeus Benedict. I only looked at a couple before I wondered why I was allowed to touch them. They're in archival sleeves now, thanks to Mr. Allen Ramsey. Both he and the deeds reside at the Connecticut State Library in Hartford.

Brian Stevens at Western Connecticut University in Danbury allowed me to see the oldest maps, from which I tried to piece together a town.

Sundry people read the book in early stages, all helping in their own way: Charles Phelps, Suzanne Neesen, Damon Martinez, Scott Johnston, and Karen Myers-Mahaffey.

My very first reader said, "Oh, it's like *Johnny Tremaine!*"

It was my daughter Marit Hughes who said it, but it still counts!

Made in the USA
Middletown, DE
18 August 2021